LOVE AND MARRIAGE

"What are you thinking when you look at me in that way?" Ian tipped his head. "And do not," he continued after half a moment's observation, "ask me *what* way. That lovely color in your complexion tells me you know exactly what I mean."

The faint flush deepened to a blush. "I do know," said Serena, turning away. "But I cannot discuss it. Please do not ask."

He came to her and put a hand gently on her shoulder. She resisted his attempt to turn her. "Serena," he said, "I am your friend. I hope you know that."

"I believe it."

"Friends can tell each other anything."

"Not everything."

He sighed. "Perhaps it is just that you have so little experience of friendship, my dear. Please believe that I am here for you. That I will do anything in my power to make you happy." He forced her to face him. When she would not look up, he put a hand beneath her chin and gently pressed her face up. "Anything, Serena."

Books by Jeanne Savery

THE WIDOW AND THE RAKE
THE REFORMED RAKE
A CHRISTMAS TREASURE
A LADY'S DECEPTION
CUPID'S CHALLENGE
LADY STEPHANIE
A TIMELESS LOVE
A LADY'S LESSON
LORD GALVESTON AND THE GHOST
A LADY'S PROPOSAL
THE WIDOWED MISS MORDAUNT
A LOVE FOR LYDIA
TAMING LORD RENWICK
LADY SERENA'S SURRENDER

Published by Zebra Books

LADY SERENA'S SURRENDER

Jeanne Savery

Zebra Books
Kensington Publishing Corp.

http://www.zebrabooks.com

ZEBRA BOOKS are published by

Kensington Publishing Corp.
850 Third Avenue
New York, NY 10022

Copyright © 2000 by Jeanne Savery Casstevens

Zebra and the Z logo Reg. U.S. Pat. & TM Off.

First Printing: May, 2000
10 9 8 7 6 5 4 3 2 1

Printed in the United States of America

In memory of Joan Shapiro

Friend exemplar.
Friendly critic extraordinary.

May there be lots of
desserts where you arc now—
all of them with chocolate!
(Save me some!)

Prologue

February, 1812

White of face, Lady Serena entered the ladies' parlor at the back of her family home, her skirts swishing in a less than ladylike manner.

Serena's mother looked up from the white work lying across her lap and paled a trifle herself. "Serena. My dear child. Can you not refrain from . . . from . . ."

"From watching my father reveal himself a monster still again?" demanded the young woman hotly.

"Oh, dear," whispered Lady Dixon. She closed her eyes in exquisite agony. "I *wish* you would not."

"That poor woman is more than seven months, Mother. She needs food and care and . . ."

"But, my dear, it is not right that we in this parish should provide for her. She is none of ours!"

"You prate Father's words without a single thought of your own," stormed Serena, her color changing from pale to something beyond prettily flushed. "Did you not listen to Vicar Morton's sermon just last Sunday? Did you, too, not hear him say that generosity to the poor—"

"You will hush," insisted her mother, sitting straighter in her chair. "It is the business of the Poor House Board to decide who will and who will not be admitted."

"No, it is not," retorted Serena, her tone acerbic. "It

is Father's business alone. He decides and the rest say, 'yes, my lord,' 'no, my lord,' and 'it is done.' There is not a single backbone among them."

"Please, Serena," begged her mother, leaning forward, "do not speak of this to your father. It will do that poor sinful woman no good. It will cause strife and perhaps"— Lady Dixon seemed to shrink—"*worse*."

"So far he has only beaten me," said Serena absently. "Why, by the way, is that woman sinful and the man who forced her *not?*"

"Forced . . . is that what she said?"

"She was ravished."

"Serena." Her mother's eyes widened. "You must not speak of such things. You ought not to know of such things." A sudden thought made poor Lady Dixon look very much like a startled hare. "Oh dear. Surely not! Serena, tell me you do *not* know what the word means, what is . . . involved?" finished her mother hopefully.

The fading red bloomed, this time from embarrassment rather than temper. "Mat was . . . kind enough to explain," said Serena.

"But," said a bewildered Lady Dixon, "Mat is at sea. At least, I believe he is at sea. Oh, is he *home?*" asked the fond mother.

"No, of course he is not. I was sixteen at the time."

Lady Dixon's eyes widened in horror. "He didn't . . . ?"

Serena's humor lightened for the first time since she'd burst in upon her mother's privacy. "Demonstrate? Of course not. Come, Mother, my brothers are exceedingly rough and unbelievably stupid, but by their lights they would protect me from harm. Unfortunately, they enjoy such terribly crude humor. Mat thought it great fun to, hmm, describe what men and women do to create babies."

"You have known since you were sixteen . . ."

"When did you know?"

"When your father, er, *demonstrated* on our wedding night," said Lady Dixon dryly and then blushed rosily. "Oh dear. Please, Serena. This is not a proper conversation!"

Serena sobered, her jaw firming. "But, Mother, that woman. I do not understand why—"

"Because it is a man's world, my dear," said her mother firmly. "You are not meant to understand."

Serena's lips pressed tightly together. With a sad, faintly baffled expression, she studied her mother. "Once again you spout the nonsense my father teaches. Why? Why do you let him . . . ?"

"My dear, he is my lawful husband," said Lady Dixon. On firm ground she spoke with more authority. "He is the head of the household, Serena. It is his place to tell us how to go on." Lady Dixon bundled the bed linen on which she worked to one side, her mood lightening. "And speaking of how we go on, my dear child, I meant to tell you immediately I saw you! We have had delightful news. Your betrothed arrives the last Sunday in the month, and your wedding will be the following day. *At last* all is in train. I assure you, *this* time nothing will go wrong! Serena? Is that not wonderful?"

"You believe he will come?" asked Serena blandly. "Before the first arrangements he went sailing, was blown off course, landed in Ireland with something wrong with the boat, and was weeks getting it fixed. The second time, he was waylaid. His horses were stolen from the traces and he and his servants tied up, left to their fate in the most isolated of regions. Do you truly believe he will arrive, hale and hearty, on this, the *third* attempt at a wedding?"

Her mother frowned. "Poor man. He has had the most appalling ill luck, but your marriage will not be postponed again, my dear. This time nothing will go wrong.

Come the last Monday of this month you will be wed! Oh, there is much to do, my dear! We will be so rushed!"

"I will make you a wager, Mother."

"Yes, my dear?"

"I will wager anything you like that James will, for one reason or another, find himself once again unable to appear at the altar."

"You say that so calmly. Why do you not gnash your teeth that you have been forced to wait so long for your husband?"

Again Lady Serena cast her mother that perplexed look. "You *know* I've no wish to wed. I am happy that, as of yet, I have not been forced to do so."

"But your father is determined to see you married before your birthday, and, my dear, you will be twenty-five in little more than six months! Really, I've no notion how the time has passed so quickly. It seems impossible."

"Somewhat more than *seven* months," corrected Serena, who counted the days. "If still unwed, I may collect my inheritance and shake the dust of this house from my shoes!"

"Dust? What dust? Oh dear!" Lady Dixon turned an agitated expression toward her daughter. "What can you mean?"

Serena bit her lip, mentally chastising herself for further upsetting her mother. "You have known forever my plans for the future."

"But you jested. Surely you jested! Your father would never allow it." Lady Dixon did her best to frown sternly. "You will behave as a lady and you will do as your father says."

"Father tells me I am no lady, so why pretend to be what I am not when something so important as my whole life is at stake?" Serena's eyes danced. "Come with me, Mother. When I leave this house, *come with me.*"

Lady Dixon blushed to the roots of her hair. The hesitation before she spoke said volumes to her perceptive daughter. Her words, however, denied the pause. "I am a married lady, my dear, and my duty is to your father. Even if you remain unwed when you reach your birthday, which will not be the case, I could not leave this roof."

"All my dependence is on James," said Serena. She picked up the sheet, found where the needle was set in a torn hem, and set herself to finishing the mending. When it was suggested she put it aside in order to help plan her wedding, she murmured, "Do what you will, Mother. It is a sham, this wedding, and I'll play no part in the planning. Vows made under duress surely cannot have legitimacy. If I am forced to the altar to wed James, I doubt vows made by *either* of us will have merit."

One

Ian McMurrey sat close to the bed on which James, his next younger brother, lay. In turn, his features expressed his love, his exasperation, and his sadness at this brother who had, all his life, been something of a rebel.

"It is his name," Ian remembered their mother saying. "I told your father not to name him James!"

The memory brought a hint of a smile to Ian's lips. *Had* James attempted to live up to, or perhaps one should say *down* to, the Pretender's tarnished reputation? He blinked away sudden tears. The night was long and chill and waiting for the end unendurable. Unbearable that James, bright, puckish, life-loving James, should lie here dying. But it must be borne. Ian sighed.

The soft sound brought a flutter to bruised-looking eyelids. "Ian?" The word was a breath of air.

"I'm here, Jamie."

"She didn't want me to . . ." The words trailed into silence, sweat appearing on the dying man's brow.

"Seems you're going to extremes to oblige her, Jamie." Ian wondered who she might be and what Jamie had done.

The dying man smiled weakly. "But, Ian, I promised . . . you must promise, Ian . . . promise . . ."

The voice faded. Jamie's breathing grew more difficult, more ragged. Tears dampened Ian's eyes. It wouldn't be long now—but now the wait was nearly over, now it was too soon.

Oh, Jamie, why? Why you? Why now? Why whywhy-why . . .

Ian sat with his father in the exceedingly masculine room which was the elder McMurrey's sanctuary. A room he rarely left. "It was an easy death, Da. If death is ever easy." Ian stared into the fire. "He said something strange toward the end."

"Aye?" said the elder, staring into the same crackling fire.

"She didn't want me to. . . . That was the first thing. And then *I promised*. . . ."

The elder McMurrey turned his head, an unexpectedly swift and decisive movement. "That was all?" Ian shrugged. "His mind was on his wedding, his bride. What else said he?"

"He wished me to promise . . . something."

"That you take his place at the wedding, of course," said his father promptly.

Ian looked up, met his father's searing gaze.

"That *you* wed Lady Serena," insisted the older man. "No question!"

Cogitating, Ian frowned, then shook his head. "That doesn't feel right, Da."

"And what else would he want?" asked the older man, agitated. "The wedding only a ten-day off and all?"

"It is true that the arrangements were in place." Ian stared into the flames of the small fire almost lost in the great hearth. "In place for the third time! Does it occur to you, Father, that, despite your *arrangements*, James had no intention of wedding Lord Dixon's chit?"

"So it was an arranged marriage, but, listen you, a good one. She is well trained and would not interfere in his pleasures but would have run his house and raised his children and been content to remain in the country."

Ian cast his father a scornful look. "And, of course, there is the fortune."

"Dinna ye be denigrating the fortune, lad! We are no so wealthy we can forfeit it."

Ian sighed softly. *When Father speaks of the family finances*, he thought, *he becomes more than usual Scots. Worse, he cries poverty when we could buy an abbey, as the saying goes.*

"You will take your brother's place," continued the white-haired gentleman, interrupting Ian's unfilial thoughts. "You will not say me nay!"

"If I deny you, will you disinherit me?" Ian's gaze sharpened, focused on the red marring his father's ears. "Is that it, Da? Is that the rod you held over Jamie's head?"

"And if it was?" blustered the elder McMurrey.

"Mother would be ashamed of you."

"Ye leave your mother out of this!"

"Because you recognize the truth of what I say?" Ian rose to his feet. "I can find no other meaning for Jamie's words, so I will wed Lady Serena in his place, Da, but not because *you* demand it. Because of Jamie's promise and the promise he'd have extracted from me if he'd had the strength." Ian turned on his heel and trod heavily toward the door. His hand on the handle, he paused. "But, Da, I ask time in which to grieve for poor Jamie, and that you cannot deny me. You may write Lord Dixon that I will arrive on the twentieth of March and that Lady Serena and I may be married on any date thereafter."

"Where are you off to?" asked the elder McMurrey, rising unsteadily to his feet.

"The hills, Da"—Ian's deep voice took on a poetic lilt—"the hills and streams, the wind and the rain, and lochs, Da. The salmon and stag and—"

"And auld James," interrupted Ian's father, distaste in his tone. "That auld shepherd, stinking with the stink of sheep!"

"Old James is who he is. Among all else he is a wise old man, Da. He will help me sort through the pain of my loss and"—a thin smile tipped Ian's lips, disappeared—"that other loss as well." When his father frowned, he added, "The demise of a bachelor's freedom!"

His father ignored the weak jest. "You will be there on the twentieth? Ye'll *not* find excuses to postpone the wedding?"

Ian moved back into the room. "So you agree that is what Jamie did?" he asked, seemingly idly.

The elder McMurrey grew more agitated. "The lady approaches her twenty-fifth birthday. The wedding must be held before then or the contracts become invalid."

"Is that so?" Across the dimly lit room Ian eyed his father.

The older man fidgeted with a squat dark bottle, *uisgebeatha* distilled deep in some hidden glen. The whiskey was McMurrey's way of dealing with grief. He had disappeared into the drink for a good six months after the death of his wife. Ian hoped it would not be so long for a mere son. Especially when the man was blessed with five of them.

Four now . . . Ian swallowed. Hard. And stalked from the room.

The hills called. The fishing and hunting and good clean air. The wind and heather . . .

There was white heather on the lea slope. Would it have blossomed out of season as it occasionally did? Unlikely . . . but if it had? An omen? If it had, perhaps he would cut some, pack it in ice, and send it to his prospective bride. Would she like it? Or would she feel it an intrusion on her grief?

Grief? Did the lass *feel* grief for Jamie? Had they loved each other?

And why, wondered Ian, was his father so insistent that a McMurrey, any McMurrey, wed the chit?

Not a chit. A woman. A woman with nearly twenty-five years behind her. And this woman, lying so long on the shelf, the woman his brother had twice—thrice if you counted his death!—avoided wedding, this woman was to be his wife. Ian grimaced. Undoubtedly she was an antidote, or a nag, or both, that she remained unwed to such an age!

Ah but—the sarcastic thought ran through his mind—*a rich antidote if m'father is to be believed.* A coat of whitewash to cover any fault!

On a blustery first of March, Ian McMurrey pulled up his curricle before his closest friend's country mansion. He looked along the facade of Tiger's Lair, as Renwick Towers had come to be called, to where a groom rounded the corner. Ian, stiff from long hours behind his team, dismounted from the lightly built racing rig. He gave orders for the care of his horses, warned the fellow a traveling carriage would arrive within the hour, and then, stripping off his gloves, moved toward the open door.

The Renwick butler bowed and condescended to give his master's friend a warm welcome. He informed Ian that Lord and Lady Renwick were in the blue salon.

"And Lord Renwick's aunt?"

"She visits friends."

Ian asked that he be shown to his room before joining his hosts. The early spring day had been windy and the roads dusty. He wished to freshen himself. Reeves, approving, directed a footman to lead Ian to the best guest bedroom.

At the top of the stairs they turned left and then right

at the first corridor. A lad racing down the hall almost ran into Ian. Ian's hands shot out, grasped the East Indian's shoulders, steadying him.

"Prince Ravi! You still here?"

"And where would I be else?" asked the young Indian with royal arrogance. His dusky cheeks were darkened by the blood of embarrassment at being caught running in the halls.

Ian grinned. "I thought Jason might have wrung your neck, scamp, or that you would run off in a huff! Ah!" He looked the prince up and down, his brows arching. He placed a hand on the lad's head. "You've grown, m'boy."

"I am not your boy." But the prince grinned, pleased at the compliment. "You will ride with me while you visit? Miss Eustacia does well for a beginner"—the prince himself had learned to ride only a few months previously—"but she rides slowly and it is a huge bore to dawdle so!"

"You should say 'Lady Renwick,'" scolded Ian. "But did not her ladyship say she did not wish to learn to ride?"

The boy's grin grew a touch wicked, his eyes sparking with devilment. "I have changed her mind. There was this little thing I did not wish to do and I said I would if she would learn to ride. I must go now." He backed down the hall. "Aaron—" He stopped, his eyes widening. "But Aaron is your brother. He will wish to see you! Sir! I will tell him you have arrived!"

"No!" Ian knew he must speak to Aaron of Jamie's death, but it was still hard to even think of it. He forced a smile. "Let it not be said that I interfered with your lessons, Prince Ravi. The dinner table will be time enough for us to meet."

The prince pouted. "But it is the essay. I think I did not do it well and would much prefer that Aaron . . ."

Ian shook his head, and the boy sighed. "You are quite as bad as Lord Renwick. You do not allow me my way. If I were home I would order the both of you thrown to the tigers."

Ian grinned. "Sahib would protect us."

The boy heaved a still deeper sigh. "True. My father did our country a disservice when he gave the magic beast to Lord Renwick." He scowled, his mercurial emotions dipping down. "Sahib should be *mine*."

"As I understand the tale," said Ian, "you yourself put Lord Renwick into a position of extreme danger or *no one* would have Sahib and Sahib's dam would have had *you*."

The prince, unabashed, grinned. "That is so. Now I will go before you give me a set down"—his brows arched—"that is how one says it?"

Ian nodded.

"A set down which I cannot forgive!"

The boy ran off, and the footman, meeting Ian's eyes, shook his head. It was obvious, however, that the servant felt a certain affection for the thoroughly spoiled only son of an Indian maharaja, who, when he wished it, was a charmer.

Soon Ian returned to the ground floor. He paused in the doorway to the blue salon when his friend's pet, a fully grown white tiger, rose to his feet and opened his mouth in a long, soft roar.

"Quiet, Sahib. It is only Ian," said Lady Renwick, rising and approaching. "Ian, we did not expect you again so soon."

"And such a burden, your arrival," added Lord Renwick jestingly.

Ian eyed his friend, studying Jason's mood, and relaxed when he judged his blind host was happy and contented. "I would not have burdened you so few months after your marriage, my friends, but . . . it appears I too am to wed, and in a very few days now. Not only is the Lair not too distant from my intended bride's home, but I wish you to attend." Before Renwick could do more than frown, Ian continued. "I know you dislike travel, Jase, and visiting, but"—Ian's lips pressed together—"frankly, I need my friends about me."

"Married?" asked Eustacia quickly. "But surely . . ."

A bleak look entered Ian's eyes. Sahib, sensitive to human moods, lifted himself from the floor and silently padded across the carpet to stare at the stranger. Ian, sitting in his chair in a misleadingly relaxed fashion, stared back.

"Our James is dead," he said, belatedly responding to Eustacia's unasked question. "I take his fiancée to wife on the twentieth."

"James! Dead? Ian, what happened?" Renwick put his hand down to his side and discovered Sahib was not there. He gripped the arm of his chair instead. "Does Aaron know?"

"Not yet, and I do not look forward to the telling. He and I will walk together after dinner." Ian's bleak look deepened. "As to how . . . Jase, you knew James. A friend lay ill of the smallpox. Jamie, careless of his own safety, went to comfort him. He contracted the disease but appeared to be recovering. Something . . . happened. The doctor said a weak heart."

"Jamie?"

Jason's disbelief brought a wry smile to Ian's lips. "Wild as he was, it seems impossible, does it not? But it seems this sort of weakness can go on for years unnoticed. Then suddenly it worsens. The doctor believes the smallpox did the damage."

"But did not *you* contract the smallpox?"

"I was vaccinated while still at university. A lecturer explained the notion, and I thought it a good one." His look of despondency deepened. "Like a fool I did not take the idea home, did not have my brothers inoculated. I could have saved him, Jase."

"If there was this weakness of which you speak, then he would have succumbed to something else. Do not blame yourself. Tell us, instead, of your bride," demanded Eustacia, turning the conversation to better things. She spoke in the wonderfully molten-gold voice which had first drawn her blind husband to her. "Is she pretty?"

"I've no notion. None of us but James ever met her, unless Father saw her in her cradle." Ian sighed. "James left us some weeks early for his wedding, which was to include just her family He'd had news his friend was ill, you see. The wedding! It had been scheduled twice before, but both times something prevented it. Then Jamie's dying . . . Her father wished our wedding too, to include her family only, but, besides Aaron, I mean to ask a few friends. We—my bride and I"—a muscle worked in Ian's jaw—"are to meet at the church."

"A pig in a poke!" exclaimed Jason. "Ian, is this wise?"

"You fear I will find an antidote walking down the aisle?" Ian grinned but quickly sobered. "Jase, I've no choice. My father wishes it, and Jamie"—Ian's eyes lost focus—"there at the end he wanted me to promise . . . something." Sahib edged closer, lay his head against Ian's knee. "I believe James regretted failing Lady Serena, that he wished me to wed her in his place. For his sake I will do this, will fulfill his last wish."

"Of course you must," said Eustacia softly, soothingly. "All Jason asks is if it is wise to wed so quickly. Before you even meet?"

Ian reached inside his lapel and pulled a much-read letter from an inner pocket. "This came in response to my father's communication explaining Jamie's death and that I meant to arrive on the twentieth, and the wedding could take place on any later day."

Eustacia perused the words. "But this is outrageous. Threats and demands and both in less than fifty words! The man is a master at putting all in a nutshell, is he not?"

"Read it to Jason," said Ian, absently putting his hand on Sahib's head. The tiger bounced the hand a little and Ian scratched his ears.

Sir,
   Too long has my child remained unwed. If your son stands not at the altar on March twentieth, he stands before a court of law and explains why not. Ian McMurrey must be at the church at ten of the clock. Lady Serena meets him there, willing to speak her vows.

                                        Yours etc.,
                                        Dixon

Eustacia frowned. "Ian, are you *certain* you wish this?"

"Jamie—"

"Ah, yes."

"Will you come?" asked the big man, his deep voice revealing a trace of wistfulness, his deep-set eyes looking from one to the other.

"Of course we will," said Eustacia although her husband frowned. "And," she added, "you will stay with us until we must drive to the church, which you say is not far?"

"Not too far, but I cannot stay. Tomorrow I'm off to find Wendover. Merwin was in London and I saw him there. Unfortunately, Princeton and Seward are not available."

"No. Princeton is in the Peninsula, and who knows where Seward has lost himself? But could you not write?" asked Renwick.

"I'd rather explain face to face, Jase."

"Yes, of course," said Eustacia. "They will come here and we will all go on together."

Ian smiled. "Thank you. I knew I could count on you." He saw that he had been petting Sahib, and his eyes widened. "Jase, I believe your pet likes me."

The Renwicks chuckled. "I think," said Eustacia, "that Sahib knows when someone is preoccupied. Then, without thinking, the person will scratch him just as he likes. Normally, people are a little afraid of him, you see."

"Is that it?" Ian looked at the tiger. "I'd much prefer to think you like me, Sahib."

The beast opened his mouth in a nearly silent roar. "You are correct and I wrong," said Eustacia. "Sahib has just told us he likes you!"

"You will wed him."

"I will not."

Lord Dixon stared at his stubborn daughter, his eyes cold, a cruel, sneering smile tilting one side of his thin lips. "You will. I know the one thing which will convince you."

Serena was thinner than before she'd received the news that she'd lost one prospective husband but that another would be provided. Her father had beaten her when she objected to wedding a stranger, and then, when still she would not agree, he had tried starving her into submission. But time was running out, and she had yet to sign the papers.

"Nothing," she insisted, "will make me wed this man. This *stranger*!"

"You will wed him, Serena. I will use this crop"— Lord Dixon pointed at the wicked whip lying on his otherwise clear desk—"on your mother if you do not. Again and again until you change your wicked mind."

His eyes narrowed. "You know, my stubborn daughter, that I never make empty threats. Ah!" The crop slapped the desktop with a sharp crack of sound. "You will not faint until after you have penned your name to the marriage agreement."

Serena stiffened her spine. Her chin came up. "You are a brute and a monster. You have no right to call yourself a gentleman."

"*You* are nothing but a fool of a woman."

"I am, at least, a Christian woman. You are evil."

Again Lord Dixon sneered. "You have listened too long and too often to that prattling fool of a vicar. Another woman!"

"Mr. Morton is a good man. You think it is a weakness, but it requires more strength to be good than to be evil. A man who beats his wife to force obedience from his daughter is evil." Serena ran from the room, slamming the door against the tirade building behind her. Knowing the first place he would seek her was her mother's room, she went instead through the kitchen, giving three knocks on the wall as she approached. It was a signal that anyone working there must close their eyes so that they could with honesty say they had not seen her.

Beyond the kitchen was the dairy, empty at this hour. And at the far end was the cheese room, where aging cheeses required turning. Serena had meant to give the order on the morrow, but it was a task requiring no thought, only effort, and the work, she knew, would help her control her temper. She lifted the first cheese, turned it, moved along the shelf to the next. And the next. Finishing the first level, she began on the second . . .

Serena soon reached the painful conclusion that she must sign the marriage agreement. Given her father's wicked threat, she was forced to bend to his will. It was the only possible decision.

Almost worse, to humble her he would demand an

apology, and she must give it as well. However insincerely. But for the moment—she *could* not. She could not yet make herself unsay words which were no more than the truth.

Working from a ladder, she attacked the third shelf. The fourth shelf held the oldest cheeses, ones which would soon be taken to market where they would be sold whole to London dealers or cut into wedges for the local trade. Her family had long been known for their excellent cheeses.

Serena finished and stood away from the wall staring at it. Her eyes narrowed as it occurred to her that she alone knew the secret of making the Dixon family cheese. She had been taught by her grandmother, and without his daughter's supervision in the cheese room, Lord Dixon would discover that, not only had he lost the income from his daughter's fortune, but another source of income would decrease as well!

But more than her mother's ignorance of cheese-making was involved. Her grandmother had allowed Serena's mother no part in the management of the house. From the dowager Lady Dixon's death, Serena had managed the whole of the Dixon household. Had it occurred to her mother that, with her daughter married and gone, she must take up the reins? Her poor mousey little mother? Her soft and yielding mother?

Could Lady Dixon manage . . . ? Somehow Serena doubted it, and a new worry entered her heart. How, she wondered, could her mother be protected from her husband's wrath when he discovered his wife was ignorant, untrained, and unable to manage? And there was no time to rectify the problem! How could Serena bear to leave her mother to face her father's wrath!

And *wrath* inadequately described Lord Dixon's reaction. Her father would not understand, or would pretend he did not, that his wife had had no opportunity to learn how to be chatelaine of his home. Lady Dixon would bear the brunt of his rage.

But she must wed, must leave . . . Serena realized she was trapped. All her plans had fallen to dust. Despite her denials and defiance, her ranting and raving, she *would* be wed. She'd fight to the end, of course, but it would happen and she would leave her home. Married. Some man's wife. And her mother left to her father's untender mercy . . .

Serena stared blindly at the cheeses. Was there nothing to be done? Nothing at all? A stool stood by the table at her side and she dropped onto it. She lay her head on her arms, hot tears slipping down her cheeks. Trapped. As was her mother. Both of them must suffer, as women always suffered, with no recourse and no hope. As that poor pregnant woman her father had denied help must be suffering—although Serena had done what she could to relieve the stranger's problems. For a day or two, at least . . .

It was unfair that women's lots should be so hard.

Still . . . perhaps she could ease things for her mother. Perhaps there was a way that Lady Dixon need not find herself at an utter loss. The cook and the housekeeper—would not those two help the countess until she felt competent to make decisions? Serena would talk to them.

As always when there was something to do, Serena faced the next step and then the next and did not falter. But as she walked toward the door intent on finding the housekeeper, she cast one last look at the cheeses. A wicked smile tipped her lips.

There was one thing she would *not* do. She would not pass on the secret of the cheeses. She would have her revenge.

A small revenge, perhaps, but very, very sweet!

* * *

March twentieth dawned damp and gray. A blustery wind whipped around, finding ways through the dormer windows of the attic room in which, for two tedious days, Serena had been locked. Her father, distrusting his rebellious daughter and fearing she might run away, had taken no chances.

Serena sat and stared out the small panes. She heard footsteps in the hall but didn't move. It would be her youngest brother, Jonathan, come to escort her to her mother's room, where her mother would bear her company on her last morning in her own home.

The key turned. The door opened. Jonathan, surprised, asked, "Why do you sit on the floor?"

"Because," she responded, "it is the only way to see out this window."

"But there is nothing *to* see! Nothing out there—"

"There is freedom, Jonny. Freedom you have known all your life and I will never know."

"There you go again, talking like a book."

Serena turned slightly to stare up at her brother. He wore a perplexed expression, and she smiled slightly. "Talk like a book, you say? How would you know? You didn't like your books."

"No, I didn't," he admitted. Almost proudly, he added, "I'll never open the cover of another one."

"No," she said, saddened by his pride in his ignorance, "I don't suppose you will." Aching from the hard bed and chill air, to say nothing of the restricted diet her father had allowed her, Serena climbed stiffly to her feet. "You are to take me to our mother, Jonny, are you not?"

He cast her a worried look. "No tricks now," he warned, reaching for her arm.

She jerked away, moving just out of reach. "No tricks. Jonny, do you truly think I would behave in such a way as would give our father reason to beat our mother?"

"I thought it a silly notion that he'd beat *her* if *you*

misbehaved, but it seems he had the right of it. Why do you care?" he asked, ducking his head under a low beam.

"Why do I care? Jonny, she is our *mother*."

"Not much of a mother," he said carelessly.

Serena glanced at him, curious. "She has not been allowed to be, has she?"

"Nonsense. What sort of mother should she be if not herself?"

Serena started down the first flight of stairs. She wanted to argue with Jonathan, try once again to get through his thick skull how idiotic it was to treat others badly, cowing them with the fear of further pain, and then expect them to behave with strength and determination, but there was no time. She sighed a second time, giving it up.

"Never mind, Jonny. Even if I explained it, you would listen to our father's ranting and immediately forget everything I said."

"You don't like Father, do you?" he asked, as if suddenly making the discovery.

She cast him a look of amazement. "Jonny, perhaps there *is* hope for you!"

He frowned. "There you go again. Saying things that don't make sense. What has what you just said got to do with liking Father?"

"It was the fact you noticed which gives me hope!"

"Why should I not notice?" He steered her toward the next set of stairs.

"Why has it taken you so long to notice?"

"I'm not as stupid as you think. I knew you didn't like Father. I just don't know why."

"Lord give me strength," she muttered.

He counted on his fingers: "You got a roof over your head. You got food. You got clothes. You even get a bit of pin money, which I *don't* understand since you waste it on stupid books." He shook his head. "No, I don't see any reason for you to complain."

"You see no reason for me to feel it is wrong to withhold from me the money which is mine by inheritance?"

"Ain't withholding it. It goes to your husband. And a right tidy bit it is, too!"

"It will go, as you say, to my *husband*"—a muscle jumped in her jaw—"not to myself. I will not have it. I will have no control over it. I will be unable to draw on it or to spend it as I wish, even though—*something no one denies*—it is mine."

"Not until you are twenty-five."

She sighed. "But I am forced to marry this man, a complete stranger, before I am twenty-five when I have no wish to do so."

"But Serena," he said, perplexed, "someone has to take charge of your money."

Serena rolled her eyes. "If I were allowed to reach my birthday unwed, Jonny, that someone would be *me*."

"Yes," he agreed. "Exactly." He smiled down at her and in a kindly tone added, "You know we can't allow that. You're a *woman*."

Two

"It is a nice little church," said the vicar complacently. "No really special features, but nothing to which one could object." He spoke to the huddled group of men standing in his churchyard ignoring the drizzle. "Shall we go in? The sanctuary will be chill, but it is comfortable in the vestry."

Lord Wendover looked at the others. When Ian said nothing, he spoke. "An excellent notion. McMurrey? Merwin? You, Aaron—you look chilled to the bone. Yes, Vicar, do lead us to this vestry."

They followed the vicar down the aisle and across the front to the vestry door. Mr. Morton had not lied. This vestry, unlike many the men had seen, was not only newly whitewashed, but blessed by the existence of a small stove in which a few coals burned.

"You are a trifle early," said the vicar, smiling at each in turn. "I must apologize that I've no notion which of you will be wedding our dearly beloved Lady Serena. We, the whole of the parish, will miss her when she has left us," he said, and there was no doubting his sincerity. "A good woman. A good Christian woman."

The men noticed the vicar said nothing of Lady Serena's looks. Ian, however, was glad to hear praise of his bride's character. "I am Ian McMurrey," he said.

"Lady Serena's intended bridegroom." He offered his hand.

The vicar shook it heartily. "As I said, we will miss her, but, for her sake, I will be glad to see her removed from her family." He sobered, his eyes taking on a cool look. "Not, as I am sure you know, the best family in which to be a woman."

"I do *not* know," admitted Ian. "My brother, who was contracted to Lady Serena, died. Our respective fathers insisted a substitute groom be chosen."

"If I were not so young . . ." began Aaron stoutly.

"But you are, pup." Ian smiled at his youngest brother, who had taken the news of their brother's death as badly as Ian had feared he would. "You have a lot to do before *you* take a wife."

Aaron forced a grin. "I admit I'd rather not do so at once, but, Ian"—he frowned, heavy ridges crossing his brow—"I recall you saying you would only wed if you found a woman to equal Mother. Yet you have agreed to marry, sight unseen, this stranger!"

"Yes, well," said Ian hastily, "I was much younger and knew little of the world." He cuffed his brother's shoulder. "Silence, bantam! The wedding goes forward in less than half an hour." It was his turn to frown. "I wonder what happened to Jase and Lady Renwick. They were behind us when we left Renwick's Lair."

"They must travel slowly over bad roads," explained Aaron a trifle diffidently. "Lord Renwick's blindness makes travel difficult."

"I am grateful he agreed to come. I just hope he arrives in time."

McMurrey stepped to the window and stared out over mossy gravestones to where one or two larger monuments stood against the brick wall bordering the cemetery. The others, politely ignoring him, talked softly in the background. Ian barely heard them. He was thinking of the changes a wife, even a good wife, would make to his way of life, but was startled from his thoughts when a smallish woman appeared, running around the corner.

She was, he guessed, heading toward the largest monument, an oversized figure of an avenging angel, set on a plinth near the corner of the graveyard. Behind her came a portly gentleman, puffing and red in the face. And, obviously, exceedingly angry.

Ian could not hear what passed between them, but he liked the way the woman raised her chin to the man, the way she stood, arms akimbo, and argued with him, and how, at the last, she turned on her heel and continued on toward the monument. The gentleman beat a crop against his palm, a thwarted look on his face, and watched her.

Ian grinned. If *that* woman were his bride, then perhaps marriage would not be so bad. His smile faded. It would not be. His bride, an heiress, was all but on the shelf. There must be something very wrong with her that she remained unwed! Ian watched the Valkyrie-in-miniature and dreamed dreams of what might have been. . . .

The woman stood for a long time before the monument. Once the sour-faced man called to her, but, although she nodded, she remained still for a little longer. When she turned Ian noted with pleasure her neat figure. The woman was slightly too tall to be considered a Pocket Venus, but otherwise her petite form fit that notion of perfection-in-miniature. A wonderful head of thick dark brown hair had been swept up, braided. It formed a neat crown around her head, on which she wore no hat. Moisture beaded it, and a sudden flash of sunlight breaking through the clouds added glints, making of it a true diadem.

Her skirts, weighted by the damp, made graceful sweeps around her legs as she returned to the church at a swift pace. Ian was again amused by the choleric man following in her steps, haranguing her.

The vicar joined Ian just then, cast a startled look toward the receding backs, and said, "Ah! Excuse me. I will return shortly, Mr. McMurrey."

Ian watched the vicar leave the room, gently closing the door behind him. "Well?" asked Ian.

"But *is* it well? Truly?" asked Aaron.

"We will make the best we can of our situation, Aaron. The both of us. Trust me, will you?" Ian smiled at his worried brother.

The vicar returned. "Now, my lords," he said in a slightly fussy way to Wendover and Merwin. "If you will seat yourselves in the front pew . . ."

Tony and Alex each shook Ian's hand and departed.

"Mr. McMurrey? If you are ready?"

Ian hesitated. "Did you notice if other friends had arrived?"

"No strangers have come, sir," said the vicar, "but, sir, if you are agreeable, I do not believe we should tarry?" When Ian made no response, the priest added, "Lord Dixon, sir, is not a patient man."

Ian had very much wished Jason to be with him on this occasion, as he had, himself, been with Jase when the Renwicks married.

"Sir?" The vicar cast a perturbed look toward the door.

"Very well. Come, Aaron."

The vicar placed Ian and Aaron near the altar and then looked toward the back of the church. Lady Serena's eldest brother escorted her mother down the aisle to join her other brothers in the family pew.

Ian was not impressed by their looks. The men were too chunky, too red in the face—coarse men who would grow old quickly. In her way, the mother was worse. A tiny mouse of a woman who jumped at her own shadow.

Ian's lips thinned, but he turned a steady gaze on the closed doors at the back of the sanctuary.

They opened. The young lady he had seen in the cemetery, her eyes lowered demurely, came down the aisle on the arm of another red-faced man, the portly gentleman who still carried his crop in a businesslike fashion. Ian turned his gaze back to the now modest-looking warrior maiden. Was this, after all, his bride? It seemed she was. Ian found himself releasing a breath he had not known he held. He turned toward the smiling vicar, who began the ceremony.

Lord Dixon handed his daughter to Ian as the doors opened again. The vicar's skin paled, and sweat popped out on his brow. Ian smiled. "Allow my friends to take their seats," he said softly, "before we continue."

Except it was impossible, for some moments, to continue. Lady Dixon, glancing back, had seen Lord Renwick's white tiger. She had screeched in a restrained and ladylike manner. And fainted. Ian heard cursing from the Dixon pew, and then, loudly, Lord Dixon ordered the ceremony to continue.

"But your wife, my lord—" objected Vicar Morton.

"My idiotic wife is perfectly comfortable."

Ian turned slightly. "They have laid her on the pew." His bride, who had not looked, merely nodded.

"Continue!" snarled Lord Dixon.

The vicar bit his lip and glanced at Lady Serena, who nodded again. Mr. Morton began the ceremony over, casting only an occasional glance toward where Sahib lay in the aisle beside Lord and Lady Renwick's pew.

Not until the rite was completed and the married couple returned from signing the register did Lady Serena see the tiger. She realized then that what had disturbed her mother was not the *wedding* but a *beast*. The new Mrs. McMurrey glanced from the tiger to Ian. Then Lady Serena's chin went up, and, although she took her new husband's arm, which she had not meant to do, she walked firmly up the aisle, passing the tiger without another glance.

"You have strange friends, my lord," she said softly as they exited from the church's small, bare entry.

"I have no title, Lady Serena," he responded in his deep, rumbling voice. "I believe we would be most comfortable if you were to call me Ian."

"You might be comfortable, sir, but *I* would not," she said with a slight bite to her tone.

"Very well." He glanced down to see her raise startled-looking eyes up at him. He held her gaze. "What would you prefer to call me?"

"I have a choice?"

"Of course, but Ian is my name. Could that not please you?"

She frowned, a puzzled, wary look on her face. "I will think about it," she said and turned to greet the vicar, who joined them just then.

"Mr. McMurrey," said the vicar after offering best wishes to the bride, "that . . . that beast. In my *church.* I cannot believe—"

"But, Vicar, does it not say somewhere that the tiger shall lie down with the lamb?" asked Lady Serena blandly. And then she again cast a quick, wary look toward her new husband. She seemed surprised when he smiled at her sally.

"Tiger or lion?" asked Ian softly.

"It is much the same, is it not?" she retorted.

The vicar chuckled. "My dear! Well, there is something of that sort, perhaps. But"—he forced a certain sternness—"I cannot have my parishioners fainting away during a service. Lady Renwick, for that is who she said she was, went to your mother's aid once we finished. She will care for her."

"Excellent," said Ian. "And the others?"

Again the vicar chuckled. "Your brothers, Mrs. McMurrey—"

"I would prefer to retain my title, Vicar Morton." The bite was back.

"As is your right," inserted Ian quickly, again inducing surprise in his bride.

"Your brothers, Lady Serena"—the vicar's frown expressed a faint but definite disapproval—"left by the side door, departing rather quickly, I thought."

"They are afraid of the beast. Good."

"Were not you?" asked the churchman, curious. It had taken every bit of willpower he could muster to edge past the lolling tiger.

"Of course. But the animal came with friends of my . . . my husband. I assume he'd not allow a wild beast to attend his wedding. Therefore, it is logical the tiger is under control. Although," she added, "no one paid it the least attention." She spoke in a thoughtful manner and frowned slightly.

"Sahib goes everywhere with Lord Renwick, as I will explain later." Ian glanced around. "Will you tell us what has been arranged, my dear?"

"If you anticipate a wedding breakfast, then you will be disappointed. My father is only too happy to be rid of me, even though he must also cede my fortune to you. He told me there are papers you must sign, but that you may do so at his solicitor's in London when convenient. As for you and I"—she tilted her head and eyed him warily—"I assume you have plans, sir?"

"I have." But Ian blinked at the notion that Lord Dixon did not want to so much as meet his new son-in-law. "If you are agreeable, of course."

"And if I am not?"

"Will you listen first?" he asked in a deep, calm, rumbling tone, his over-large frame relaxed, his deep-set eyes looking down at her.

A *kind* look? Serena realized he waited for her agreement. "Of course." Her lips thinned. "I have promised to obey, have I not?"

Ian ignored her provocative tone. "Since there is to be no celebration, we will return to the Renwicks' where the supper Lady Renwick planned will provide us a meal in place of the nonexistent wedding breakfast here. We will, if you are agreeable, proceed from there to a house on the coast. Lord Wendover's grandmother lends us the use of it for a month."

"Lord Wendover?"

"That is I," said his lordship from behind them. "This serious-looking fellow on my right with the sharp chin is Lord Merwin. Beside him is Ian's brother Aaron. On my left is Lord Renwick and Sahib. But before you do anything else, Mrs. McMurrey, say hello to Sahib. *Please*," he added, his face contorted into a comical look. "It is important, you see, to introduce all new friends to Sahib. At once!"

"So he knows," said Renwick, staring at nothing at all, "that you *are* our friend. Sahib," he finished softly, and the tiger pressed gently against his leg. Renwick waved an over-long cane in Lady Serena's general direction. "Sahib, this is a friend."

Serena, a certain amount of strain revealed in the tension about her mouth, stared at the beast, who stared back. "What do I do?"

"Merely tell Sahib hello. Use his name," said a smiling Lady Renwick coming up on Sahib's other side.

"Hello, Sahib," said Serena.

She flinched when the tiger moved forward a step, but she held her ground. The animal stared up at her, blinked, and then opened his mouth in a silent roar of welcome.

Lady Serena flinched slightly. "You are very beautiful, Sahib," she said with unmistakable sincerity, "but I think I will like you better from a distance."

The men chuckled and Lady Renwick laughed. "Oh, I *will* like you. I hoped I would. We hadn't a notion, you see, what to expect . . ." She trailed off and blushed. "Ah! My most abominable trait, you'll find. That I speak with utter frankness and, far too often, with too little thought!"

"It is unnecessary to apologize," said Lady Serena. Her smile, weak as it was, faded as she looked beyond the small cluster of strangers toward the church where her father, his hand holding her mother's arm too tightly, appeared. "Excuse me."

She moved in the swift, graceful fashion Ian had noticed earlier. His new wife ignored her father, in fact appeared to avoid coming too near him. She hugged her mother.

"He looks a good man, Serena. Do not judge him too quickly, my love."

Serena's eyes narrowed. "He is a man, Mother. That is enough to make him unacceptable."

"No, dear. Please." Lady Dixon glanced to where her husband spoke to Ian, who had followed her, and she whispered, "Not all men are like your father and your brothers. Think of Vicar Morton."

Lady Serena nodded, although she thought the vicar was brave only because of his faith, and she, as yet, had no reason to believe that her new husband was blessed with a similar character. What she knew was that religion played no role in the lives of the men of her family and that at least some tonish men were equally evil. Witness that poor pregnant female her father had scorned.

"Stop your whispering," growled Lord Dixon, turning. "Your husband awaits you, missy, and I for one want to return to a good fire and a drink."

"Mother—"

"Go, child. I . . . I will manage."

Serena sighed, hoping her organization of the household would prevent her father from finding too many excuses to be angry with his wife. One more hug and she turned to face her husband. Her chin rose that significant bit. She looked around for the others. One carriage had departed and three men were entering a second. A third, smaller carriage, piled with luggage, awaited her pleasure.

But Serena was *not* pleased. When she and her new husband were seated in the last carriage, she asked Mr. McMurrey to excuse her and, cuddling into her corner, pretended to sleep. It rather shocked her that she was allowed to do so. Was it possible her mother might be correct?

Serena could not make herself believe it.

But Lady Serena was allowed the same privilege when, some hours later, she reluctantly entered the carriage again. Lord Wendover's grandmother's estate was, she'd been informed, less than three hours along the coast. That she would be allowed to ignore Ian McMurrey for those hours was beyond belief. So she was startled when, this time, she was wrapped gently in a travel rug, a pillow was placed behind her head, and she was again left in peace.

When, after they had gone perhaps half the distance, she dared to peek at the stranger . . . her husband . . . *him* . . . she discovered he watched her through narrowed eyes, the merest hint of a smile hovering around his lips. What was he thinking? she wondered, and realized it was the first time it had crossed her mind to question how their marriage might affect *his* life.

"May we talk?" asked Ian.

"Why? What is there for strangers to say to each other?"

"Perhaps *because* we are strangers and must not remain so? Is that not reason enough?"

Serena sighed. "I do not understand you."

"And you will not if you make no attempt to learn anything about me."

She didn't respond, her lips pressing tightly together.

"Then too, I'll learn nothing of you. Which, much to my surprise, I am impatient to do."

"Surprise?"

Her disgust that she had succumbed to speaking was obvious to the watchful man. "Yes," he said, "surprise." Ian chuckled, a low bass rumble which, because he'd been told, he knew was infectious. Very nearly, he noted, it drew a smile. Perhaps this odd marriage could come right. If he were careful. "You are nearing your quarter century, Lady Serena. An heiress, but still unwed. I admit I assumed there was something"—he drew in a breath and substituted another ending—"some reason."

A sudden, instantly choked back laugh was reflected in her dancing eyes. "At the very least you expected an ugly bride!" She sobered. "And yet you wed me. Your father, too, is a tyrant?"

"A tyrant, my lady?" Had Jamie described the elder McMurrey so? "When you meet him, you must tell me what you think. My sense of him is colored by memories from when our mother yet lived. I realize he has changed greatly, but I see him through the screen of the past and I cannot tell you if others would consider him a tyrant. But," he continued just a trifle sternly, "it was not for my father's sake I wed you."

His eyes lost focus, and Serena read pain in his expressive features.

"I was with Jamie when he died," he said softly. "At the end he did his best to speak, attempted to elicit a promise from me. He was, poor lad, too far gone to do more than try, but I have wed you, Lady Serena, for the sake of my brother, for the promise he made you, and no other reason."

"For James's sake! But . . ." She eyed him, her consternation obvious. "Oh, no. No! You are wrong. So very wrong!"

Suddenly, knowing that James had tried to save her, had, at the end, tried to explain, all the starch went out of her. Tears welled and fell. Hating to cry, hating still more that someone knew she cried, she turned from him.

Jamie tried to save me. He did not fail me . . . except, of course, he did, she thought, bitter.

"My dear," said Ian tenderly, "I was unaware you loved him so much."

"Loved him . . ." Serena's quick mind grasped at that. "Oh, yes. Of course." She sat up and wiped her face with a corner of the travel rug. Once she composed herself, she glared. *"You*, Mr. McMurrey, are not *he."*

Ian eyed her, not quite believing this sudden attack. He could not put his finger on what was wrong, but something . . .

"You can never be he," she added when he didn't respond.

"It is impossible to argue that, of course," he said pacifically.

Lady Serena cast her new husband a look of bafflement. "I do not understand you."

"Which explains why we need this month alone together, does it not? That we may come to understand each other?"

Serena gritted her teeth. The man had a soft answer for everything. When would he show her the iron under the velvet? When would he lose patience?

Her plan for later that evening filtered through the barriers she had built against revealing it, and panic filled her. He was so big . . . would she be able to . . . could she . . . ?

Her chin rose that revealing notch, although she did

not know it. Nor did she know that, even in the fading light, her husband read determination in her expression. *What,* Ian wondered, *is she up to?*

Three

Serena paced the bedchamber allotted to her, her skirts swishing around her ankles. When would he come? What would he do? He was so big. Fear welled up at the thought of the beating she would deserve if she carried through her plan. Or perhaps he would turn her over to the local magistrate.

She chuckled a rather watery chuckle. That would surprise the poor magistrate, would it not? A bride, on her wedding night, accused of attempted murder? The door opened and she swung around, crouched, her hand fisted around the leather handle of the long-bladed knife she'd stolen from her youngest brother. She watched her husband's brows climb.

Her chin rose that significant bit. "I will not be bedded."

"Will you not?" he asked in that soft, rumbling voice which ruffled up and down her spine every time she heard it. Even now he showed no sign of temper. No anger or even irritation.

Baffled, Serena watched him approach. She put both hands before her as her brothers had taught her to do. Determination filled her. She would *not* become a meek little mouse like her mother. Nothing he did would bring her to her knees as her father had brought her mother. She waved the knife back and forth, the point upward.

She knows how to use that blade, thought Ian, surprised. "Who taught you?" he asked, the thought becoming words even as it crossed his mind.

"My brothers. They were bored."

"Bored and taught you something a gently bred woman would never know. Interesting. I wonder what else they taught you. Do you know swordplay as well?"

His words startled Serena out of her concentration. Swordplay was the way one of her brothers referred to his activities with the local whore! Did this man mean he thought *she* . . .

"Oh! To the devil with you!" Serena stared at her wrist, held firmly but without pain in his huge paw.

"Drop it."

"I will not."

Ian sighed. With far more gentleness than Serena thought possible he uncurled her fingers. The knife fell with a thud muffled by the carpet. They stared at each other, the incriminating blade lying between them.

"You have lived, I think, with men who have had no care for you. You must learn that I am different. I came—" He slowly released her . . .

. . . and stepped on the dagger when she dropped to catch it up.

"—to suggest we spend a week or two learning to become comfortable with each other before we come together. Much to my surprise, my dear, I am impatient to discover more about you. You are an intriguing woman, Lady Serena." He turned and left the room.

Lady Serena crouched, gaping. Finally she closed her mouth, glanced at the knife lying mere inches from her hand, and then looked at the door. Did he mean it? He would not insist on bedding her?

At least . . . not immediately?

Could she turn this to her advantage? But even as the thought crossed her mind, she saw in her mind's eye that broad back—a broad, *vulnerable* back—walk away from her. Had he known she would not pick up the knife and throw it? Had he guessed it had taken every ounce of her not inconsiderable will to *face* him, knowing she might hurt him, determined to do so if she must? Surely he had *not* known, so how could he know she would not stab a man in the back?

The answer was that he could not know, but even so he had turned his back to her. He had walked at a normal pace out her door and he had closed it. Softly.

The door!

For the first time, Lady Serena noticed there was a key. She rushed to it, turned it, and swung around. A key! Her back to the door, she pressed her hands against the panels. Her father had allowed no keys, but here it was different.

For the moment, surely, she was safe. With only months until her birthday. Six months, one week, and two days and then—

That firm little chin rose once again.

—she would sue for an annulment. *She would be free.*

In his lonely bedroom, Ian paced. The chit had not been frightened . . . not of joining him in that huge bed. He was almost certain of that, so what reason did she have for such resolution? For such a determined effort to keep him at arm's length? Because *determined* she certainly *was*.

He searched his mind for clues to explain his bride's action and remembered her denial that Jamie had wanted another brother to wed his fiancée. She had implied she loved Jamie, but that was a sham, a thought he had put into her head at only that moment. Never would he believe she had loved his brother.

Or, he asked himself, *is it that I don't wish to believe it?* A tender smile curved his lips, only to be replaced by a frown as he recalled Jamie's words. *She didn't want . . .* what? Once, Ian had thought it might be that she did not wish to leave her home. Having met her family, however briefly, he decided it could not be that. Any sensible woman would wish to leave such a home!

So. Not want *what?*

Not wish to wed? Nonsense. Every woman wished marriage. But Lady Serena was not "every" woman. So, if she had not, then had the delays to the marriage been other than the accidents they appeared? Had Jamie, twice, come up with a dramatic means of postponing their vows?

Neither father was the sort to give in to a demand that the contract, signed when the two were children, be set aside. Had Jamie and Lady Serena plotted to prevent the marriage? To what end?

Ah! Obviously so that Lady Serena might reach her twenty-fifth birthday when the contracts would be null and void. But what sort of woman *preferred* to remain unwed? That she was passionate, hot-blooded even, was obvious to the least observant, which Ian rather prided himself he was not. Surely it was not that she dreaded their union—or any union, for that matter. So, if it was merely that she wished to remain unwed, why had she agreed to *their* wedding?

Ian's unruly brows clashed over his deep-set eyes as it occurred to him that, somehow, Lord Dixon had forced her. He recalled how thin her wrist was when he'd grasped it there in her room . . . but many women were naturally slender, were they not? Surely her father had not starved her?

On the dresser stood a decanter. Earlier Ian had ignored it. Now, his thinking bogged down in surmise and suspicion, he went to it, pulled off the crystal top, and sniffed.

Brandy.

He poured a modest portion into the waiting glass, lifted it. Sipped. Astounded, he stared at his glass. Not *mere* brandy. The best brandy he had ever tasted. Taking the glass with him, Ian moved toward the windows looking out over a long, gentle lawn toward the water.

The water . . . and France not all that far beyond. Unhappily, Ian gave the glass a last longing look, returned it to the dresser, and, wishing ill to all smugglers, took himself to bed. His empty bed.

How long, he wondered, *will it remain empty?*

Two days passed in which Lady Serena did her best to avoid every possible situation where she and Ian might meet. Only at dinner had she been forced to accept his company. And there she remained silent, uncommunicative. Now, on the third day, she slipped through the door as she had the previous mornings. She closed it gently, and turned . . .

. . . to face her husband, who leaned against one of the pillars supporting the roof over a long terrace. Serena glared. Ian chuckled, that soft, rumbling laugh which under other circumstances might have drawn a smile from Serena. But this situation was too serious for smiles. Her scowl deepened.

"We cannot become acquainted, my lady," said Ian softly, "if we spend no time together." He watched her lips compress into an intriguing pout. "Which direction do you walk this morning?"

"I take the sea path. Alone."

He shook his head.

"Like all men, you will demand that I obey you."

"I recall," he responded gently, "that you *promised* to obey me. Did you not?"

She curtsied derisively. "And how may I obey you this fine morning, oh master?"

He laughed, again shaking his head. "You will not give an inch, will you, my dear? Very well. One more day, wife, but then you must spend each morning with me." His expression grew pensive. "Somehow, my love, we must weave a future together."

"You will not call me that!"

"My love? I would like to call you that and know it true, but, my dear, I will desist if you insist."

"I am not your dear, either."

"So bitter. Is it truly so terrible that you and I are wed?"

"Yes."

Ian frowned, pursing his lips. "My dear Lady Serena, tell me—no lies and no evasions—do you love a man of whom your father disapproved?"

Serena blinked rapidly. She tried very hard to lie to him, but could not. She sighed. "No."

"But there is something."

"Something which puts me off marriage?" she asked, overly sweetly. "Oh, there *is*. To wed, there must be a man. I have yet to meet one I can respect, let alone one I wish to call lord and master. Not, of course, that I was allowed to meet all that many . . ."

Ian's brows rose. "You had no season?"

"Waste a season on a woman betrothed practically in her cradle? What would be the use of it?"

"I am sorry. At the proper time, Jamie should have suggested that you be brought to London so the two of you could meet in an unexceptional fashion. I suppose he was too young to think of it. But still, surely your region is not so lacking in happy families that you know nothing of successful marriages."

"Successful? I know several. From the husband's point of view. Happy? Perhaps one or two, but those are among the lower orders, where such things are different than in ours. One I envy?" Her chin rose. "Definitely not."

Ian wondered what else he might ask which would help him understand the way Serena's mind worked. "Did you," he asked, "dislike Lady Renwick?"

Serena, prepared to contradict everything he said, closed her mouth with a snap.

"Did she seem cowed or broken or unhappy?" insisted Ian.

"I saw her for less than two hours," said Serena, speaking defensively and hating herself for it. More firmly, she added, "One cannot judge another in such a brief visit, and certainly not the inner workings of a marriage."

"As you cannot judge me in a few hours."

She could not contradict that, either. "You said I might have my walk."

"Yes . . . Lady Serena," he added as she edged a step to the side. "I have been warned we should not go beyond the stone fence lying to the east. You have, perhaps, seen where the wall has begun to crumble away into the water? Just where the land begins to rise?"

"I was warned. I go inland at that point." *Why*, she wondered, *do I bother to tell him anything at all?*

"Enjoy yourself, my dear."

"And you?" Serena frowned. Again she'd spoken when she'd had no intention of doing so. Why? Why prolong the time spent in his presence? Why not just *go*?

"I will take out a gun." He gestured toward the north and west. "There is unenclosed wasteland up on the downs which is overrun with rabbit and fowl. Cook said she would appreciate any game I supply."

"Very well. Good-bye."

Serena drifted more to the side as she moved forward. Quite obviously, it was not a conscious maneuver, but more a habitual attempt to put herself beyond reach. He watched her stroll toward the water.

Her pace, thought Ian, *is deceptive. She covers a great deal of ground without seeming to hurry at all.*

What had she feared? Perhaps that he would stop her as she passed him? He had said she could go, so, if she had not believed him, what did that say of her family? Had her father, for instance, *wished* to instill fear in her?

Ian reentered the house, where, still thinking of his wife, he selected shot, powder, and a gun. As he left by a back door, a white and brown, silky-haired dog ran up, his tail wagging. The animal hesitated, one paw raised, a hopeful, questioning look on his doggy countenance.

Ian eyed him. "Yes, you wish to go with me, but would you be a help or a hindrance?" He glanced around, saw the gardener at work clipping hedges that protected a vegetable garden from the sea winds. Ian approached the man. "Your dog?" he asked.

The gardener glanced at the dog, grunted.

"He is trained to hunting?"

A quick judging glance, taking Ian's measure, and another grunt.

"Would you object if I take him with me?"

A wry chuckle answered that. "Try, you, to leave him behind!"

Ian grinned. "I don't think I will. Good day to you."

The dog, Ian discovered, was a well-trained animal. He returned with a good game bag and, as thanks, gave a brace of pheasant to the gardener's wife before taking the rest to the cook.

Serena, watching from an upper window, was surprised to see him hand the birds over to the woman who had a shy toddler hanging onto her skirts. As she dressed, she wondered why he showed such generosity to the wife of a mere worker, but, she told herself sternly, she would not ask. What he did was of no interest to her. *None whatsoever.*

She repeated that thought as she went downstairs. For

two evenings she had avoided conversing with him at dinner and she would continue to do so. She would sit at her end of the table, the centerpiece between them, and concentrate on her food, eating quickly and . . . The epergne was gone!

Serena hesitated, then decided to return to her bedroom and order a tray as she did for breakfast. She turned away.

"You are not a coward, Serena McMurrey." Ian spoke softly. He stood there beside his chair, tall, broad . . . and just a trifle stern.

No man would have reason to call her coward! Serena's chin rose. Only a step or two into the room, she stopped, stared at the place where she usually sat.

"We cannot talk at such a distance," continued Ian. "I suggested your place be set beside mine." He gestured.

Her lips pursed, but, forced by his challenge to her courage, she moved closer and Ian held her chair for her. She accepted the courtesy awkwardly, since it was not one performed for her in her old home. He moved to his place and nodded to the butler, who set a neat roast before him. Ian picked up the carving knife and a long-handled fork.

As they ate, Ian spoke of this and that, ignoring her lack of response. Finally, toward the end of the meal, he said, "I had a rather interesting day hunting. The gardener has a dog which insisted on accompanying me. I wonder if the dog has sired equally talented pups, one of which I might acquire."

Serena said nothing, eating steadily and silently.

"The common land is, as promised," he continued, "overrun by rabbits. We'll have rabbit pie. At least I hope we have a pie. I'm fond of it."

"Is that a hint?" she asked, her voice cool.

"That when you plan our meals, you remember I enjoy a good meat pie? I had not thought of it as a hint, but would appreciate it. I am told that yesterday you went to the village. A rather longish walk, I'd have thought, but you were not overly tired last night."

"A compliment? Or complaint?"

He chuckled. "Oh, surely a compliment, do you not agree? I am not the sort of man to appreciate a namby-pamby miss who lolls all day on her couch pretending to set a stitch in this or in that."

"I must learn to loll," she retorted, and then wished she had not. She bit her lip, cast him a glance . . . and frowned to see him grin.

"I handed you that one for nothing, did I not?" He chuckled.

She looked at him fully, her fork suspended. "Why do you laugh? I do not understand you."

"You did not mean for me to laugh?"

Serena's chin rose. "I meant an insult."

"An insult." He eyed her thoughtfully, beans dropping from his own fork onto his plate. "If you expect a reprimand or—"

She paled, and his eyes narrowed.

"—perhaps worse?—"

She swallowed. Hard.

"—you will be disappointed." Exasperation mixed with shock that she had, indeed, expected retaliation. Ian's dislike of her father hardened. "Serena, you made an excellent rejoinder to an opening I thoughtlessly provided you. Why should you suffer for being quick with words?"

She didn't respond.

"Time passes," he continued doggedly, "far more amusingly when a conversation includes unexpected by-ways and turns. And repartee is what gives a discussion spice, is it not?"

"I wouldn't know." Her chin rose that significant notch. "Repartee was not encouraged in our household."

He stared at her. "How," he asked, startled, "does one survive without it?"

Serena was not required to answer that extraordinary question because, just then, the butler offered a tray from which she took her time choosing a sweet. Her finger hovered over a beautifully glazed tart, moved toward a slice of Chantilly cake, returned, and then, with a sigh, she indicated *both*.

"A sweet tooth?" asked Ian, chuckling. "So have I, but I dare not indulge it." Ian took a pear from the tray and reached for his fruit knife. "I have, I fear, a tendency to put on weight when away."

"Away . . . ?" Again Serena admonished herself. She had *promised* herself she'd do nothing to prolong any conversation.

"At home I spend long hours in the hills. I hunt. Fish. Or simply roam the hills if I've no other reason for going out. And there is a shepherd with whom I have interesting conversations. I would like to introduce you to him. He is a poet, and I have encouraged him to write down his verses."

Serena cast him a disbelieving glance. A shepherd who could write? Surely that was nonsense. She said so.

"In Scotland we encourage the education of all, my lady. You will see, but we were discussing those very tempting sweets. Unfortunately, when I am in your soft southern climes, I tend to be far too sedentary and, if not careful, I grow fat." He eyed her. "I suspect you are one who may eat as you will and never gain an ounce." He sighed. "I envy you that."

Serena frowned. "A man envies a woman nothing."

"Is that something your brothers told you? How very stupid of them. One envies another regardless of gender. It is the *thing* which is envied, rather than the person."

Serena sighed. "Then I have been unlucky in my associates. I have often envied men this or that, but never had reason to envy a woman anything."

"Why should you? You are lovely to look at. Your long, thick hair is, I suspect, especially beautiful." He eyed it, wishing he could get his hands into it, but forced his mind to more prosaic thoughts and dropped his gaze to meet hers. "You have intelligence beyond the ordinary. You have your health. Your wealth. What is there to envy anyone?"

"Freedom," she blurted.

Appalled by what she revealed, Serena pushed back from the table and bolted from the room. She would have been astonished to see her husband rise, politely if slightly belatedly. She would have been far more astounded by the thoughts racing through his head.

"Freedom?" he repeated softly.

When he did not reseat himself but merely stood there lost in thought, the butler asked, "My lord? Should I clear the table and set out the decanters?"

"Decanters!" exclaimed Ian, recalling his suspicions concerning the brandy. "That reminds me. I meant to ask if there are wines *not* supplied by the local, hmm, industry? I have no intention of asking impertinent questions, but I will not drink smuggled goods. The war, you know. The price of every keg, every bottle, costs the lives of our men in the Peninsula."

The butler's ears turned bright red. "I will check the cellar, my lord. I believe there is some older wine laid down by the master." Ian nodded. "Shall I clear now?" he asked again when Ian continued to stand.

"Yes. I think I will take a stroll."

Before he left the house, Ian took a cigar from a hidden pocket and lit it. He stood under the veranda roof until he had it burning well and then walked out onto the dew-wet grass. Splotches where the dew was disturbed caught his eye, and he grinned. His pace picked up as he followed the trail his wife thoughtfully—or thoughtlessly—left to tell him the way she went.

Guessing her direction was more difficult when he reached the path. The well-trod surface left no trace of her passage, so he hoped that she had gone toward the wall of which they'd spoken earlier that day. At least, he'd had the impression it was her favorite walk. . . .

Ian allowed his mind to play with the notion of freedom. He knew what he meant by the concept, but what would it mean in a woman's mind? Freedom to do something? Freedom *from* something?

From *someone*?

With her twenty-fifth birthday the marriage contracts would have been voided and she freed from wedding Jamie. But women needed to wed. How else could they live comfortably? Men cared for, cosseted, supported. . . .

Supported!

Ian stopped. Once she was twenty-five, Lady Serena would have been rich and able to support herself. Had she plans? Notions of what she'd do? Had she relished the *freedom* it would give her?

Ian walked on, wondering what form such freedom might take. Had she thought to go to London so she could finally experience the tonish pleasures which had been denied her when she should first have enjoyed them?

Or had she meant to remove her mother from her father's domain, to care for her herself? Ian recalled the woman who had fainted at the sight of Sahib. Perhaps that was not so surprising: Most people feared Sahib. But if Lady Serena hoped to rescue her mother, would such a little mouse have the courage to *be* rescued? Ian thought not. Lady Serena was not stupid. She, too, would know that her mother lacked the resolve to leave her husband.

What else might a young woman desire? Ian scanned his surroundings, searching for his bride so he could question her. He wanted answers.

And, by God, I'll have them! She will, finally, talk to me with no roundaboutation! Ah!

Ian stared at the slim figure seated on a rock that had tumbled from the boundary wall. Her back rested against a young tree which, conveniently, grew on the landward side, and she stared over the water. The setting sun lit the side of her face, revealing a pensive expression.

On what, wondered Ian, *does she muse?* He threw away his cigar and approached cautiously, aware that, like a doe, she would spring away from him at the slightest noise, startled by his most mundane actions. When he was still some distance away, he perched himself on another chunk of wall. It was not particularly comfortable, being too small for him, but he suspected she'd feel safer if he did not loom over her.

Serena reached for a pebble and tossed it into the water lapping gently against the shore. Ian found another and tossed it after, letting it fall almost exactly where hers had.

She twisted around. "You."

"Hmm. Serena, my dear, you must know you left me with questions much in need of answers." She didn't speak, and he frowned. "Freedom. Freedom from what or whom? Or freedom to do? I need to know what you meant."

"What difference does it make? I am a woman. I am bound by the rules men make and enforce."

"But not all men enforce the same rules. What would you have done with your fortune if you'd managed to reach your birthday unwed?"

"You wouldn't understand."

"Try me."

She merely shook her head and stared pensively over the water.

"Travel perhaps? Naples? Or a visit to American cousins? Did you wish to explore a world you have had no opportunity to see?"

"I've no desire to see the world. It would only be more of the same."

"Very likely mankind is much the same everywhere, inside, but there are many ways of living. So you are both right and wrong when you suggest it would be more of the same. What of London, then? Have you no desire to visit London?"

"I had not thought of it."

"We go there next, so you might wish to think on it," he said with just the barest hint of humor.

She flashed him a look he could not interpret.

"Perhaps," he suggested, "you want to go elsewhere? We can do that after a brief but necessary sojourn in London. The Lake District will, in a month or two, be at its most beautiful. Or, if you wish, I could take you home to meet my father . . . ?"

She shuddered.

"Yes." He chuckled. "We will postpone that meeting until you trust me to support you. My father is . . . my father." Ian sighed. "Not an easy man."

"I have never met a father who is."

He grinned at the acid in her tone. "Ah! But you admit you've not met so very many. Lord Wendover's father is a man of great understanding and sensitivity. He and his wife have a marriage I wish you would study, my dear. I would like something similar."

"Another order?"

"Order?"

"That I study that marriage so that I may model myself on the wife?"

"My dear, you could not."

Serena stiffened.

"That is not an insult. Tony's mother was crippled in an accident."

"Poor woman. I suppose you speak of her marriage as it was before the accident when you say it is one I should study?"

"You mistake. A carriage overturned when she was twelve. She was crippled before she wed."

Serena turned. "No man would . . ."

Ian interrupted. "That particular man would and did. He recognized her strengths, her intelligence and wonderfully generous nature. They love each other deeply, Serena, and she'd not thank you for pitying her."

"Love. A fairy tale for children. It does not exist."

"If you believe that, then *you* are to be pitied! But you have led me from what I wish to discuss. Or do you deliberately avoid talking about freedom and what you mean by it?"

Serena shrugged. "In six months I would have had my fortune." She spoke dreamily. "I would have been responsible, could have made decisions. I would have started with a home for . . ." She seemed to wake up. She glanced at him speculatively and turned away. "I still could."

"How?"

Serena drew in a deep breath. "If you were to demand an annulment . . . ?"

"Deman . . ." He eyed her. "Now I understand the knife! You would remain a virgin, is that it?"

"Yes."

"But . . ."

Virginity was not enough! Did the chit not know that the only grounds for an annulment were a man's impotency or if a woman proved unfruitful? The one he could not attest to, and the other took years to determine.

Still—Ian's eyes narrowed—*if she believes it possible . . . there would be time. . . . Time? Why,* he wondered, *do I need time? Ah! That is obvious, is it not? I need time to change her mind. Time to entice her into falling in love. Time to win her . . .*

And, Ian realized, he very much wished to win her! He nodded. "Very well."

"What?" Lady Serena rose to her feet, staring down at him.

"I agree we will not"—Ian chose his words carefully—"hmm, come together as man and wife."

Disbelief turned to joy.

"But how will your father react to your renewed freedom?"

Serena's color faded, and she put her hand against the tree to steady herself.

"Not well? My lady, I suggest that, for the time being, we do nothing. That we pretend our marriage is satisfactory—"

She raised her eyes to his as if she would demur.

"—until *after* your birthday. Once you turn twenty-five we can discuss ways and means."

She stared, her eyes painfully wide open. "You would do this for me?"

"For the two of us, my dear."

And you may, he thought, *interpret that however you like.*

Four

"But . . ."

"Close your mouth, Serena. You look far too much like a fish stranded on the beach."

Her mouth snapped shut. She eyed him. Very slowly she reseated herself. "Why would you do this?"

"Because I am a gentleman?" *Not*, he thought. *No gentleman would take advantage of your ignorance in such a way.*

"I cannot see how it is to your advantage."

"Have I not said? I wish a marriage of love and contentment. Of equals."

"No woman can be a man's equal. No man would allow it."

"There it is again. You think all men are like your father." He shook his head. "We are *not* all alike. But, Serena, you must agree to certain things. Together, we must decide on the rules which will guide our behavior over the next few months."

"Assuming you mean what you say, it is simple, is it not? Hire me a house and leave me there."

Yes, thought Ian, *if I meant it, it would be that simple*! He dismissed the rueful thought and asked, "Would that not rouse suspicion in your father? You *would* like that, would you not?"

She blanched. The deepening dusk almost hid her ashen complexion, but not quite.

"That was not well done of me. It is not my intention to frighten you," he said gently. After a moment he asked, "Will you listen?"

"Have I a choice?"

"We always have choices, Serena."

"So *you* say." She shrugged and picked up several pebbles.

"Does your silence mean you'll attend me?"

She nodded.

"First," he said, "we must appear to the world to be happily married."

"Why? I would think the authorities would be more likely to grant an annulment where there is unhappiness."

"The one has nothing to do with the other. Certain things must be sworn to in order to achieve what you want. Nothing else is important."

"Is that true?"

What a suspicious lady was his bride! Ian knew it would be difficult under any circumstances to overcome her suspicion. Since he was aware he was tricking her, it would be still more difficult. Still, *this* question he could answer truthfully.

"I assure you, my dear, it is the truth. Occasionally proof is demanded that the woman has not been violated, which is, I fear, a rather embarrassing procedure, but usually a man's oath is all that is required."

She eyed him and then seemed to accept what he said. "But to pretend to be happy"—she stared over the water—"I don't think I can."

His craggy brows drew together. "Serena, have you never had a friend with whom you were comfortable?"

"No."

He stared at her. "From the time I first read the letter he sent my father I disliked the sort of man I guessed yours to be, but now I begin to detest him. How could any man allow a child to grow up friendless?"

"My brothers have friends."

"But you do not?"

"I am a mere female and unworthy of consideration. I exist only to see to *his* comfort."

"Nonsense."

"Is it?" she asked wistfully, wanting to believe him. *"I* have always thought so, but whenever I acted on my belief, he had a firm way of, hmm, dissuading me."

"His methods?" asked Ian coldly.

"His favorite is his whip."

Ian winced at the thought of weals on Serena's lovely skin.

"He also advocates locked rooms and bread and water. Occasionally he stooped to blackmail." Her lips trembled. "With me gone, I fear for my mother." She brushed a sudden and unexpected tear from her cheek, but another fell to take its place.

"Serena, hear me well," said Ian sternly. "I swear to you I will never raise a hand to you. To any woman. Or to my children, if I am lucky and have any. That is not my way. Nor," he added, smiling slightly, "is blackmail or starvation. Serena, did he threaten your mother if you refused to wed me?"

She turned shiny wet eyes up to his, their blue turned to gray in the diminishing light. "How did you guess?"

"I can think of nothing else which would have convinced you," he muttered. Soberly, he asked, "Can you agree, Serena? *Can* you play a role for the next few months?"

"That of loving wife?" She grimaced.

Ian chuckled. "I don't ask so much of you, my dear. Merely that we present a contented facade to the public and that you might be my friend? Friendship is also something I wish of marriage. And friendship is, I think, possible between us, even if marriage is not. You see, Serena, I like what I know of you. Your courage. Your intelligence. Your willingness to sacrifice yourself for another as you did for your mother. The fact you've a sense of humor. Ah, yes! Humor! Although I've seen little of it yet, I have great hopes of it." It was his turn to shrug. "There are other things I like as well. But, Serena, friendship takes two. Although you have not learned to trust me, is there anything you have discovered in me to dislike?"

"That you constantly surprise me, disconcert me, make it impossible to know how best to go on? I dislike it, but" she sighed as if she regretted what she was about to add— "I cannot say that the behavior which causes me to feel that way has been bad."

Ian chuckled. "You have thrown me off stride on occasion as well, my bride. I did not, for instance, expect to face a blade on my wedding night."

"No. Merely swordplay," she said, and once again wished she could learn to control her tongue. Her father would have reacted instantly and not with softness so, with no delay, she added, "I'm sorry."

"Cant language is something else your brothers taught you?" he asked. "My dear, some things would, perhaps, be better for the forgetting. There are tonish ladies who, assuming they understood you, would give you the cut direct for that particular locution!"

"You are shocked. I truly am sorry. Perhaps you recall that, before you disarmed me, you asked if they had taught me swordplay. *You* meant with dueling weapons, but my eldest brother has used the phrase the other way. I was flustered or you'd not so easily have rid me of that knife!"

"I believe you. My dear, you are an attractive woman, and any man may be forgiven for thinking of, er, *swordplay* when in your presence."

That, Ian thought ruefully, *is becoming increasingly true!*

"What you must believe is that I came to your room for exactly the reason I gave you. I believed we would both be more comfortable if we waited, if we knew each other better first. At that time, of course, I had no knowledge of your dreams."

"I do not know if I can trust you. My life has not been such that I find it easy to believe any man's words." She sighed. "I will try to behave in a friendly fashion, but I promise nothing. Experience has taught me that suspicion is the safer course."

"A promise is more than I would ask of you, my dear. Only that you will try, as will I, to enjoy the other's company." He rose to his feet. "Are you ready to return to the house?"

Instantly she shook her head. "No."

"Then I will see you in the morning. Good night."

Serena watched Ian walk away. It had been, she realized, truly a question of her wishes. Instant contradiction was her habit when responding to her father's or a brother's demands, despite the fact the result was forced obedience. She had retained some bit of independence that way. . . . Rising and adjusting her shawl, Serena ran after Ian.

"I changed my mind," she said . . . and, with a sideways glance, fell abruptly silent.

Ian glanced down, noted her confusion, and smiled. "I am glad," was all he said before offering his arm.

Serena hesitated, but, after a moment, she took it.

Ian felt that, under the circumstances, her laying her hand on his arm might be considered a major victory and not merely a successful skirmish in what he suspected would turn into a battle worthy of Wellington.

* * *

The next morning, not quite certain why she did so, Serena forbore eating alone and went down to breakfast. Just outside the door to the room to which a footman directed her, she stopped. Ian sat with a piece of toast in one hand and a letter in the other. Once a quick smile brought a twinkle to his eyes. Once a hint of a frown creased his brow.

He folded the missive and sighed softly. Serena wondered why. Then wondered why she cared. Pretending a carelessness she was far from feeling, she entered the room. She went directly to the sideboard, where she checked the morning's offerings.

"Good morning, my dear," said Ian, looking up. "You've a letter." Ian held it out but not so far that she was not forced to come to the chair at his side. He laid the crisp paper at that place and rose, pulling her chair out for her.

Serena had had no intention of sitting next to him, but somehow it seemed overly crude to ignore his polite gesture. She seated herself and looked at the wax-sealed paper. Ian poured her tea, asking if she wished milk or sugar, and, when ignored, pushed her saucer near her hand.

Staring at the envelope, Serena lifted the cup, sipped. "What would you like for breakfast?" asked Ian.

"Hmm?" Her head snapped up. "Breakfast? Oh, anything. It is all so good and such a change from the porridge Father insists is all a woman needs." She turned her attention back to the letter, staring at it.

Ian, watching her, gestured the attending footman nearer, whispered in his ear, and matched the footman's grin with one of his own. Then he opened his next letter and pretended to read.

Serena touched her missive with one finger, poking it as if it were alive and might bite. The thought brought a smile to Ian's face. He forced it to fade, again pretending to read. The footman brought a plate laden with a little of everything and set it before Lady Serena.

Ian wasn't disappointed, exactly, when his mild jest brought no response. In fact, he wondered if she knew what was on the plate. She appeared to eat without thought, without tasting what she put into her mouth, and her eyes never left the letter which she did not, again, touch.

"I believe it is from Lady Renwick, is it not?" asked Ian.

"I don't know."

Ian knew. Renwick had signed the outside, franking it. "If you were to open it," he suggested, "you might discover . . . ?"

"I've never had a letter."

"Never! No, of course not. When you've no friends, who would write you? Another point against your father. Serena, do you mean to leave it unread?"

"I don't know."

He chuckled at that unexpected bit of honesty. "When you finish breakfast, you might take it somewhere where you could be alone."

She looked up at him, surprised. "You will not wish to read it?"

"My dear, it is your letter."

"But—"

"You must cease this looking like a bewildered fish, my dear. It is not at all attractive, which is amazing. Since you are a very attractive woman, it must be difficult to achieve the reverse!"

Serena felt heat rise up her throat. "Nonsense." She looked at the stacks of mail on either side of his plate, a pile of letters already opened, the others yet to be read. "You received all that this morning?"

Ian glanced down. "It is considerably more than usual,

ut that is because it was collected over several days and
orwarded here."

"You mean you have mail every day?"

"Why do you look so wary, my love?"

Serena drew in a deep breath, telling herself he was
not like her father. "Because at home when Father re-
ceives mail it always puts him in bad sk . . . er, a bad
humor. If you have mail in each day's post, then I must
remember always to have in mind the nearest shelter!"

Ian grinned. "Ah! There it is again. That lovely dry
humor. I hope to hear more of it each day, my lady, as
you become more comfortable with me. As to shelter,
shall I promise to inform you when I receive a letter
which puts me in *a bad skin*? Better yet, I shall read
such missives to you so you may help me decide what
to do. I have one here. It is from my brother, the next
younger to Jamie—"

A fleeting sadness drifted over Ian's broad features,
deepening the arctic blue of his eyes to a more somber
shade. He shrugged away his grief.

"—who," he continued, riffling through his letters for
the right one, "has got himself into difficulties. *Not*,"
said Ian hurriedly, "with his university work. Robert is,
I believe, the brightest of us. But not when it comes to
people. A classmate inveigled him into a card game. I
fear the fellow is a sharp and Bobby the flat, but I doubt
it can be proven."

"Sharp? Flat?" interrupted Serena. "I have not heard
those terms before."

"Your brothers do not gamble? I am glad to hear some
good of them. They are cant words, of course, which I
assumed they would have taught you. A *sharp* is a man
who cheats at cards, particularly when he can find a *flat*
who is too naive to see him for what he is. He then
proceeds to take the flat for all he can. Such a man makes
his living that way."

"He cheated your brother?"

"Bobby is, as I said, intelligent. He is *very* good a
cards. He is also overly trusting, and since the sharp i
a classmate, Bobby will very likely not accept the notio
the fellow might cheat." Ian sighed. "It is not such
huge amount, but I hate allowing the man to win."

Serena swallowed a bite of coddled egg. "I don't sup
pose you know a sharp of your own?"

"Hmm?"

"You could send your sharp to win back from tha
sharp the money he won from your brother."

Ian stared.

Very dryly and with great courage, Serena suggeste
that Ian close his mouth. "It seems we neither of u
emulate a gasping fish to our advantage," she finished

Ian shut his mouth, his lips spreading in a smile. "Oh
yes," he said softly. "Yes, yes, yes. Do give freedom t
your joking side, my love. Please!"

Serena felt her heart rate speeding up at the look i
his eyes. Admiration was not something with which she'
had much experience. She found she liked it. A lot. And
that frightened her. "I don't understand you!" sh
blurted.

"You will," he promised.

Or threatened? Serena was uncertain. It was safer t
return to their discussion of his brother. "Could you no
send a sharp to take the edge off that other sharp?"

"I might if I knew one. Or, that is, if I knew one
trusted, which is rather a contradiction, is it not?"

He flipped his brother's urgent request for funds back
and forth against his fingers. Then he sighed. "There is
no help for it. Bobby promises he'll not gamble again i
only I will help him now, and I must leave it at that. I
will suggest that my brother discover if the fellow wins
too regularly and if he often plays against inexperience

men. Perhaps Bobby will see him for what he is and not be caught out in future by another such."

"He is more likely to insist that his sharp friend cease and desist, is he not? Then he'd be faced with a duel!"

Ian felt tingles under his skin and knew his color faded. "My dear, I believe you have just saved me from an egregious error. Thank you."

"Egrig . . . egreg-ous?"

"Egregious. Shocking, glaring, flagrant . . . in other words, a terrible, perhaps disastrous, mistake. You are correct that Bobby would challenge the fellow's honesty and very likely would have received a challenge of a different sort." Ian sighed. "Very well. A lecture on the evils of gambling and a reminder of his promise he'll not play again. At least, not beyond a social hand or two. And, of course, my note of hand. And"—Ian glowered—"the devil gets off with a whole skin, ready to skin another flat!"

"Perhaps when you go north, you yourself might do something about it?"

"Perhaps." Ian had slit another letter and begun reading it. His lips pursed.

"More trouble?" asked Serena, wondering at herself for speaking.

"A letter from our father. He rants about the weather and complains of a gillie's insolence." Ian looked up. "A worker on our estate," he explained. "More than likely the man had reason! When our mother died, my father became a sot. He has since given over excessive dependence on the bottle, but now he is a grouch, a miser, and the worst sort of recluse. My dear, perhaps the sort of problems you have with your father and brothers are less complicated than the sort I must deal with with mine!"

"I would argue that."

Ian glanced up and grinned. "Yes, I am certain you

would! And do an excellent job of debating your side, too. Shall we agree to disagree?"

"We will certainly disagree, agree or no!" Serena realized she'd responded without thinking and, apprehensive, waited for the ax to fall.

Ian chuckled. "You are a delight."

Serena's eyes popped open. He was not offended. He did not mean to retaliate. He read his letter and didn't even glare at her! Serena could take no more sudden ups and downs, such fiercely emotional swings. She rose to her feet, excused herself, and forcing her feet to obey, hurried from the room.

Her previous explorations had revealed a cozy parlor at the back of the house tucked into a protected corner with a lovely little knot garden just outside the window. Safely alone, Serena seated herself. Then, holding her letter in rather unsteady hands, she stared at it.

Why had Lady Renwick written? What could the woman possibly say to her, strangers as they were? Did she mean to warn the new bride? Or lecture her? Trembling, Serena slit the seal. Carefully, she unfolded the thick paper. She turned it right side up and had no further excuse to delay.

. . . short acquaintance, but I wish you to know that my husband and I approved Ian's marriage. We'd no idea what to expect. All sorts of notions ran through my head, everything from the fear you were ugly as sin to the notion you were the biggest shrew alive! I am glad neither is true. Ian is such a nice man and deserves a good wife, a woman who will help him and care for him and become involved in the things which interest him. I don't suppose he has told you much about his work yet, but I'm convinced you will not think him strange or outrageous or otherwise odd for feeling so

strongly about the subject. I suspect this letter is an impertinence, but I wanted you to know we were happy to have met you and that I look forward to a time when we may spend hours together getting to know each other.

All best wishes,
your servant,
Eustacia Renwick

Serena stared until the words blurred. The baroness liked her? She was *glad* they had met and *wanted to know her better*? But why? To what purpose? Serena's confusion faded into the suspicion with which she'd learned to meet any new situation. The baroness's words were very pleasant, but easily penned. Time alone would prove if they were to be trusted.

But what was this about Mr. McMurrey's work? What work? He was not a clergyman. Was he a solicitor, perhaps? What else did a well-born man do, if he did not go into the army or navy? Government service? Was he a diplomat? Serena frowned as she realized she'd no notion in the world what her husband's life was like, how he'd spent his days before their marriage, how he would spend them once they went their separate ways. And why should she care? That she did, that she wanted to know . . . oh, so many things! . . . was nonsensical.

He is a man, and that is sufficient knowledge, she insisted silently. Something would prove her right, that in some way he was as difficult as she knew he must be. She wanted nothing to do with him.

Nothing.

The door opened, and she looked up, her lips tightly compressed. "You," she said, recognizing the inevitability of his arriving at just that particular moment.

Ian's brows rose. "My dear, I thought it was agreed we'd spend our mornings together."

"Did you? I've no recollection of agreeing to anything."

"Just the mornings?"

How, she wondered, could he sound so wistful? Coming from such a big man, it was more endearing than if he were childishly small. She sighed. "What have you in mind?"

"You enjoy walking. I wondered if you would come with me when I went back up onto the downs with a gun." He came a step or two farther into the room. "Do you shoot?"

"Shoot? . . . Oh, yes." Serena nodded. And then with a touch of mischievousness added, "My brothers were *often* bored."

Ian grinned. "I shall enjoy discovering the things they taught you. Come." He held out his hand and tipped his fingers coaxingly. "We will see if there is a gun suitable for your use."

Much to her surprise, Serena enjoyed the morning. Ian didn't comment on the fact she never once attempted to shoot anything—a forbearance her brothers would *not* have had! And she especially enjoyed the company of the dog. Her father firmly discouraged pets. Any show of softer emotion had been rejected as weakening, and love for a pet was, therefore, to be avoided.

"He truly is an excellent animal," said Ian, who enjoyed watching Serena drop to one knee to take a bird from the retriever, pet him, and tell him what a good boy he was. Serena looked up, her face glowing both from the exercise and from pleasure. "And you are truly beautiful," said Ian softly. "That wonderful hair. Do you never cover it?"

Instantly, Serena's smile faded. She rose and turned

away, her back stiff. "It is unnecessary to pour the butter boat over me."

"The truth was startled from me by what I saw."

"The truth?"

"My dear, has no one told you how lovely you are? Best of all, it is not a surface beauty which will fade in a few years, as happens to all too many young women. In you it is bone deep. You will only improve with the years."

"Nonsense!"

"Modesty is all very well, my love, but you must accept compliments with more grace. Not that my words were, at that instant, a mere compliment. As I said, the truth was startled from me by your glowing complexion, by your happy mien. I must apologize if my speaking spoiled your mood."

"I do not understand you," she said, each word distinct.

He stared down at her, his deep-set eyes hooded. "Perhaps," he suggested, "if you were not always looking for hidden motives behind my every word, if you merely accepted the truth for the truth, you would find I am easily understood."

"It cannot be truth. It is impossible you speak truth."

"In this case, my dear, all you need do is look in your mirror."

"I look in a mirror every time I do my hair."

"Exceptionally lovely hair it is, too. Someday I'd like to see it let down, flowing around you . . ." Ian sighed. "Enough, my lady. We might spar all day and get nowhere. Besides"—he smiled a quick smile—"we need another bird."

"There is always far more food on the table than necessary. *One* bird is sufficient for the two of us."

"For *our* table, yes, but what of the servants'? Besides, this is for the brace I mean to give the gardener's wife."

Serena frowned. "Why do you kill birds for the servants?"

"Do they not work hard, deserve good food?" he asked in that calm tone she was coming to associate with him.

"They can be fed far more cheaply if . . ." Serena closed her mouth with a snap. "That is my father speaking." She smiled. The smile broadened. "Indeed, *yes*. *Do* let us find another bird, Ian McMurrey." She chuckled. "Lots of birds!"

The dog had lain quietly panting at Ian's feet. Appearing to approve her words, he jumped up and led them up a narrow track bordered by brush and high grass. It was a difficult path for Serena, but she managed, determined she would not show weakness before this man who had yet to show her his temper.

And since he was a man, he must have one. Serena spent some time wondering what would bring it to the surface.

After dinner Ian excused himself and disappeared down the hall to the room he'd adopted for an office. He must, he said, answer his correspondence, particularly the letter from his brother. Serena watched him go and realized, with amazement, how ambivalent she felt. She was far too honest not to admit *why*. She had enjoyed their morning. The blasted man was a mystery, one which teased her convictions and confused her expectations, upsetting her no end.

Serena wandered outside and stared blindly at the lead-gray Channel, so changed from yesterday's morning-blue and, later, when clouds drew in, darker greens and deeper blues. She sighed, very nearly wishing she did not have long hours to fill before she would see Ian again. She *had* enjoyed their walk on the downs. Had enjoyed watching him bring down his birds, enjoyed the dog's

antics before Ian called him to order and he behaved,
very seriously, as a proper hunting dog should. Would
Ian allow her to have a dog?

But what am I thinking? Shock brought her up short.
Once free, she could have a dozen dogs if she wished
and with no need of any man's permission!

After a moment Serena strode off, heading along the
path toward the boundary wall. When she reached it, she
leaned on an untumbled portion and stared out onto the
wilder land of the headland beyond. Here and there a
sheep munched course grass. Several ewes had lambs,
and she smiled to see them play.

And then she heard a faint bleat which sounded somehow desperate. Her eyes searched systematically for a
sick or hurt animal. The sound came again—from the
direction of the water. There were low rough cliffs along
the shore just here, climbing higher the farther along one
went. It occurred to Serena that a sheep might have
slipped over the edge, might be trapped somewhere. She
looked around for help, but no one was in sight.

She frowned, debated with herself, and decided that
until she knew the problem, it was silly to go for help.
Sheep were stupid. It was quite possible this one would
discover a simple solution to its situation and there would
be no need to waste someone's time coming to its aid.

Where the tumbled wall was low she might easily get
around the end, but she recalled the warning that the
coast just there was not to be trusted. With a sigh, Serena
bundled up her skirts, climbed the barrier, and dropped
to the far side . . . hearing the sound of tearing cloth as
she did so.

She twisted around to check the damage, but gave it
up when another desperate bleat called her back to duty.
She soon discovered the difficulty. A rough path led
down the cliff side, and the half-grown animal had fallen

from it to a narrow shelf from which it could not scramble up.

Serena studied the situation. A young animal and not large . . . could she rescue it herself? Very carefully, watching each step, Serena made her way down the path. She talked to the sheep as she went, which only made the idiotic beast cry more loudly and more often. Reaching the path's end, Serena realized she'd been misled when looking down from above. The ledge was far lower than she'd thought, and it *would* be necessary to go for help after all. She sighed, turned . . .

. . . and slipped on grass wet from sea spray.

Almost gracefully, although she grabbed and grasped at everything in reach, Serena slid over the edge and joined the sheep on the ledge. Once she was certain she'd not fall further, down into the low but determined waves, she waited for her heartbeat to steady. The sheep, sheeplike, was huddled as far from her as it could get.

"Stupid beast. See what you have done!"

The sheep blatted.

"Yes, it is all very well to insist it is my own fault, but now what do we do?"

She stared at the sheer walls trapping them. Suddenly she was pushed from behind. She fell to her knees, very nearly over the edge, but caught herself by scrabbling and scrambling and rolling against the back wall. The sheep poked his nose into her face, and Serena, already panicked by the near fall into the water, screamed.

Carefully, moving slowly, she pushed herself up until her back was against a wall. One hand hurt rather badly and she looked at it, discovered it was scraped bloody. She checked the other. It had scratches and two broken nails. Why, she wondered, had she not put on her gloves? But she had not, so there was no help for her poor hands. Still, she could prevent more damage, perhaps. As she belatedly and with care drew on her gloves, Serena looked at the sheep, who stared at her.

"*You* are no help at all," she said.

The sheep blatted.

"In fact, I wonder if I dare allow you to remain here with me if you mean to behave in such an unsociable fashion. Do you think I might lift you up so you, at least, may escape?"

Planning every move, Serena captured the creature. She lifted the kicking animal and shoved it until its front feet reached the path. She swore, using every word she'd ever heard her brothers use, when the sheep's flailing hooves raked along her arms and shoulders. Dirt, dust, clods, and stones rained down on her, powdering her face and hair, getting in her eyes, and adding more dirt to her gown.

But the sheep disappeared, and, despite sore places, despite the dirt and the bruise on her cheek which had been hit by a rather large stone, Serena felt a modicum of satisfaction. Except . . . although the sheep was safe, she herself was still trapped.

How long, she wondered, before someone missed her? Serena reverted to her own favorite swear word.

"Oh, piffle!" she shouted into the wind, which relieved her feelings a trifle. But only a trifle, for what could she do? The afternoon was her own. It would not occur to Ian McMurrey to miss her until she was late for the evening meal.

If then.

The panic she'd pushed aside returned: Perhaps he would think she was avoiding him, as she had given him every reason to do. He'd have no reason to feel concern. Serena looked over the edge at the rolling waves and wondered if the water was a trifle higher than when she'd first seen it.

Was the tide coming in? How high would it rise?

Serena's heart banged harshly in her chest as it occurred to her that high water might cover the ledge. How did one know? Lying down, she leaned out and studied the cliff below her. Ah! Was not that change in color an indication of the tide's highest point? At least she need not worry she'd be swept from her perch by waves!

But then a sudden chill breeze swept along the coastline, lifting spray to dampen her. To the west, a different sort of cloud appeared and quickly piled high. Serena, noting them, shivered. Perhaps she need not fear the tide, but what of wind? What of rain? Rain and wind she could bear, but—she swallowed hard— what if it stormed?

Storms meant thunder and lightning. She hated storms. More truthfully, she feared them, irrational as she knew it to be. Serena shivered again, not entirely from fear but partially from the cold wind. Perhaps she would come down with an inflammation of the lungs simply because she'd been silly enough to try to rescue a stranded sheep.

Ah! But she *had* rescued the creature, had she not? So in that, at least, she was successful.

But was such success worth finding oneself carried off by illness? Definitely not. Serena turned back to the bit of wall below the path and studied it. Perhaps if she tugged that stone out . . . and that one . . . could she form a means of climbing up?

She worked carefully, but even with the gloves, she broke another nail while digging out a recalcitrant rock.

Five

Ian glanced up when for the second time a flash of distant lightning broke his concentration. He went to the window and looked west. Thunderheads boiled higher, roiled, the wind driving them. Ian turned on his heel and went to the hall.

"Has my wife returned?" he asked the footman on duty there.

"Haven't seen her ladyship, sir."

Ian's frown deepened. "Discover if anyone has. Send a maid to her room. The weather is worsening, and I don't like to think of her out and about."

"No, sir. Promises rain before nightfall, it does. I'll see if her ladyship has come in."

Ian paced the small entry, irritated by its lack of space. He was convinced his wife was in difficulties. He sensed it deep inside just as, long ago he'd felt that need to cut short a walking tour and return home to his mother's deathbed. As, more recently, he'd been forced to go to Jamie. And as in the deep past, when a mere boy, he went out into driving snow to find his favorite dog and discovered the animal caught in a trap.

He'd rescued the dog—Ian smiled wryly—and then needed rescuing himself. How his father had scolded!

The smile faded. Now another storm brewed. *And somewhere out there his wife was in trouble.* He knew it as he knew his own name. The baize-covered servants' door opened, and he turned.

"No one has seen her ladyship since you ate, sir."

"She must be found." Ian's heavy brows drew together. "We must organize a search party. Tell the men to assemble on the terrace."

The terrace was what Ian needed for pacing, but every time he turned west he saw the clouds piling higher at such an alarming rate that his fears intensified. Wind. Very likely buckets of rain.

Where was she?

The dog Ian had befriended raced flat-out up the lawn toward him, catching his attention. Something hung from the animal's mouth, and Ian paused in his pacing, waited, wondering. Anything was better than the near panic seething in and around him much as the clouds did in the western sky. The dog approached. Ian reached for him. Playfully the dog backed off.

"Here boy," said Ian sharply, having had a better look at the thing the dog carried. It was a lady's glove and very like those Lady Serena wore. "Come," said Ian, in a firm demand for obedience.

The dog crouched. Ears down and almost on his belly, he crawled close. His big, moist eyes begged forgiveness as he gave up his prize. Absently patting the dog's head, Ian stared at the "S" embroidered on the hemmed edge of the mangled cloth. Lady Serena's? It must be. But if it belonged to his wife, where had the dog found it?

The gardener rounded the corner of the house as three male indoor servants came out the front door. At the moment, Ian was interested only in the first. "Your dog brought me this. I believe it is my wife's. Will he lead us to her?"

The man frowned, his thumb and forefinger going to his chin, which he tugged gently. "Don't know, do I?" he asked. "Never tried him *finding* things."

Ian sighed. He dared not trust to the dog altogether, although the creature's help was their best hope of finding Serena quickly. He'd take the dog and the gardener and send the others off in other directions. "Do any of you ride?"

"Ta groom's coming, sir," said the oldest indoor man in a slow southern voice. "Bringin' the old saddle mare. Thought it might be needed."

"Very good. He must ride to the village. You men go that and"—he pointed in each direction—"that and that way. I'll go along the coast to the east."

"Knows not to go beyond the wall," said one man. "Warned her."

"Yes, but it is her favorite walk, that direction. If anyone finds her, return with her and ring the alarm bell. Everyone within hearing will know to come in. Now. Off with you."

"And me, sir?" asked the gardener.

"The dog is yours." Ian clutched Serena's glove. "I hope you can make him take us to her." Reluctantly, he handed the bit of cloth to the gardener, who knelt beside his dog. Resenting every moment's delay, Ian watched the two have what appeared to be a serious discussion. It seemed forever, although it was likely only a minute or so, before the man rose to his feet.

"Sassy will do his best, but I don't promise . . ."

"I know. Let's go."

The gardener waved the glove near the dog's nose. "Find, boy. Find her."

As Ian expected, the dog set off toward the wall. They reached it as lightning flashed again and the first cold drops of rain fell. The dog jumped up on the stones, looking back at the men as if telling them to hurry. Then he jumped down into the rough land beyond.

Ian frowned. "She knows she's not to go out there."

"Sass, boy!" The dog paused but did not return. He

looked at them, moved on a bit, looked again. "He wants us to follow, sir."

"She knows . . ."

"What should we do, sir?"

"If she went on, why over the wall where it is difficult rather than near the shore where the wall has tumbled?"

"Avoiding where the land might give way?"

"Yes. A reasonable notion, that." Ian, thinking, looked at where he'd placed his hands. He noticed a wisp of blue threads caught in a crack, and his head rose. He scanned the pasture. Sassy barked. Twice. Ian crossed the wall, wind-blown rain pushing him toward the blurred figure of the dog who ran on, disappeared . . .

"Serena!" yelled Ian . . . and, faintly, heard a reply. "Where are you?"

"Ian!" His name. *She had used his name*! Ian picked up his pace.

"Careful, sir. Pretty close to the edge here."

"Serena, where are you?"

"Nearly down to the water," came her call, louder now.

"Down . . . Why the devil . . . ? No, now is not the time," he muttered. "Where'd the dog go?"

"Good boy," they heard. "Oh, you very good dog. No! Oh, now see what you've done, you silly beast."

Ian chuckled. Already chilled by the wind-blown rain, irritated now that he was no longer fearful, still he could not refrain from chuckling at his wife's words.

"Here, sir," said the gardener. "A path of sorts."

"Careful," called Serena. "It ends suddenly."

"That'll be wet, sir," warned the gardener. "Slippery like."

Ian gave the crude path a grim look, nodded, and, careful of every step, started down. "Serena?"

"It was a sheep."

"What? A sheep? No, tell me later! Describe your situation."

"I'm on a ledge just too far below the path for me to get up to it."

Ian heard that he was near. Giving no thought to what the wet would do to his trousers, he knelt, walked his hands forward until he felt the edge, and then, inching forward, looked down just in time to receive the dog's wet tongue and be scratched by one scrabbling paw.

"Yes, all right," he said irritably. He grasped Sassy by his scruff and hauled him up. He heard Serena laugh. "I am glad you find humor in this," he said.

"Oh, yes. You cannot know what a relief it is to be aware that one must close one's eyes when helping an animal up over a cliff edge! Last time, I got a face full of dirt and a bit in my eyes, which was *most* uncomfortable. This time, I merely got my face dirty."

With the dog on its way up the path, Ian again looked over the edge. Less than a yard below was that damp and dirty face. Even so she glowed.

"We have a small difficulty here," he said

She lifted her arms. "Can you not pull me up?"

"Very likely I could, but you'd be scratched and your gown tattered beyond repair. Would you not prefer that I get ropes and retrieve you with a trifle more of your dignity intact?"

"The gown is long out of date, already torn, and no great loss. As to scratches, what are a few more to add to what I've got?"

"Very well." He looked over his shoulder to where the gardener, hugging the cliff wall, shivered. "I will inch back as I pull Lady Serena up. Warn me if I move toward the edge."

For once in his life, Ian was glad he was oversized and strong with it. It took nearly every bit of muscle he had to lift Lady Serena straight up. "Put your arms around my neck," he ordered.

When she hesitated, he repeated himself sternly. Reluctantly, Lady Serena submitted. She felt his warm breath on her forehead, and on her ear as she was pulled higher. His quickening breath made her heartbeat speed up as her predicament had not. A pulse pounded at her temple.

Once Ian had her arms around his neck, he pushed against the ground with his hands and slowly reared back onto his knees. When she was on his level, he pulled her close, his forehead pressed into her shoulder.

"Serena, Serena, Serena," he muttered into the dirt on her dress. "What am I to do with you?"

"Get me home?" she asked in a shaky voice, uncertain why she suddenly felt exceedingly trembly, but quite certain it could not be good for her.

Ian chuckled. He pulled her up as he rose to his feet and, one arm holding her close, put a hand under her chin. He stared down at her and laughed. "You will not be happy to have others see you as you are now." Very gently he wiped a finger across her cheek, the rain and dirt smearing into mud. "No. Not at all."

She shivered.

Contrite, he frowned. "You are soaked to the skin and cold, and I should not tease you. We must get back to the house, get you warm and clean again."

She brushed a grimy hand across her rain-wet face, adding to her unladylike appearance. "You cannot know what a relief it is just to be up off that shelf! I want to savor it."

"Hmm. Do you think it possible," he asked with a rumbling laugh, "that you do your savoring while moving toward more comfortable surroundings?" One brow arched as, he smiled down at her affectionately. "Perhaps you have not noticed it is raining?"

She chuckled that warm, lovely laugh he was coming to love. "I am being inconsiderate?" She tipped her head.

"Very," he said with overdone solemnity.

"I see," she said just as gravely. The two grinned at each other, and she held out her hand and then flinched when lightning flashed and thunder rumbled. "Perhaps you will help me up? Frankly, I'm not certain I can do it myself."

That, thought Ian, *is an admission you once would not have made for all the tea in China.* When they reached the top, Ian told the gardener to get himself home quickly. He was to ring the alarm bell, calling in anyone near enough to hear it . . .

". . . and then," Ian called to the man's receding back, "tell the kitchen that hot water is needed. We, at least, will want baths. Get yourself dry and warm. And," added Ian loudly, "tell Cook to give Sassy the very best bone in the larder!"

Ian put his arm around Serena, felt how she shivered, and took it away. He removed his jacket and insisted she put it on before he took her back under his arm.

He was pleased she came willingly. Could this be considered a victory? Only, he decided, to a skirmish. She had been frightened and was cold and wet and had the sense to know his body heat would help.

But she allowed that help! So, yes, he'd won a skirmish, and that was good . . . but how many battles must he face in order to win her trust? Her *love*? Deep inside, Ian grimaced. When, he wondered, had it become so very important that he win her love? A love to match his own.

Love.

Self-awareness twisted the secret inner grimace still more. Because *of course* he had fallen in love. He had ever been a romantic, had he not? So, in this situation, wed to a strikingly lovely and intelligent woman, a woman who needed him . . . how could it be otherwise?

An hour later, Serena was tucked into her bed, a fire roaring in her grate and a warm brick at her feet. She wore her warmest nightgown, covered by a Scottish wool robe Ian had donated to the cause.

Ian, also in night attire, sat at ease in an oversized chair. He was secretly amused by his bride's determined nonchalance as she sat in her bed, hands folded primly in her lap, and told him of her adventure. *She makes*, he thought, *a good tale of it, too.*

She told of discussing the situation with the sheep and the sheep's reply. And her long talk with the dog. "Sassy thought it a game and would drop my glove back down to me. I'd given up making steps, you see. The earth was too crumbly and I feared I'd slip into the water, so when Sassy appeared I was relieved. I assumed someone, you perhaps, was with him. Only"—Lady Serena sobered—"when I called, no one answered." She sighed. "I almost gave up trying to get Sassy to take my glove to you. And, of course, I wasn't certain that was what he did even when he ran off. And that storm . . ."

When she didn't go on, Ian took a closer look at her pale skin and staring eyes. "You dislike storms?"

"I . . . of course not. Why would one dislike storms?" She cast him a quick worried glance.

"My mother," said Ian, "feared storms." He made silent apologies to that long-dead, once fearless woman. "My father fretted when one rose up and he was not home to comfort her."

Serena's breath whooshed out. "I too fear them. I was almost certain you would not scold me."

"Scold you? For what?"

"Father considered it a weakness. Knowing I was afraid, he shoved me out of doors into every storm that came. When I grew older and could pretend indifference, he stopped. After that"—she cast Ian a conspiratorial glance—"I made certain he was elsewhere when I indulged my ridiculous terrors."

"What a very stupid man your father must be," said Ian calmly.

Inside he was anything but calm. How could the man have been so cruel? Or was he the sort who found a perverted pleasure in another's fear, another's pain? Such people were rare, but they did exist.

After a brief silence, her tone careful, Serena asked, "Stupid?"

"Hmm? Oh. Your father. A person's fears, such as yours of storms, would, I think, be worsened by his treatment. It seems to me a stupid thing to do. That is all." It wasn't all, but he wasn't about to go into his true thoughts on the subject.

"I disagree," she said firmly. "He is not so much stupid as knowingly cruel—"

Her words reinforced Ian's thoughts and reminded him she was a strong woman who did not like or need subterfuge.

"—a vicious man," she finished. A bleak look entered her eyes, and her lips compressed into a thin line.

"You are thinking of your mother."

Ian had not made it a question, and Serena cast him a wondering look. "Yes," she admitted.

"You fear for her." He wanted to reach out to his wife, comfort her, but he dared not touch her. Particularly here in her bedroom, where she might easily misunderstand. Instead he said, "Once we are settled in London, I will invite her to visit."

"He will not allow it."

"Nevertheless, I will invite her. And when we visit them, I will give her a purse of money which she can hide. If things become more than she can bear, she may use it to escape."

Serena's eyes rounded. "I wonder if she'd know how . . ."

"How to escape?"

"Hmm." She continued to stare at him as if he were a freak in a fair.

Ian chuckled softly but ignored her unasked questions, saying instead, "Then together we will make a plan. We will write out instructions so she will know exactly what to do!"

"If my father never discovers the existence of purse or plan, then it is an excellent idea. Except"—she pursed her lips for a moment—"could she keep such a dire secret?"

"She is your mother, of course, but"—Ian frowned— "Serena, I have known such mousy little women. I cannot *know* she is the same, but in my experience, the one talent such women have is keeping secrets from their brutes of husbands."

Serena thought about it. "Perhaps. Besides, Father believes her utterly cowed. He is unlikely to suspect."

"Excellent. Serena," he added, "I wonder if, given our situation, you would prefer to go to London earlier than I'd meant to do."

She cast him a quick suspicious look. "Does it truly make a difference what I wish?"

"Of course it does. If you are enjoying our stay, then we will remain here. If you think you might find more to amuse you in London, then we will go to London."

"And it makes no difference whatsoever to you?"

"I like the country, Serena. I live on our Scottish estate much of each year. But I also live in London. I've friends here in the south, and I've bits of business to which I must give my attention with some regularity." He resettled himself in his chair, trying very hard not to reveal that a recent letter suggested some of that business could use immediate attention.

"Business?" She reminded herself it was none of *her* business what he did! "Never mind," she added before he responded. "Ian, you will allow me to think about it until morning, will you not?"

"Of course." He rose to his feet, towering over her. "Serena, you are all right, are you not?"

"Except for the scratches and one or two bruises, I got off lightly."

"You will tell me if you begin to feel ill?"

She frowned. "You mean an ague?"

"Yes." Ian saw again that look of confusion which bothered him so much.

"If you insist," she said, hesitantly.

"Why do I suspect your father would not allow you to admit to illness?"

Her lips tightened into a hint of a smile. "Because it would be true?"

"I happen to believe illness should be treated promptly." One brow arched. *Before* it has time to take a good hold of a body."

"Then I will tell you the instant I feel the least sign of . . . of anything adverse."

"Excellent," he said. Pensively, he stared at her . . .

. . . until she plucked nervously at her bed covers.

Then, noticing her fidgets and recognizing them for a nervous reaction to his staring, Ian gave himself a slight shake, told Serena a brisk good night, and took himself off to his own room. Had he really hoped she might ask that he remain with her until the storm passed over?

Or that, when their supper trays were brought up, she would suggest they eat in the cozy intimacy of her bedroom? Ian sighed. If he had, then it was a *forlorn hope*, as was said in the military of the predestined failure of some tactically necessary attack. The greenest recruit, surveying this particular battlefield, would have told him that!

With such depressing thoughts in his head, Ian would have been surprised to discover that, after he left her,

Lady Serena stared blindly at nothing at all for a very long time. Alone, she could no longer push from her mind those moments on the cliff path when she'd been held in his arms. That soft, warm breath on her temple. The strength of him and the welcome heat of his body . . .

. . . And that odd tingly feeling that began deep inside and spread until she trembled and quivered and was very shaky indeed. As she did now . . . ? A bit? It was not an entirely bad feeling, was it? Nothing like the shivers one suffered when merely wet and cold.

What, she wondered, caused it? The problem teased her mind to such a degree that she was quite surprised when her guttering candle brought her back to the world . . .

. . . and the discovery that the storm had passed, becoming no more than a distant, no longer fearsome, thundery mutter.

The next morning, when Ian finished perusing his letters, Serena said, "I have decided London might make an interesting change. On two occasions, I was taken into Tunbridge Wells for a day's shopping, but that is the only city I know. Is London *very* much larger?"

"Much," said Ian dryly. "For several years now, I've rented a house and kept it staffed. It isn't the largest of dwellings, but should be sufficient for our needs unless you decide to hold a ball."

She blinked at the notion she might even consider such a thing. Why would he think she would hold a *ball*? Ah! But the house was too small, so of course he knew she could do no such thing!

"Still, one can always rent a ballroom if such is your desire," he continued, compounding a confusion she'd thought satisfactorily explained. "I must see to providing you an allowance, must I not? You will need far more pin money than in the past. The bills from your modiste and others of that ilk will be sent directly to me. . . .

What else? Ah! The housekeeping. You are accustomed to keeping household accounts, are you not?"

She nodded.

"Then you will know what to do in that capacity."

"Why did you assume I have done such a thing?" asked Serena, her shock at his generosity fading as her suspicious nature roused.

"My knowledge of your mother makes me doubt she had charge of the household. Not when an intelligent, competent, and generous daughter was willing to take up the burden."

Serena frowned. "It is true. But I do not see how, when you have never spoken to my mother, you can know her so well."

"Serena, I am thirty-six. I am, I hope, not unintelligent and pride myself on being observant. And I *like* people. I freely admit I make a study of them. Your mother is, unfortunately, a not uncommon type."

Serena pounced on the word. "Unfortunately?"

"Yes. I am horrified when someone is not allowed to exercise their God given talents. Your father is an extreme case, of course, but far too many men believe themselves less manly if their wives or even their sons have too much power. Witness our king's feelings toward Prinny! Such men make every decision, take away all independence, and generally act as if others were put on earth only to serve them."

"You disagree?"

"Have I not said so? I know many strong, capable women, so how can I think the female naturally inferior? Besides, it demeans me."

"Demeans *you*?"

"It is a blot on humanity and, therefore, a blot on *me*."

"Such women are not your responsibility . . ." she muttered and then, with a quick glance his way, bit her lip.

"I have never quite managed to believe I've no responsibility if I am in a position to offer help."

"My father . . ."

"Your father would, of course, disagree," he said when she paused.

"Vehemently!" She winced.

"Don't look as if you expect to be slapped. I have told you I will not use violence toward you." He sighed. "I would not in any case, but toward my wife? Never."

"Not? Never?"

"I am a big man, Serena—"

He grinned when she nodded firm agreement.

"—and, frankly, it is a nuisance."

"A *nuisance?*"

"You are surprised? But, my dear, *think*. When young I grew rapidly. All my friends were smaller than I. Serena, can you not see how *unfair* it was? I could not, you see, fight with them without gaining the reputation of a bully!"

Serena thought of her eldest and largest brother, who used his size and strength with pleasure *because* of the advantage it gave him. She sighed. "My world is topsy-turvy. Or perhaps it is merely that I dream. You cannot be real."

Ian grinned a slow grin. "Not real? Oh, yes, Serena. Very real." *And someday I will prove it in the time-honored way of a man with a woman!* Wondering how long it would be until that day came, it was Ian's turn to sigh.

Uncertain why his tone unsettled her, Serena drew in a deep breath. "We have traveled far from the original topic," she said. "When would you wish to leave for London?"

"Day after tomorrow," he responded promptly. "It will rush you, I fear, since a woman's packing is such a finicky chore, but I believe you will like London and I look forward to introducing you to it. Besides"—his eyes glinted and his expression was that of one asking another to share a joke—"I am informed last night's storm is only the beginning and that we may expect any number to follow. Storms over a city are far less disturbing than in the country, so you will prefer to be there for that reason as well."

She found nothing humorous in this topic. "Less disturbing? How can that be?"

Ian tipped his head, considering exactly what he did mean. "I suppose the crowding of individuals all together makes it a sharing sort of thing, or perhaps the everyday, to-be-expected, noise of town life makes the storm's clamor less noticeable?" He shrugged. "I do not know *why*, but I believe it true." He rose to his feet, gathering up his post. "I've several letters I must answer immediately, Serena. Will you have any to add to the pouch I'll send to the village to be taken up by the coach?"

"Letters?" Serena looked, she was certain, as startled as she felt. "I think—"

It crossed her mind she should respond to Lady Renwick's kind letter and that she should try to send a reassuring note to her mother even if her father was unlikely to give it to her.

She changed *not* to "—yes."

Perhaps she could write to Mr. Morton, who, knowing the situation, might make an encouraging comment to her mother. Serena adjourned to her bedroom. She sat at the small desk and tried to remember the last letter she'd written. It had been years, more than a decade, since she'd penned a stilted thank-you note to her godmother for the present of a dress her father had never allowed her to wear.

Far too fine for a hoyden, he'd sneered. A muscle jumped in Serena's jaw. She had *wanted* to wear that dress. Wanted so badly to be seen in it, looking pretty and demure and proper and *like all the other girls who came to church each Sunday!* She sighed at the memory and then tucked it away into the past where it belonged.

The note to her mother was quickly penned. She could say so little, since her father would, of course, read it first. But her note might ease her mother's fears. Assuming she was allowed to know of it.

The letter to the vicar was nothing more than a masterpiece of the commonplace and soon done since she could not explain *why* she wrote it.

The letter to Lady Renwick was more difficult. Serena had no notion how to respond to her ladyship's generous offer of friendship. She reread the words and was still unsure how to interpret them. Ian's friends had wondered if she was ugly? Well, she was no beauty, but certainly not ugly. A shrew? Hopefully she was not that either . . . but how could Lady Renwick know on such short acquaintance?

That Ian McMurrey was a nice man . . . well, he *seemed* to be. Still, he was a man and, for that reason alone, Serena could not bring herself to trust him, although she admitted, in the privacy of her mind, she *wished* she could.

And what did her ladyship mean by his "work," his "feeling so strongly" about the "subject"? So far, Ian had not explained, as Lady Renwick seemed certain he would. But neither had Serena asked him to do so when he mentioned business. But—Serena's chin rose a notch and her mouth firmed—why should she? Why, in fact, did she want to?

Because, she admitted, she wanted to learn more about this man to whom she was married. Temporarily married, she reminded herself. It was none of her business *now* and, in a very few months, would be none of her business *ever*! Not if Ian actually gave her her freedom. No, she need know nothing about Ian McMurrey.

So why, she wondered, did she so often find her curiosity roused, so often wish she knew more? Serena sighed, pushed the disturbing thoughts away, and drew paper close. She dipped her pen and . . .

. . . allowed the ink to dry as she searched her mind for words proper to the occasion. She dipped the pen again, and again could find nothing to say. Irritation filled her. This was ridiculous. Lady Renwick was merely a pleasant lady who had written kind words. A simple thank you was required if nothing else.

Serena found it was not so very difficult after all to pen such words. She went on to mention how surprised she'd been to be introduced to a real live tiger, and still more surprised to find the creature responding. From there it was easy to mention the gardener's dog and describe how Sassy had helped rescue her from yesterday's predicament . . . and then to explain that they were off to London sooner than expected . . . and, finally, squeezing the words in at the bottom of the page, Serena's hope they'd meet again.

She stared at those last few words, exceedingly surprised to discover they were true. She did hope to meet Lady Renwick again. Serena, wiping the pen nib, began reading from the top . . . and felt renewed amazement that once she'd begun, she'd found so much to say.

But was it acceptable? *Did* one tell perfect strangers such things? Even though one had made a humorous story of it? Oh, dear, what if Ian didn't wish his friends to know they were cutting short their month alone? That thought roused a familiar anxiety, and Serena, who if she were a rider would be the sort who always faced her fences, picked up the letter, gathered up the notes to her mother and the vicar, and went to find her husband.

He was standing by the window in the room he'd chosen for his study and turned as she entered. She thrust the letter at him. Looking at her face rather than at the page, he took it.

"Read it."

He frowned ever so slightly but obeyed. "Well?"

"Is it proper? Did I say anything I should not?"

"Perfectly proper, and what did you fear you should not have said?"

Serena explained, and he chuckled. She shook her head. "I will never understand you."

Ian turned back to the window. He found it easier to speak half-truths if he did not look at her. "Merely believe that I am not naturally underhanded nor usually a sneak and perhaps you will find it easier."

Not a lie or half-truth after all. It was extremely *unnatural*, this tricking her into getting to know him, leading her into being easy in his presence . . . and, if he were very lucky, guiding her toward a growing love for him! Would it fall out as he wished, or had he placed himself in a position where he would, one day, perjure himself before the archbishop, fulfilling what had been an implied promise but not a true one?

"Leave your letters on my desk," he said a trifle gruffly. "I will address and seal the one to Lady Renwick."

Serena walked to his desk and glanced down at the address on the letter lying there. Her brows rose. Headmaster? Of a School for Deserving Boys? Forcibly, she tore her gaze away. She turned it toward Ian and found him staring out the window. There was something in his posture—a sadness, despair? Or perhaps it was grief? Was he remembering Jamie? Serena discovered she wanted to cross the room, wanted to touch him, let him know she was there if there were anything she could do.

Frightened by such feelings, Serena turned on her heel and, even more quickly than usual, removed herself from his presence. She went directly to the sitting room she'd adopted as her own. Once there, she paced from corner to corner, moving aside a small table in one spot and, in another, pushing an exceedingly ugly Sheraton chair out of her way. Then she began to scold herself thoroughly for weakening toward Ian in the slightest way.

He was a man. He was *not* to be trusted, and she would *not* fall into the trap of thinking he was. *She would not.*

It was quite simple, really. All she need do was survive the next few months until he did whatever must be done to get the annulment! Then she'd be free and could do something for women who were forced from their homes by fathers and brothers who considered them "fallen" *when the truth was they'd been tripped or pushed!*

Had that woman she'd seen not so long ago survived? And her baby? Had the few coins Serena managed to slip her helped? Serena felt again the anger and horror she'd experienced when her father had decreed that the stranger be carted into the next parish, where, very likely, she received the same treatment and was carried onward.

It was so unfair! She would *do* something. She *would* . . .

Serena sighed. She had no notion what she could do beyond buying a house and somehow getting the word around that help was available to those who needed it. That there were problems with her simple plan she readily admitted. For instance, she'd no desire to waste time or money on sluts who freely chose their way of life. Yet, how did one distinguish the truly fallen women from the unfairly treated ones she wished to aid? Still . . . somewhere there must be a solution, and somehow she'd find it.

It occurred to her that it was not impossible that, in London, there might be like-minded souls with whom she could discuss the problem. Among the clergy, perhaps. But if they existed, how would one find them?

Serena bumped into a chair, stubbed her toe, and decided this was no room for proper pacing. She found a warm shawl and went to the terrace, where there was space for vigorous movement.

Not ten minutes later, Ian, looking for the same freedom to move, came to the door. His brows arched at the sight of his bride's swishing skirts as she strode steadily away from him, her head bowed and her hands loosely clasped behind her. The faintest of smiles tipped one side of Ian's mouth, a sardonic expression narrowing his eyes. *If my wife makes a habit of tramping back and forth in this energetic fashion, then it behooves me to see that our every residence provides space for it. Lots of space.*

Ian, after all, all too often required room for the very same activity!

Six

London, Lady Serena discovered, was fascinating. It was also hurried, dirty, and noisy. And frightening. So many people. So many carriages and carts. So much confusion.

But there were shops and bookstores and museums, to say nothing of historical edifices side by side with modern squares. Ian took her here and there and back and around and, best of all, introduced her to one or two ladies she liked quite well on first acquaintance.

One of them sat across from her at that moment.

"Yes, Lady Serena, you were correctly informed," Mrs. Ralston responded to a comment. "It is extremely dangerous to venture into such areas. The filth and sickness are obvious deterrents, of course, but pickpockets would have your reticule before you walked ten yards, and the women steal the clothes off your back. And what would happen *then*, my dear—well!" Mrs. Ralston's mouth primmed. "My dear, you must *not* go into the slums, however curious you may be."

Serena bit her lip, thinking. "But how does one learn what is needed if one does not look for oneself?"

"You may accept that there is *everything* to be done." Mrs. Ralston sighed. "And nothing."

"That is a contradiction."

"You do not understand."

"Exactly! I do not understand. And I cannot unless I see for myself."

"Then, my dear," said Lady Serena's visitor repressively, "may I suggest you ask your husband to arrange it? If it is truly important to you, perhaps he will organize a drive through a slum so that you may observe from behind the carriage curtains."

"Behind the curtains?"

"You would not wish to be seen, of course. If those poor wretches ever learn you've an interest in the poor, and your face becomes known, you will be besieged by beggars whenever you leave your door!"

Serena frowned. Was it so very difficult to do good? "Mrs. Ralston, when Mr. McMurrey introduced us, did he not say you are active in various charities and good works?"

"I do what I can, my lady." A more lively expression crossed Serena's visitor's face. "Perhaps you would join one or more of my committees?"

"Committees?" *Of what possible use is a committee?* "Perhaps you would explain?"

The lady's eyes glittered. "The one of *most* interest to *you*, Lady Serena, supports a certain boys' school—

Why— Serena withdrew a trifle—*does she look at me in that odiously coy fashion?*

"—here in London. I am sure you know—"

Is that merely an expression, or does she truly think I've knowledge of such a thing?

"—it is run in the new style where the masters teach the older students and, as they reach the higher levels, the older boys help in the teaching of the younger. In this way, many more are reached than by any other method yet devised. It is a wonderful opportunity for the lads, and, as well as taking in paying students, it rescues many a child from the streets, setting his feet on a path to solid citizenry."

"It sounds worthwhile, Mrs. Ralston, but my particular interest is in women who, through no fault of their own, have been ruined by the unthinking or selfish or vicious behavior of some man."

Mrs. Ralston's response was cool. "It is impossible to determine which women have come to that life by choice and which were forced into it. And, my dear, you cannot have thought . . . once a woman is ruined, how else may she earn her bread but . . . but . . ."

"On her back?" asked Serena sweetly.

"Exactly. No decent woman would hire her as a servant. She couldn't be allowed to work with children, of course. And even if she were the best seamstress ever, she would find it difficult to get a place with a *good* modiste. And how else could she earn her bread? Marriage? All too often such girls were badly trained in their own homes, so it would be impossible to *buy* them husbands, even from a class lower than their own! No, it is better to do what one can for the deserving poor than attempt the impossible."

Too intelligent to argue directly, Serena asked, "These charity students of whom you spoke. The ones from the streets. How old would they be?"

"Often it is difficult to determine exactly, but usually between five and nine. No more than twelve at the outside."

"And they have survived pretty much on their own?"

"Yes. It is pitiful. The poor things. Cold and hungry. With pinched little faces. And so eager to learn."

"But they have been earning their bread even at that tender age?" Serena adopted an expression of innocence. "How?" she asked.

"We do not ask. It is better if we do not know exactly how they managed to survive."

"But, of course, an unmarried woman who becomes pregnant—one needn't *ask* how she survives."

"Exactly. It is obvious."

"But, since it is not obvious that the boys you help are thieves or, in some few cases, worse, one may ignore that they have, er, fallen?"

"My dear Lady Serena!" said Mrs. Ralston. The shocked tone turned icy as the woman rose to her feet. "I cannot determine if you are merely obtuse or if you think to bait me. In either case, I fear we must terminate this discussion. Good day."

Mrs. Ralston turned on her heel and found her nose nearly touching Ian's cravat. She glared.

Ian, obviously amused, stepped back and bowed. He watched the lady stalk from the room, her nose in the air, before turning to Serena. He grinned, clapping his hands softly. "Bravo, my excellent wife."

Serena stared after her departing guest, a worried look putting creases in her forehead, but, at his words, she turned. "Ian, I am so sorry. I did not mean . . . well, I did, but still . . ." She put her hands over her face. "Oh, dear."

"Why are you suddenly inarticulate?"

"But you know! I insulted a guest in your home—"

"Our home," he interjected.

"—and it was very wrong of me."

"To the contrary. I'd say you behaved toward her exactly as she deserved."

"She is your friend." When he shook his head, Serena's frown deepened. "I do not understand."

"Lady Cartwright is my friend, my dear. Unfortunately, when we met her ladyship at Mirabele's, she had been accosted by Mrs. Ralston. I was forced to introduce the both of them but should have warned you. Mrs. Ralston likes the cachet of being thought a great philanthropist, but she herself is the first to explain that she has no money and all her efforts go into prying it loose from those who do." A pensive look creased Ian's forehead.

"On the other hand, she gives hugely elaborate parties, is always dressed in the latest fashion, and her husband spends lavishly on his hunters, his dogs, and other sport." He shrugged. "Hers is not the sort of charity I understand."

"I would guess"—Serena was nobody's idiot and her voice was dry as dust—"that she is also careful about the charities with which she allows her name to be associated."

"Oh, yes. Only those already having important names attached to them may expect to enjoy *her* patronage!"

Serena eyed her husband. Was *his* name important? Was it attached to a charity? *A school for deserving boys, for instance?* Dared she ask?

Trying to force the question from a suddenly tight throat, Serena swallowed. Even then she could not bring herself to voice the question. Her father's response to what he considered impertinent queries was quick—and invariably hurt. He had, she decided, taught her well, since she dared not ask if Ian was a patron of the school to whom he'd addressed that letter, even though she was certain he'd not react as her father would have done.

Well . . . *almost* certain.

"Have you plans for this afternoon?" Ian asked when his wife didn't respond to what he'd thought a provocative comment. He had hoped it would be an opening for introducing a discussion of his own charity work, but it was not to be. It seemed Lady Serena had too little interest in him, in his life, to care to know.

Would she ever?

Although Serena wasn't ready to ask about his work, she did need to understand why he didn't scold her. "Ian, I was rude. You will admit it was exceedingly impolite of me to point out her hypocrisy. Should I apologize?"

"Only if you wish to continue the association."

"I've no desire to become intimate with her." Serena

frowned. "Nevertheless, I dislike it in myself that I deliberately baited her."

"Put it from your mind. I only wish Lady Cartwright had been here to enjoy your performance."

"Her ladyship would *approve?*" Serena cast her husband a surprised, almost shocked, look.

"We will ask her. She is in my study, if you'd care to join us?"

"In your *study?*"

"Her ladyship discovered, barely in the nick of time, she claims, that Mrs. Ralston arrived before her. She asked for me instead. I came to oust your guest only to discover you had done so yourself, and very neatly, too. Come?" He offered his arm.

"Should we not," suggested Serena, "ask her here to the salon?"

"My study is more comfortable—"

From her experiences in her father's study, Serena questioned whether that was possible.

"—and we've much to discuss. You will discover that Lady Cartwright is far more knowledgeable about true charity than your late guest will ever be." Ian grinned, his deep-set eyes twinkling. "Just now she has high hopes she can convince me to help her start a school for girls, particularly the female offspring of common soldiers who have died fighting Napoleon and, assuming enough money can be raised, orphans from the poorer classes as well. Come. I will let her explain it to you."

He held out his hand in that coaxing way he had, and somehow, uncertain why, Serena found herself rising and taking it.

Lady Serena retired early that evening. There was much she wished to think about, and she could not bring herself to pretend she would enjoy Ian's proposed visit to the Royal Opera. Hesitantly, fearing a refusal would make him angry, she suggested, "Another night perhaps?"

He merely nodded. She had *almost* expected that mild reaction, but was shocked to be proved correct.

When his wife went to her room directly after dinner, Ian decided to go to his club and, needing the exercise, chose to walk rather than call out his carriage. Once across Piccadilly, he turned into St. James and strolled toward Brook's, nodding to the occasional friend but, by his steady pace, avoiding the necessity of speaking to anyone. Why, he wondered, when he felt less than sociable, had he chosen to indulge in a convivial evening among men? Even men he liked would not, he feared, distract him from his thoughts, his fears, *his hopes* for the future.

He handed his hat and cane to the porter. "Who is in the rooms tonight, Timothy?"

Knowing that a gentleman's query of this sort was not a *general* question, the lackey sorted through his knowledge of Mr. McMurrey's particular friends. "Lord Wendover dined and I believe he now plays at piquet," he offered.

Ian was not in the mood for Tony's insouciant style. Besides, his friend was unlikely to remain long but would soon take himself off to a ball or soiree.

"Anyone else?"

"I believe Lord Merwin may be found in the reading room."

Much better, thought Ian, and flipped the man a coin. He passed the gaming room where the undecorated walls rose starkly bare, offering nothing in the way of distraction to the men seated, nerves at the stretch, at a baccarat table. He started up the graceful cantilevered staircase, turned at the landing, and continued up to the first floor where he went directly to the room in which he was almost certain to find his friend.

"Ian!" exclaimed Lord Merwin. "I had not thought to see you for some time yet."

"We've been in town several days. Lady Serena fears storms, and a weather-wise country man informed me they were in for a series of them. The one we experienced was quite violent enough, so she was more than content to come away."

Lord Merwin leaned back in his chair, extending his legs and crossing them at the ankles. "Do I hear a tale?" he asked, his fingers caressing an old-fashioned quill pen.

"Why do you still use those things?"

"Hmm? The quill?" His refusal to convert to the use of a metal-nibbed pen was one of Lord Merwin's few eccentricities. "Touching them, running my fingers over the feather—" He demonstrated. "I like to think it helps me think."

"And does it?"

"Are you leading me away from the story?" One of Merwin's brows arched. "I am convinced there is one."

"As usual, you have the right of it." Ian grimaced but proceeded to describe Lady Serena's adventure with the sheep and her subsequent rescue. "But it isn't that." He frowned, lounging deeper into the deeply padded, leather-covered chair beside Lord Merwin's desk.

After a long silence, his lordship gestured a waiter nearer and ordered claret and glasses. Ian, surprised when he was offered a glass, looked up. He grinned ruefully. "Not good company, I fear. What have you been up to while I've been"—his brows arched—"occupied elsewhere? Is there news I should know?"

Lord Merwin cast Ian a knowing look, but did not make the sort of ribald comment concerning bridegrooms which Ian might have expected. "News, you ask?" A muscle jumped in Alex Merwin's jaw. "Bad news, actually. Jack's back."

Ian froze. "Wounded?"

Alex nodded.

"Badly?"

"It isn't good." The jaw muscle rolled over again. "He took a ball to his thigh. It is festering, but he refuses to have it amputated. Frankly, Ian," said Alex bleakly, "I cannot believe he'll survive. He's in town, by the way. At the home of a fellow officer who helped him return to England."

"Who? Where?"

"You remember Templeton."

Ian searched his mind. "One of Lord Freeman's twins? Roland or Alaric?"

"Rolly."

Ian frowned. "I was unaware either twin had joined the army."

"An impulse." Alex grinned, his tilted brows and narrow chin giving him a puckish look. "Rejected by the great love of his life, or some such thing, and in a royal snit as a result, Rolly trotted off to take the king's shilling. His father put a stop to his becoming cannon fodder, of course, but insisted Rolly remain in the army. Lord Freeman, it seems, has grown tired of the twins' erratic behavior. Alaric is, hmm, shall we say, *equally eccentric?*"

Ian ignored that bit of wry humor. "Jack will be well cared for, at least. Is he allowed company?"

"Brief visits only. I've stopped in twice." Merwin grinned a wry, nearly sardonic grin. "He's got a dragon to watch over him."

"Old nurses are like that," said Ian. He didn't note and would not have cared that Alex, grinning, very nearly contradicted him. "Life is full of rum goes, Alex. Have you noticed?"

"Oh?" Once again Ian fell silent and the quill's feather was in danger of damage as Alex brushed it back and forth in a rapid slashing movement. Finally, softly, coaxingly, he asked, "What particular glass of grog has *you* feeling low?"

"Grog? Oh. *My* rum go." Ian debated. He sighed again. "Nothing with which you can help, my friend."

"We feared it." The tips of Alex's brows clashed together, their upward curve deepening into a vee. "You and your bride have not come to an accommodation. Jase and I worried that might happen."

"Because we wed in such a scrambling way? You are wrong, old friend. Because we have come to an . . . you called it an accommodation?" Ian's harsh bark of laughter held not the least touch of humor. "Accommodation!" he repeated. "An excellent word for it."

"What is it, Ian?"

Merwin's true sympathy brought Ian to a partial confession. "It seems my brother and Lady Serena laid a plot. He was to discover ways of preventing their marriage until it was too late. Which he did. Twice."

"Too late?"

"Unmarried, she would, upon reaching her next birthday, come into possession of her fortune." Ian shrugged. "So?"

"Unwed, she could have done as she pleased. Married, the fortune goes to her husband."

Lord Merwin digested that bit. He frowned into his drink for a long moment before asking, "What did she wish to do with her fortune once she had it?"

Ian shrugged. "I haven't a notion. I have tried, politely, to discover an answer to that vexing question." He pursed his lips. "Perhaps it was nothing more than to escape from her father's heavy-handed control. He's the worst sort of tyrant. Vicious, but cunning with it. The sort to whom nothing may be done, even though he perpetrates more misery on this earth than another half dozen men may do!"

"That can't be it, Ian. Had she wed when it was first planned, she would long ago have rid herself of her father's management."

Ian's features took on a bleak look. "She doesn't wish to be married. Not to any man."

"Ah." Lord Merwin was silent for a long moment. "I see," he said with compassion.

Ian glanced up and caught his friend's sympathetic expression. "Yes," he agreed. *"Far* worse than mere control. Vicious to the point that I wonder if she will ever again trust that *any* man will treat her decently."

"She'll learn. She was lucky it was you and not some other who wed her."

"Was she?"

Alex chuckled. "You cannot convince me you would ever do aught to upset her."

"I have done my best not to," agreed Ian. He sighed. "Alex, I have always believed myself a patient man. I begin to wonder, however, if I've the patience to undo the damage that man did to her. She lived far too many years under his boot."

Again a certain desolation cued Ian's friend that Ian had yet to delve to the root of the problem. "What are you *not* telling me?"

Ian sighed. "I lied to her. I implied that I'd . . . do something. She will think me as bad as any other man when she discovers the truth." After a pause he added, "If she discovers it. You see, I may find it necessary to fulfill my implicit promise. I don't want to."

"Hmm?"

"Alex, if you know how to convince her that not all men are devils, then spit it out." Ian flashed a quick grin. "However, if your thoughts will *not* help, then please keep them to yourself!"

"I doubt I can advise you unless I understand the whole. And," Merwin added after a moment, "you do not mean to tell me, do you?"

Ian's full lips compressed, nearly disappearing. "It would be wrong to tell when it is not wholly my secret."

Alex nodded. "Then of course you cannot. But this much, Ian. Is she reconciled to the marriage?"

"Not in the least."

"You answered that promptly enough. You do have a problem, do you not?"

A wry, self-deriding expression settled onto Ian's broad features. "More than you know, Alex. More than you will ever know."

Alex straightened, his brows again forming that severe Mephistophelian vee shape. *"You haven't."*

Ian quirked one brow.

"Tell me you haven't!"

A sardonic smile twisted Ian's features. "Tell you I haven't fallen deeply in love with her?" Ian pressed his lips tightly together and sighed. "Of course I have. You met her, and even in that short time together you must have recognized her worth. And you know me, Alex. So, my friend, romantic fool that I am, was there ever a possibility I would *not* fall in love with her?"

Alex shook his head slowly. "I am glad I don't know myself as well as you know yourself. It must be unsettling to be so very aware of one's strengths and, even more, of one's weaknesses!"

Ian chuckled, his low, rumbling laugh drawing eyes. "You humbug! You are more clear-sighted than any of us."

"Clear-sighted enough to know that what the two of you need now is time." Alex always knew when a subject should be dropped. He changed it. "Ian, will you come with me to see Jack? Tomorrow?"

"Yes, of course. Lady Serena has a fitting in the

morning, and Lady Cartwright arranged to take her to a meeting of the Philanthropic Society in the afternoon." He sighed. "I admit I am not happy to see her go south of the river without me, which is where the society meets, but I must trust to Lady Cartwright's good sense, which I can, of course. In the evening I mean to take Serena to the opera. A production of Mozart's *Le Nozze di Figaro*, which I believe she will enjoy."

Merwin reached for the bottle. "I too go to the opera," he said. "Grandmother begged my escort. She would enjoy additional company in her box, so why do I not pick you up and we all go together? Or will your bride object to the intrusion of my grandmother and myself?"

"I suspect," said Ian in a dry, grumbling tone, "that she would prefer it. I've a suspicion she still fears to be alone with me, although she conceals it well." He grimaced when his friend looked doubtful. "You do not believe me? Come to dinner and you may judge for yourself."

Alex nodded. "I will do that."

Ian, wishing to distract his mind from unsolvable problems, settled more comfortably in his chair. "So, tell me," he said. "What have you been up to? I was deprived of news while gone, so, has there been a riot? Has the roof been too weak to support all that hot air and fallen in on a goodly number of Parliament's wordiest ornaments? Has Prinny made a royal ass of himself in some new fashion?"

"Are you sure you wish to hear it all?"

When Ian grinned, Alex threw his quill onto the desk, crossed one leg over the other, and began. His recitation went on for some time. Quite long enough for them to consume, between them, the rest of the claret and much of a bottle of brandy. They ended the evening by sharing a hack.

Ian, not quite steady on his feet, was relieved he'd left orders that the servants, including his valet, were not to wait up for him. He'd just as soon no one saw him in the unusual state of inebriation he'd reached.

He would have been chagrined to know that, through the barest slit of an opening, his wife watched in growing consternation as he stumbled to the door to his room, fumbled for the knob, and entered.

Nor would he have been happy to discover that, recognizing his condition, she sat rigidly upright in her bed, her painfully wide eyes staring at her door.

And still less happy that she feared his anger when he discovered it locked. Which he would do. She *knew* he'd come. Her father, whenever he got into such a state, invariably invaded her mother's room. She had listened to his voice coming from behind the closed door, demanding she knew not what of her mother. And heard her mother's distress. Worse, she would sometimes see bruises on her mother's person the following day.

It was a long time before pure weariness forced Lady Serena into a restless sleep, still unconvinced he would not come.

Ian was greatly perturbed by his visit to Jack Princeton. He was glad Serena had not yet returned home, so he could go directly to his study. He poured himself a goodly tot of brandy and, tossing it back, poured a second, which he carried to the window to sip.

Jack was a strong man, but no one, surely, could survive such infection. Still, did anyone have the right to interfere in a man's decision that he'd rather not live if it were to be as a one-legged creature who could do nothing without help.

Although that was not strictly true, of course. It was

merely that he'd be unable to do things he had in the past found important. In particular, his riding. Jack was unbelievably good in a saddle and truly happy nowhere else. Ian recalled a long-ago visit to Astley's Amphitheater after which Jack emulated the rider who stood on the back of her horse as it galloped around the ring. He'd also learned to ride hanging off one side, vaulting back up into the saddle, his horse never pausing. There had been other tricks . . .

How terrible that they'd never see their friend ride like that again. Ian's stomach churned as it occurred to him that, if Jack died, he would be the first of the Six. Six boys who met at school, aided and abetted each other throughout those years, had great fun at University light-heartedly exploring slightly more dissolute pleasures, and then, only a little more mature, had come down on the ton arm in arm.

The first to die, that is, if Miles Seward did not lie unmourned in an anonymous grave in some unknown corner of the world! But Ian had faith that Miles would turn up eventually, hale and hearty and wondering why anyone worried about him.

So Jack . . . would be the first. Ian sighed, hugely.

"What is the matter?"

He swung around. His thoughts had been so dark, so morose, he'd not heard his wife enter. He stared at her for a moment and then, jerkily, his eyes moved away from her, looked down and off to one side. He turned away.

"Should I go?"

"What?" He turned back. "Go? No." With great effort he put aside his melancholy. "Did you enjoy your outing with Lady Cartwright?"

She waved that aside. "Yes, of course, but you . . ." Her lips compressed. "No. It is not my concern. I am sorry I intruded." She backed toward the door.

He lifted his hand. "Stay, Serena," he said contritely. "I am sorry you find me so maudlin, but I had a bad day. An old friend." His lips compressed into a hard line. He swallowed. "Home from the Peninsula. . . ." Ian glanced at his brandy, finished it off.

"Wounded?" she asked, sympathy for his pain drawing her toward him.

"Badly. His leg. He will not allow them to amputate."

"It is infected." It was a statement rather than a question.

"The room stinks of it," he blurted, appalled all over again.

Lady Serena bit her lip. "Ian . . ." she began.

"Yes?"

"I fear saying it"—her lips twisted in a grimace—"because it sounds so nasty. Almost as nasty as the smell of decay. An old wives' tale. Perhaps nothing but a tale . . . except . . ."

Ian set aside his glass and came to her, grasping her upper arms. "If you've any notion at all which might help, then tell me." He shook her gently. "I will not be angry, my lady," he added when she cast him one of those glances he'd come to recognize and which he believed hinted at her fear of a man's temper.

"It may be nothing but rural nonsense," she warned. "I think that must be all it is. Still, Mr. Morton, our vicar, you know? It was he who told the tale of a woman who'd had the courage to try a remedy she'd heard of somewhere."

"Tell me."

Serena's breath caught in her throat and she swallowed. "It occurred where Mr. Morton was curate before he came to us. There was an odd sort of spinster who raised horses. A wounded soldier was brought to a neighboring estate and everyone believed he would die. But she had heard of this cure . . ." Again she cast him that worried look.

"Spit it out, Serena! Nothing could be worse than what I saw today!"

She looked doubtful. "I'm not convinced you'll think that when you hear! What the vicar claims is that she took maggots from rotting meat and dropped them into the decay in the soldier's body." Her eyes widened. "He claimed the maggots ate the decay!"

Ian looked rather green, swallowed hard, and then laughed harshly. "You were correct, my dear. Some cures do seem worse. Still"—he eyed her hopefully—"it helped?"

"The vicar swears the soldier lived."

"In what condition?"

Serena's brows drew together and she pursed her lips. "I don't believe he ever said," she admitted, searching her memory. "He just said that everyone was amazed, especially the doctor. And also, of course, the soldier who had resigned himself to death!"

"But . . . he lived," said Ian slowly.

For a long moment he stared at nothing at all, wondering if he dared. Wondering if he had the right to interfere if he *did* find the backbone to try such a thing. Then the faint hope there might actually be something he could do allowed him to pull away from his dazed thoughts.

He shook himself slightly and spoke more firmly. "Serena, I've a confession. I forgot to inform you that Lord Merwin, whom you met after our wedding, has invited us to attend the opera this evening along with his grandmother. I asked him to take dinner with us beforehand and then, idiot that I am, failed to tell you of it."

Serena's eyes opened wide. "Oh dear."

One brow drew down. "You fear you will be shamed

by the meal presented? I doubt it. Alex is an abstemious diner and does not care for long-drawn-out dinners. Nor is he a fussy man. He will eat and enjoy whatever you have ordered."

"For the sake of my nerves I must believe you!" She made a tstching noise with her tongue. "I had forgotten we were to attend the opera. I must change." She backed toward the door, feeling behind her for the knob.

"My lady," said Ian quickly, wishing to keep her by him. "You came to me for a reason and, preoccupied, I failed to see it. What is *your* problem?"

"Problem?" She looked startled. "Oh, nothing. It is just that on the way home Lady Cartwright"—Serena's eyes narrowed in a suspicious look—"had her coachman drive us by *your* school."

Ian grinned, his mood slightly lightened by the compliment. "Her ladyship called it *my* school? How kind of her. It was, I admit, my idea, but, like Mrs. Ralston, I looked elsewhere for a great deal of the funding!"

"Your idea? To help poor boys better themselves?"

"You do not believe me?"

For just a moment, she looked much like a startled hare and, for just that moment, a bit like her mother. "Of course I believe you. Why would I not? It is just that I—"

They spoke together.

"—do not understand you."

She cast him still another look of wonderment and was chagrined when he smiled.

"My dear, your father made it very difficult for you to think of men in any but a negative way, did he not? You will begin to understand me when you accept that men, like women, come in all sizes, shapes, and temperaments. Yes, some are stupid. Some are vicious. But, my dear, *only* some."

She sighed. "I will try to believe." Quickly turning the

subject back to a safer one, she asked, "Will you take me to see your school? Mrs. Ralston spoke of such a place and hinted at the existence of yours, certain I would know of it. I did not, of course."

This time they both sighed, simultaneously and deeply. They smiled when each heard the other. Ian's smile was wide and cheerful, a sharing smile. Serena's was far more tentative. She was unused to that sort of sharing.

"Of course I will take you. I am pleased you are interested."

"I am, but now I must go," she said. The sensation of feeling in harmony with her husband was, she discovered, more than a trifle unsettling.

Ian nodded, and she slipped from the room. Lady Serena had a word with Ian's butler, who promised to speak immediately with the cook, even before seeing an extra place was laid. Serena then went to her room, where, waiting for her, was a bath, the hot water steaming gently in tins placed near the fire. She stared.

The maid bit her lip.

"I did not order this."

"No, my lady."

"Then you—?"

"Oh, no, my lady! Mr. McMurrey's valet said the master said you'd want it." When Lady Serena didn't respond, the girl wrapped her hands in her apron and asked, "Should I have it taken away?"

"No." Realizing that was rather abrupt, Serena added, "Oh, no! I *do* want it." She bit her lip and then blurted, "I just wonder why a husband would think to order it for his wife." Certainly her father had never once been so thoughtful.

The girl frowned, taking the question seriously. "Perhaps, knowing you were out, my lady, and fearing you might be late and that there might not be enough hot water and no time to heat more, well, he sent his valet down with the order?"

"I . . . see."

Serena sighed a rueful sigh. Knowing they meant to go out, it should have occurred to her to give that order before leaving the house with Lady Cartwright. It had not. She had been far too hopeful that her new friend might know how to go about setting up her own particular charity and had had no room in her head for anything else.

Certainly nothing so frivolous as the opera! Still, Ian said they would hear a new and exceptional voice, a woman who had come from the Continent and was all the rage. Perhaps it *would* be interesting.

But Serena was ambivalent about joining Lord Merwin and his grandmother. In the brief time she'd talked with his lordship at the Renwicks', Lord Merwin had struck her as a sharply intelligent, overly serious man who carried the weight of the world on his shoulders. Which was suitable in a politician, of course, but would it make for good company?

Still, Ian liked him, so perhaps she was wrong. But his lordship's grandmother! A member of the old nobility! *She* would be cold and haughty.

Or selfish and shrewish?

Or crippled with the aches and pains of old age and a dead bore on the subject? Or, perhaps, one of those poor women who seemed to grow more and more dusty with age until they seemed to have blown away. . . .

Serena's thoughts rampaged around in this manner until she was even more doubtful about the coming evening and, as a result, far fussier than usual when dressing, checking and rechecking everything from the gown's fit to the exact placement of each lock of hair. Her maid, who had felt a trifling contempt for a woman who was more than a little careless of her appearance, was forced to change her mind!

As it turned out, Lady Serena worried about the evening for good reason . . . but for none of those which had crossed her mind.

Seven

Lord Merwin's carriage was a town carriage and not overly large. Lady Serena moved her knees half an inch to the side, removing them from contact with her large husband. "I'm sorry, Lady Merwin," she said. "Something caught my attention and I missed that." She glowered when her husband moved his leg back into contact with hers, but his teasing smile disarmed her and, hesitantly, she returned it.

The dowager's brows rose.

"I am new to London, and easily distracted. Please," Serena coaxed, "tell me again, what it was you said?"

Mollified by Serena's obvious contrition, Lady Merwin nodded. "It was unimportant, really. I merely reminisce. So *many* years since I was, like you, a new bride. More than fifty now. So much has changed! Still, through it all, the theater in all its forms continues to be my passion." She sighed dramatically. "Often and often I have wished I was born of a class which might have indulged that passion."

"As if you had not!" Lord Merwin's eyes sparked in the light of a lamp they passed. "My grandmother, Lady Serena, went so far as to have a theater built onto Merwin Hall. She has organized some memorable performances there"—the white of his teeth showed in a quick, slashing grin—"*in all of which she starred!*"

"It is no such thing, you Banbury man!" scolded his elderly relative. "I took minor parts, my dear, for the fun of it, but I hired professionals to play the major roles." She tapped her grandson with her fan. "As you know! Now, you mustn't tease me so, Alexander. You are aware how serious I am. Why, I saw the first performance of Sheridan's *The Rivals*. And"—she spoke sadly—"watched as Charles Macklin, that dear old man, was led from the stage when he forgot his lines. The very last performance of one of our greatest actors ever."

"That was in 1809, as you've told me"—Lord Merwin grinned wickedly—"on more than one occasion."

"You will stop your funning, you bad boy!"

Serena was surprised to discover this lighter side to a man she had thought overly stern and preoccupied with matters of state to the exclusion of all else. Such drollery was unthinkable in the man he'd appeared to be. How was it possible that two such utterly different character traits existed side by side? Her father—

Serena clamped down hard on her jaw. She must, she reminded herself, remember that it was her father who was the exception. *Not* Ian and not his friends!

"Alex"—Lady Merwin changed both tone and, slightly, the subject—"give me your opinion. Do you like this new music director?"

"Henry Bishop? He seems to make a competent job of it."

"Competent!" The dowager grimaced. "Tell me, Lady Serena, how do you deal with a man like this one? Forever roasting one. Competent, he claims! Ah, well, Bishop is young. Perhaps he will grow into his position. Do *you* enjoy the theater, Lady Serena?"

"I don't know."

The dowager was silent for half a moment. "Don't? Know?" Her voice rose. *"Don't know*? But how can this be? Mr. McMurrey, where did you find a lady who cannot tell if she likes the theater? Or not, as the case may be?"

"Her father does not indulge his womenfolk, my lady," rumbled Ian's deep voice. "I mean to change that for Lady Serena and show her much that she would already have experienced but for him."

"You would say you have *never* attended the theater? How I envy you."

Simultaneously Serena smiled and frowned, uncertain whether Lady Merwin was teasing or if she was serious. "My lady, *you* envy *me*? How can that be?"

"Why, you will enjoy the awe of experiencing *for the very first time* something extraordinary. I can barely remember my first taste of theater. It was Garrick. Incredible man. I will never forget it," she contradicted herself. "Ah! We have arrived, and there, Alexander, is a new flower lady. Buy me a posy, my boy. Violets if she has them. Oh dear," she added, moaning softly as, with her grandson's help, she awkwardly clambered from the carriage. "It is such a nuisance, this growing old."

"Perhaps," Merwin teased, "but think of the alternative."

Lady Merwin whacked her grandson with her fan, this time with more force. "Flowers, Alexander," she said sternly. "At once."

Lady Serena reluctantly took Ian's hand, preparing to descend from the carriage. She glanced over Ian's head to where Lord Merwin chose from a pale woman's posies. Suddenly her fingers tightened around Ian's.

He saw her eyes widen, caught her when she missed the iron step. "What is it?" he asked softly.

Serena never took her eyes from the woman. "It is she. I must . . ."

"Serena, tell me." He grasped her shoulders, holding her back.

"Let me go, Ian." Serena tried to shrug him off. "I must—"

"Not until you explain," he interrupted softly. "Now tell me."

"Arguments and the two of you barely married?" interrupted Lady Merwin. "This will never do. Here is a posy for you, Lady Serena. Come along now. We will miss the opening scene if we do not hurry, and, though it is common for the *ton* to do so, I do *not* approve."

Serena literally dug in her heels and tried very hard to shake loose from her husband. "You do not understand! Ian, release me. Please."

"It is you who will not understand. This is a dangerous area, Serena. You must tell me what you wish to do."

He would never understand. Still less would he approve! Despair filled Lady Serena, and she compressed her lips. "That woman." She hadn't removed her gaze from the flower lady. "She is the one—"

"Lady Serena," called Lady Merwin loudly from some steps on. "Do not dawdle."

"But I only want to help her," said Serena helplessly and in such a low voice Ian had to bend down to catch her words.

"Help the flower girl? You know her?" Serena nodded, and Ian thought quickly. "Go with Lady Merwin, Serena. I will tell the chit she is to come tomorrow to an address to which I will escort you. Go along with Alex and Lady Merwin. I will catch up with you."

Serena stared up into Ian's softly encouraging face. "Tell her . . ." She drew in a deep breath, and her chin came up in that way she had. "Tell her I am ashamed of my father and I will do what I can for her."

"Ashamed of your . . . ?" Ian's brows climbed upward. Then he shook his head. "My dear," he said with wry humor and a twinkle in his deep-set eyes, "this is a tale I *must* hear. But *not now*." Ian almost lifted her from her feet, half carrying her to where Lord Merwin assisted his grandmother, who could not move so quickly these days. "I will catch up with you, Alex. Watch over Lady Serena for me."

What is he going to do? Serena glanced over her shoulder. *Oh, why did I allow my emotions such freedom? I could have found an excuse to come back out. Or I could have come some night when Ian was elsewhere. But he said . . . ? Dare I believe he will help me help that woman?*

Her thoughts in turmoil, Serena reluctantly moved forward with the others, looking back whenever she dared. "I wonder," she muttered, "what became of the baby. . . ."

Lord Merwin, overhearing, cast a startled look down at her and twisted his head around to look for his friend. But they had, by then, passed well under the portico, and Alex could no longer see Ian among the crowd. As they entered the theater, he decided it was none of his business and tenderly helped his grandmother up the steps, protecting her and Lady Serena as well as he could from the press of people.

The steps were crowded and their progress slow. Absentmindedly, Serena lifted her nosegay to her nose and sniffed. And then smiled. It was clear why flower girls did excellent business outside theaters: The lovely fresh scent of the posies helped one ignore the less than fresh scent of too many people massed too closely together in the heat from the chandeliers.

Finally they achieved the first floor and it was somewhat easier to move. Unfortunately, from Lady Serena's point of view, Lady Merwin seemed to know everyone and everyone knew her. Serena, who wished for nothing so much as a corner in which to hide and think, found she was forced to do the polite to dozens of people she was unlikely to remember meeting.

For once, she was appreciative of her husband's perceptive nature. He took one look at his wife and told Lady Merwin, "I will take Lady Serena to your box, my lady. She is unused to crowds and feels more than a trifle bemused, I think."

He smiled down at Serena, who weakly smiled back. Gladly, however, she allowed him to take her arm and lead her away from the chattering group surrounding the Merwins.

Once he'd seated her in the Merwin box, Ian whispered, "I had a little difficulty convincing your flower girl that our interest is benevolent, but she will come tomorrow to a Long Acre coffee house not far from here. It is clean and stays decent, since it is commonly used by Bow Street Runners. I will send a message that she is to be taken to a private room if we have not arrived before her."

"And supplied with food and ale."

"Ale?"

"She is nursing." Lady Serena frowned. "Or *should* be."

Ian looked thunderstruck. "Serena, you will not convince me"—he lowered his voice as heads turned their way—"that your father"—the door to the box opened and, perforce, their conversation was terminated.

"Have they begun? Ah! Not! We are in time." Lady Merwin seated herself beside Serena, leaned over, and patted her hand. "My dear, you will enjoy the performance excessively."

Serena, wondering if that was an order, smiled pleasantly and nodded. She cast a look over her shoulder to her husband, who was seated somewhat behind her, noted his encouraging smile, and smiled weakly in return.

I will never understand him, she thought. *Never.*

But, since she was a sensible woman who knew that

nothing could be done just then, she settled into her chair and prepared to enjoy the performance. *Excessively . . .*

. . . and, much to her surprise, she did.

The following morning Lady Serena paced the drawing room wondering when Ian would arise and when they would leave for Long Acre. What if that woman came and, not finding them there, left? How would she ever find the flower girl again? *Oh, why,* she wondered, *does he not get up?*

"Ah. There you are. And impatient, I see."

Serena spun on her heel. "We must go."

"We must *not* go until you have explained." Ian chuckled when she dared to glare at him. "My dear, that poor woman will have been up half the night selling her flowers. She will need sleep." Serena did not look convinced. "I assure you, she cannot possibly arrive until the hour I suggested, which is two of the clock."

"Not until two!" Serena plopped onto an exceedingly ugly backless sofa designed in the Egyptian mode.

"You needn't look so glum. The chit will come, I assure you."

"How can you be so certain?"

Ian shrugged. "I gave her a pound and promised another today."

"A . . . whole pound?"

"You stare." He frowned. "Ah! I see. Serena, we will get along ever so much better if you will cease comparing me to your idiotic father. I am not he. In no way am I like him. And, frankly, I find it insulting that you continually expect the worst of me."

Serena felt her face flame. "I do not mean to insult you . . ."

"I know." He sighed. "It is merely that you've had little or no experience of decent men." He eyed her for a moment. "Did you *know* any? Other than Mr. Morton?"

Serena smiled sadly. "Poor Mr. Morton. Father thought him a weakling because he could bully the poor man. Father dislikes anyone he can bully. On the other hand, he will have nothing to do with those he can*not*."

"A lonely man, I'd think."

"Not entirely. He has his sycophants who will say him yea and nay as he demands."

"Yes, he would need those, would he not? How else could he continue to deceive himself that he is a great man? Serena, tell me about your father and that woman."

"Father is on the poorhouse board."

"Ah! *Now* I understand!"

"Understand what?"

"Your message to the flower woman. I have been trying and trying to see your father with a mistress and I could not manage it."

"Mistress? Oh, no!" Serena broke into a trill of laughter, surprising herself more than she did Ian. "That anyone would think such a thing of him would first have him dying of mortification, and"—she smiled a quick smile—"as *that* faded, he would die all over again from a surfeit of rage. At the very least, he would suffer an apoplexy if he knew what you suspected."

"Merely suspected? Do you suggest," asked Ian blandly, "that it is because his sins might have been found out that he would feel anger?"

Lady Serena frowned. "He is hypocrite enough that that could be true, and perhaps it *is* what I meant. But I cannot think when he would have time to . . . to . . . Well, a mistress must require his presence, must she not? To be of any use, I mean?"

It was Ian's turn to chuckle. His warm, beguiling laugh drew a smile to Serena's face.

"What did I say to amuse you so?" she asked.

"It was the way you, hmm . . . *understated the case.*"

Serena felt heat in her face. "It is bad of me that I said anything at all. My mother suffered, often, from my habit of speaking of things about which I should know nothing."

"In public it would make sense to curb your tongue, but to me or, for instance, to Lady Cartwright, who also likes plain speaking, you may say anything which pops into your head. I do not know her well yet, but I believe Lady Renwick is also that sort." He shrugged. "That is not relevant at the moment. Explain to me why you were in a frenzy about that poor woman."

Lady Serena almost absently described the poorhouse meeting on which she had eavesdropped, retold the woman's story, told how near her time she was, and how worried she, Serena, had been for the poor deceived woman. And also how, taking care her father would not catch her, she had given the woman the remaining bit of pin money in her reticule.

"It was so little. If I were a truly good woman, I would have stolen from the household monies and given her more, but Father checks that weekly and he would instantly have discovered the discrepancy. I would have been forced to confess I'd taken it, to save whatever servant he wished to be rid of!"

"Wished . . . ?"

"He often perceives insult and insolence where there is none. Except for the family, he does not issue a reprimand instantly but awaits his chance and, when it is totally unexpected, takes his revenge. And not just among our servants, but in the community among our neighbors as well."

"Your eyes glitter and your lips have thinned," said Ian, his tone judicious. "You are angry."

"I am angry that I must admit the man is my father.

We'd Like to Invite You to Subscribe to Zebra's Regency Romance Book Club and Give You a Gift of 4 Free Books as Your Introduction! (Worth $19.96!)

If you're a Regency lover, imagine the joy of getting **4 FREE Zebra Regency Romances** and then the chance to have these lovely stories delivered to your home each month at the lowest prices available! Well, that's our offer to you and here's how you benefit by becoming a Regency Romance subscriber:

- **4 FREE Introductory Regency Romances are delivered to your door**
- **4 BRAND NEW Regencies are then delivered each month (usually before they're available in bookstores)**
- **Subscribers save almost $4.00 every month**
- **Home delivery is always FREE**
- **You also receive a FREE monthly newsletter, *Zebra/Pinnacle Romance News* which features author profiles, contests, subscriber benefits, book previews and more**
- **No risks or obligations...in other words you can cancel whenever you wish with no questions asked**

Join the thousands of readers who enjoy the savings and convenience offered to Regency Romance subscribers. After your initial introductory shipment, you receive 4 brand-new Zebra Regency Romances each month to examine for 10 days. Then, if you decide to keep the books, you'll pay the preferred subscriber's price of just $4.00 per title. That's only $16.00 for all 4 books and there's never an extra charge for shipping and handling.

It's a no-lose proposition, so return the FREE BOOK CERTIFICATE today!

Say Yes to 4 Free Books!
Complete and return the order card to receive this $19.96 value, ABSOLUTELY FREE!

If the certificate is missing below, write to:
Zebra Home Subscription Service, Inc.,
P.O. Box 5214, Clifton, New Jersey 07015-5214
or call TOLL-FREE 1-888-345-BOOK
Visit our website at www.kensingtonbooks.com.

FREE BOOK CERTIFICATE

YES! Please rush me 4 Zebra Regency Romances without cost or obligation. I understand that each month thereafter I will be able to preview 4 brand-new Regency Romances FREE for 10 days. Then, if I should decide to keep them, I will pay the money-saving preferred subscriber's price of just $16.00 for all 4...that's a savings of almost $4 off the publisher's price with no additional charge for shipping and handling. I may return any shipment within 10 days and owe nothing, and I may cancel this subscription at any time. My 4 FREE books will be mine to keep in any case.

Name _____

Address _____ Apt. _____

City _____ State _____ Zip _____

Telephone ( ) _____

Signature _____
(If under 18, parent or guardian must sign.)

RN050A

Terms and prices subject to change. Orders subject to acceptance by Zebra Home Subscription Service, Inc.
Offer valid in U.S. only.

ⅠⅠ...Ⅰ...ⅠⅠⅠ...ⅠⅠⅠⅠⅠⅠ...Ⅰ...ⅠⅠⅠ...ⅠⅠⅠ...Ⅰ

REGENCY ROMANCE BOOK CLUB
Zebra Home Subscription Service, Inc.
P.O. Box 5214
Clifton NJ 07015-5214

PLACE
STAMP
HERE

I am angry that I am expected to love and honor such a monster!"

"No."

"But I am. Mr. Morton has given many sermons on the Ten Commandments. They are nearly his only source for sermon topics. He begins with the first and goes on to a new one each Sunday and when he has finished, he begins again."

"The Commandment says nothing of love; it only demands that you *honor* your parents. Nor do I believe it is honor as one honors a hero so much as that one live a decent life. You will do him no *dishonor* unless you behave in a way that would shame him. I am, therefore, certain you will never show him dishonor."

"I am not certain I understand."

"In other words, my dear, *you* will never act as *he* does!"

"Oh, I *hope* not!" Another sudden and unexpected chuckle burst from her.

Ian grinned and suggested they explore the Tower before going on to the coffeehouse and their meeting. "I do not know how it is that we have yet to visit it. The menagerie is worth a look, and there are exhibits of ancient armor."

"And the royal jewels?"

"Oh, yes. If you wish."

"If I wish!"

Ian grinned. "I had hoped you were unaware they were housed there and that I might give you a pleasant surprise. Or perhaps you will find it *unpleasant*. They are ill displayed and rarely cleaned! Shall we go? We'll not have time for everything, perhaps, but may return another day."

Lady Serena enjoyed their jaunt, but that did not prevent her, whenever Ian's attention seemed occupied elsewhere, from checking the tiny watch he had given her

soon after their arrival in London. It was pinned to her
pelisse and she only needed a second to tip it up and
look at the face of it, but the fourth time she did so, Ian
chuckled.

Her face flamed that she'd been caught, and habit had
her apologizing. "I'm sorry."

"Why do you apologize? My dear, I brought you
here"—he gestured around the green where sleek ravens
strutted, one bird perching on the stone for beheadings—
"in the hope it would distract you and make the time go
faster until we meet with your protégé. I did not succeed
in that aim, I fear."

Lady Serena bit her lip. Then she sighed. "I am very
sorry, but I cannot help but fear that she will disappear
and I will never find her again."

"There you go again, apologizing. You've done nothing
for which you must apologize," he added a trifle sternly.

Lady Serena wished she could believe it, but her father's training could not be discarded merely because Ian
claimed it unnecessary. "She must have been afraid of
you. How could she not?" Serena cast a quick glance
from his feet up to his head.

Ian eyed her in return, a grim look around his mouth.
"As *you* fear me? No, my dear," he added quickly, "do
not answer that. I'd rather not know. But have you no
notion how important a whole pound is to such as she?
She will come."

Serena, again feeling her face hotter than she liked,
darted him a quick look. "It is less than an hour
now . . . ?"

His pensive look disappeared and Ian grinned. "Is that
a suggestion, my love?"

"I would never dare suggest—"

"So you merely hint," he interrupted on a gentle sigh,
and wondered if he dared count as a plus the fact she
had not objected to the endearment. "I wonder how I

might convince you that you need *not* fear me; that I am your friend."

Serena stared. "Friend?" she asked after finally remembering that long-ago discussion about becoming friends.

"Yes," he said firmly. "Friend. Come along. We will go, and you will discover your young woman awaits us at my coffeehouse."

Obediently Serena turned toward the gate. "Are women allowed in coffeehouses?" she asked as he helped her into the carriage. "I thought they were places where men met for discussions and debates and to read the newspapers and . . . and I don't know, do I?"

"They are all of that, my dear, but we will enter by a side door. You will not be seen by the regular patrons. Lady Cartwright often meets people there. People who will not come to her home. Or those to whom her neighbors would object, assuming such folk were brave enough to appear in an area such as Upper Brooks Street where her ladyship lives, so near the Grosvenor Gate just off Park Lane. Some people do not approve of her charity work."

Serena nodded. "Like my father." Lady Serena's lips pressed together. "I do not understand people. Why, when they have so much, do they object to helping those who do not?"

"My dear, it is a subject one could debate endlessly and still find no single answer. Perversity in some cases, greed in others, and a dislike of exerting themselves in still others. You can think of other causes, I'm certain. Ignorance, for instance. Or a deliberate closing of the eyes to the suffering of others so one need not feel guilty."

"And those like my father who get a perverse pleasure from seeing others suffer."

"Ah! We have arrived," said Ian. He tuned to inspect

her. "Pull your hat more forward." Ian reached for the brim and tugged. "Yes. Like that." They descended from the carriage. "Perhaps if you could pretend to a modesty you do not feel and keep your eyes on the paving? Yes. Exactly like that," he said. When he chuckled softly, she turned a quick glance on him. "Oh, my dear, do not look daggers at me. It is only what is done, after all, when a woman is behaving discreetly in attempting to avoid discovery."

"And why," spluttered Serena, "must I be discreet when I am doing nothing of which I am ashamed? *And* while in the company of my husband?" But, although she spoke with emotion, she looked down as she'd been bid.

"Because, my dear, you avoid the necessity of explanations if questioned by someone who has no business knowing your errand, even if he recognizes you, in a part of the city in which you've no business being!"

"Then it is for *my* benefit I hide within my bonnet?"

"But of course. What did you think?"

"For *yours*, of course," she retorted, and then gasped. He chuckled. Less surprised by his reaction to her less-than-tactful response than she would once have been, she entered the building and climbed the stairs. They were directed to a room near the main staircase where, much to Serena's surprise, since she had truly feared the woman would not come, they found the flower seller.

"I don't know you," said the woman abruptly, staring rather rudely at Lady Serena.

"No. You wouldn't. Nor do I know you. By name, I mean. But perhaps you will recall that I gave you a few coins before my father had you carted from our parish into the next—?"

"Ah! That I remember. You saved my life. What may I do for you?" she asked as shortly as she'd disavowed knowing Lady Serena.

"It is not what you may do for me, but what I may do for you. Where is your baby, and was the tale you told my father true?"

For a moment the woman's jaw trembled. Then, visibly, she shook off her grief. "The infant was born dead. But the tale? That I was forced?" She shrugged. "It was a lie."

Serena's eyes widened. "Oh dear," she breathed, having no notion what to do under these new circumstances.

"Will you," asked Ian kindly in his rumbling and most tender voice, "tell us the true story? Because you were not born to work in the streets. Your voice belies it. You are of gentle birth, are you not?"

"Of the gentry." The woman wiped a somewhat grimy hand across her face and drew a deep breath in through her nostrils. "It is an old tale. I loved but not wisely. I was deceived." Again she shrugged. "Now I pay for my stupidity."

"Tell us," said Serena, regaining her poise. She seated herself and gestured toward a chair on the other side of the table.

Ian sat with his back to the window and told the stranger she need not name names if she did not care to, but that if she did, they would not be bruited about the ton. "Perhaps first you will tell us how we are to call you?"

For the first time, the woman hesitated. Then, still again, she shrugged. "Why not? My name is Miss Henrietta Clapton. I was reared in comfortable circumstances near Lord Freeman's estate in East Sussex." She paused, her eyes going blank with memories, but after a moment she drew another deep breath. "There was a house party at the big house. I was not a guest, of course, but was invited to several entertainments."

"And there you met your seducer?"

A grimace crossed her face. "As good a term as any,

I suppose. When the party broke up, everyone went away to other parties or to tour the Lake District or up to Scotland for the fishing. Several months passed. My seducer, as you call him, did not return as promised, and I resigned myself to my loss, I suppose, only to discover . . ." She blushed rosily, glancing from Lady Serena to Ian and back again.

"The baby?"

"Yes." She grimaced again. "Actually, I lie. *I* merely thought I was getting fat. My grandfather . . . guessed." Her chin came up, and she stared at Lady Serena. "You will not know what it is to live under the heel of a tyrant. You will not know how awful it all was."

"If you saw the scars on Lady Serena's back, you would not say that."

Serena cast Ian a startled glance. She was unaware he knew of those fine white lines. Had her maid spoken to Ian's valet, who then commented on the oddity to Ian? And how, she wondered, had Ian responded? . . . Oh, dear! Did the whole household know they kept to separate rooms? *Of course they did.* Suddenly embarrassed, Serena looked at her clasped hands.

"Truly?" The woman bent a look of curiosity Serena's way. "I apologize." When Serena did not raise her head, Miss Clapton turned to Ian. "I do not understand what you want of me. I am a fallen woman. I am shocked you allow your wife to speak to me, let alone that you yourself hold civil conversation with me."

"You expected *conversation* of a different sort?" asked Ian, grinning as he hinted at one of the cant terms referring to fornication. His brow arched, and the faintest of dimples appeared. "You need not fear that of me, Miss Clapton. As to my wife, I know no more than you what she means to do. She saw you last night outside the theater and insisted she must speak with you."

Serena was *glad* to see Miss Clapton's startled expression at Ian's words. Here was another who could not believe her ears when Ian made one of his incredible comments.

"Serena?" Ian turned toward his wife.

"But I don't know, myself!" she exclaimed. "Only that *something* should be done." Serena's features fell into an expression revealing her confusion. "Except, at that time I believed the tale you told my father, that you had been forced. Now . . . Oh, I don't know what to do."

"Miss Clapton," asked Ian, "how have you managed to survive since you were ejected from your family home, which must have been months ago?"

Miss Clapton sighed. "My mother gave me the funds necessary to reach my great-aunt's home where she told me to go. Not knowing what else to do when my grandfather would not have me in the house, I went. Moreover, I stayed"—her lips thinned—"as long as I could bear it."

"Bear . . . it?" Lady Serena flinched, and her skin paled as she thought of her father's whip.

"Not beatings," Miss Clapton hastened to assure Lady Serena, "but *lectures*. Morning, noon, and evening. Telling me over and over how sinful I was, how my child would be born steeped in evil and"—her voice rose as she continued—"how I must give it up immediately it was born and devote the whole of the rest of my life to doing good works in order to atone for my mistake and that I must ask forgiveness for my sins on my knees for hours at a time and . . ." She burst into tears, searching her person for a nonexistent handkerchief. "I could have borne the rest if only she had not insisted I give up my baby. It was all I had, you see, of my lover."

"You left her roof?"

With some difficulty Miss Clapton regained control. She looked from one to the other and then down at the table before admitting, "When I insisted I would keep my child, she threw me out."

"When was that?"

"A week or so before your father hastened me onward," said Miss Clapton, brushing away her tears and straightening in her seat. "I had some coins left of those my mother gave me and, living with my aunt, I had a great deal of contact with those who live in poverty. I learned much from them," she said, her eyes glittering. "Most importantly, how to survive on nothing at all! I hoped to reach my grandmother, my mother's mother, before the baby came. I hoped *she* would help me . . ."

"But she would not?"

"I like to believe she would have."

"Would have?"

"My great-aunt had kindly refrained from informing me of Grandmother's death. She had been ill, which was why my mother did not send me to her in the first place. I was unaware how ill . . ."

"Oh dear." Lady Serena wanted nothing so much as to reach for Ian's hand, to hold it and, even more, be held by it, comforted by it . . .

A ghost of a smile crossed Miss Clapton's thin face. "Oh dear indeed."

"But what did you do?"

"I do not care to remember those days, my lady." Her dry voice demanded that one not probe. "You will recall how it was with me. But the baby was dead, so I came to London. I used the coins you gave me to set myself up in the flower business and discovered in myself a rare talent for survival. I have kept myself fed and housed for some time now. And"—her chin rose—"I will continue to do so as long as necessary."

Ian saw something in the woman's grim look which made him stiffen slightly. "As long as necessary?" he asked softly.

She cast him a scornful glance. "Until they take me up for murdering the man who deceived me, of course."

Ian's eyes widened, and Serena gasped. "Oh, no. You cannot think to . . . to . . ."

A wry chuckle escaped Miss Clapton. "Do you think I cannot? Or is it that you think suffering has driven me insane? It is neither. Merely that I will prevent this one villain from harming any other girl as he harmed me. The way to do so is to kill him." She shrugged.

"Which," said Ian slowly, "explains why you became a flower seller outside a theater. You think, eventually, to see him there?"

"Of course."

"Oh, dear," said Lady Serena again. She sighed, staring pensively across the room. "Perhaps Mrs. Ralston was correct. Perhaps it is impossible to help wronged women as I wish to do."

"How had you thought to help?" asked Ian, curious.

"How? Oh, I have had only the vaguest of notions. To buy a house somewhere where the girls might go to have their babies. To train those who are trainable. To find husbands for those who would make good wives despite their"—she tactfully changed what she'd been about to say—"fall from grace. I'd thought perhaps I might set the most deserving up as widows in isolated villages. But I've no real notion how to go about it."

"Mrs. Ralston said you could not do it?"

"She said it would be difficult, perhaps impossible, to determine which women were deserving pity and aid. She didn't put it that way, of course." Serena's lips compressed. Then she frowned, a pensive look coming into her eyes. "Now I don't know what to do."

"The first thing we must do is help Miss Clapton," said Ian firmly. "Will you come with us to our home?"

"You are in need of a maid?" asked the woman suspiciously.

"I meant," said Ian gently, "as our guest—"

The woman's chin rose and she straightened her spine.

"—or if you think that mere charity," Ian continued smoothly, "and your pride cannot stomach it, then come as Lady Serena's hired companion. Miss Clapton, if you seek your gentleman seducer, you will have more opportunity as Lady Serena's companion than while forced to earn your living as you search faces for the one you seek."

"You shock me," said Miss Clapton in that abrupt manner which was so much a part of her. "You would hire *me* as companion for your wife? Do you dare? I am a fallen woman. I am a murderer." At Serena's gasp Henrietta huffed a short laugh. "Not yet, of course, but I *will* be when I find the devil!"

"Or perhaps"—Ian's brow arced—"you will feel differently and some arrangement can be made?"

"Wed him, you mean? After he lied to me? Abandoned me?" She laughed harshly. "Are you a fool, Mr. McMurrey, or merely a blinkered optimist?"

"When you are decently clothed, when you've food and no worry about your next meal, when you need no longer fear the motives of every man who looks at you"—Ian shrugged—"perhaps then you will reassess your plight, come to another decision."

"But to hire a fallen woman as your wife's companion!" repeated Miss Clapton. "It is not the thing."

"No, but who, excepting ourselves, will know of it?"

"The villain who—"

Ian nodded, interrupting. "Yes. There is that, of course. Will he remember you?"

"Remember me?" Miss Clapton's eyes widened. "Oh, yes. He will know me."

"Then I see no problem."

"No problem!" Miss Clapton stared at him.

"Serena, I have spoken without consulting you. Are you willing to have Miss Clapton as your friend?"

"I . . ." Serena thought of her old life, of her father and how she'd have been treated under similar circumstances. "*Yes*. I am." She extended a hand to the young woman. "Will *you* have *me?*"

Tears ran down Miss Clapton's face. "I shouldn't," she demurred. "It isn't right . . "

"But," said Ian, smiling and rising to his feet, "you will. Is there anything you need from your lodging? Any relic of your old life, or bits or pieces you wish to remove to your new home?"

Miss Clapton touched her chest just below her breasts, pinching a bit of the cloth around something hidden there. "I would dare leave nothing of value there. Besides, I've only one other dress, and it is in worse condition than this, so I don't suppose I need even that."

"You are about my wife's size. She can provide you with a dress or two, and money to buy dress lengths which you may sew for yourself. You do sew?"

"*Of course*." Miss Clapton looked insulted at the notion she could not.

Ian chuckled softly. "You might be surprised," he said, "how many cannot." And then he laughed outright at Lady Serena's rosy cheeks. "Aha! My wife has kept a secret from me!"

"It is not that I cannot *sew*. But I cannot, to save me, cut a proper sleeve!"

"There is a trick to it," said Miss Clapton. With only the barest touch of diffidence, she asked, "Perhaps I can show you?"

"You can *try*. My grandmother failed in the attempt, and so did my mother. We will see."

"You two wait here," said Ian, smiling at these initial

signs of friendship. "I will return when I have paid our shot and seen that the carriage is brought around."

Ian left the room, and the two women stared at each other.

Eight

"Did he really beat you?"

Miss Clapton spoke in that curt manner Lady Serena had decided was a habit with her new acquaintance. "Yes," she responded. "From when I was very little. Only rarely was it more than a couple of stripes, but on occasion, when I was particularly stubborn, he drew blood." Serena shivered as she remembered the last time. "Unlike you, who wished to wed, I did not. Not only did he attempt to beat me into submission, but when that failed, he tried to starve me." She sighed.

"And succeeded."

The ghost of a smile crossed Serena's face. "No. He soon knew I would not give in. Only when he threatened to beat my mother did I accede to his demands."

"That was unfair of him!"

"He is a man." A muscle jumped in Serena's jaw. "Nothing is *unfair* when it comes to a man's women-folk."

"I will not believe that."

"Do you not? You of all people? Betrayed in the worst possible way?"

Miss Clapton blushed and then looked surprised. "How strange."

"Strange?"

She touched her cheeks with both hands. "I had not

thought myself still capable of coloring up this way."
Then she smiled. "Your husband did me a very good
deed, I think."

"How so?"

"He has allowed me to know you, my lady. I have for
too long thought only of my own life, my disgrace. I
have brooded and forgotten there are others who suffer."
She shrugged. "I doubt I can do you anything in return,
but I will try." A hard look returned to her face. "That
is, until I find my . . . seducer."

"If you mean it," said Serena quickly, "make me a
promise."

Miss Clapton stiffened. "You will not ask that I not
kill that man once I've the opportunity!"

"Not that. I've no right, I think, to demand that. Only
that you discuss it with me or Ian first? That you tell us
who it is and how it came about you have seen him
again?"

"Those are two things. Two promises."

Lady Serena, distressed, stared at Miss Clapton.

Henrietta sighed. "Very well. When I find him, I will
tell you."

"If you were to tell Ian the man's name, perhaps he
could discover him for you."

"He'd be abetting a murder, would he not? I think not."

"Thank you," said Ian, who had opened the door on
the words. "I would not care to help plan a murder."

"It wasn't planning," said Lady Serena. "I merely suggested that if you knew the rake's name, you could help
Miss Clapton find him."

Ian smiled the least little bit of a smile. "We will," he
said, his eyes twinkling, "leave that to Miss Clapton.
Now if the two of you are ready . . ."

He offered his wife his arm and then his other to Miss
Clapton, who, again blushing and this time furiously,

shook her head. "It is not right. I should not be treated as a lady."

"Would you have the whole world know I allow my wife to have what they would call an improper friend?" asked Ian, his steady gaze holding her defiant one. He joggled his elbow invitingly.

Miss Clapton, her lips compressed, accepted both the warning and his arm. She vowed to do her best that she not fail him . . . Except, of course, that she would kill her lover. She *would*.

Once seated in the coach, Lady Serena furtively observed her husband and wondered why he'd offered the wronged woman a roof. And, tactful man, work with which to salve her pride. The woman insisted she meant to kill a man. Surely Ian knew that Miss Clapton truly meant to kill her seducer!

Serena's gaze shifted. Where, she wondered, would Miss Clapton find the courage, the necessary resolution? Or perhaps that was not so difficult to understand. Had not she herself meant mischief on her wedding night? Although she could not have gone so far as to kill Ian, still . . . she *might* have.

Ian might have died!

Serena stifled a sudden pang. She'd no wish to delve into why the feeling was so intense. Instead, she wondered why it had never occurred to her to kill her father. Now, *that* was a murder for which there was sufficient reason to suffer the embarrassment of a public hanging! Think of the good she would have done if only she'd had the courage to rid the world of the man!

"What are you thinking?" asked Ian.

"I was wishing I had Miss Clapton's resolution." The words were startled from Serena by her husband's question. She ventured to smile at Miss Clapton.

"Resolution?" asked Ian.

"Perhaps it is merely that I am stupid." Serena's chin

rose. "If I were not I might have thought to murder my father, which would have rid the world of a villain far worse than Miss Clapton's. Unfortunately"—she sighed—"I fear I do not have the necessary courage."

Ian, simultaneously horrified and amused, patted his wife's hand and, unsure how to treat her words, allowed the rest of their journey to pass in silence.

Lady Serena looked at herself in her pier mirror and wondered if Ian would approve. The thought ran through her mind without her permission, and when she realized the implication, she was appalled. Why should she *care* what her husband thought? What did it matter what he thought? Of what possible use were *his* thoughts . . .

Honesty made her pause there. Because, if not for Ian's *thoughts*, Miss Clapton would still live in a horrid little room under the eaves of a house which, from her description, might tumble to the ground at any moment. She would walk each day to market to buy flowers. She would compose those flowers into nosegays and then, having walked miles, walk more to reach the theater of her choice where she hoped to sell enough to provide food and rent and the money to buy more flowers. Rain or shine. Cold or hot. She'd had no choice but to do this or be forced into a less honorable trade. Somehow, through all she'd suffered, Miss Clapton had avoided becoming a common whore.

But thoughts of Miss Clapton were not relevant. Serena paced her room, her skirts swishing about her ankles. What was relevant was that she found herself softening toward Ian, and she must not. That he could show mercy to Miss Clapton . . . yes, that was good, but one must remember to ask *why* he did so? What motive had he?

Lady Serena's thoughts whirled around well-trod cir-

cles, leaving her confused, bemused, and extremely unsettled.

Was Ian McMurrey, she wondered, the good man he
appeared to be, or was he acting a role she neither understood nor, she told herself fiercely, wanted to understand? He was, after all, a man, was he not? It was
important that she not be taken in.

She could not trust that his behavior was *not* pretense!
Even if it were not, she must not soften toward him. She
would never control her fortune unless he freed her;
could never use it for the good of others.

She must be free . . .

Angry with herself, with Ian, with everything, she
paced. Her pacing brought her back to her mirror, where
a glint of candlelight caught her hair, sparkling off the
new jeweled pins. Gifts from Ian. Her maid had used
them to catch up Serena's hair in a delightful manner.

Her hair . . .

Serena stared at her hair. More than once, Ian had
given her compliments on her hair. He thought it beautiful. It gave him pleasure, he said. And he'd spent a
great deal of money on the pins which glinted against
her dark locks.

A tap-tap had Serena swinging around.

Looking very nearly demure in Serena's least favorite
gown, Miss Clapton hesitated in the doorway. "I wasn't
certain," she began, "just where I—"

Lady Serena grabbed her companion's arm, pulling her
into the room. She closed the door and leaned against
it. "Cut my hair."

"Hair?" Miss Clapton's hand went to her own short
locks. "Cut it? But it is lovely just the way it is."

"I wish it cut. Short."

"You want it cropped? But what will Mr. McMurrey
say?"

"I do not care what Mr. McMurrey will say." Serena

drew Miss Clapton to her dressing table. She seated herself and began pulling the pins from her hair, dropping most onto the table, not caring that some fell to the floor.

"Why?" asked Miss Clapton. She picked up the fallen pins and folded her arms across her chest.

"Why? Does it matter why?" Lady Serena caught her companion's reflected gaze in the mirror. "Is not the fact I wish it sufficient?"

"I think it does matter." The faintest spreading of Miss Clapton's lips and the twinkle appearing in her eyes deflated Serena. Her new acquaintance's next words finished her rebellion. "You would spite your husband."

Lady Serena sighed. "I suppose I would."

"You would anger him."

"Would I?"

Was that what she wanted? To see Ian lose that confusing control? That impossible control? Finally? Surely not.

"I doubt he cares enough to be angry with me."

"I think he does, but if not, men can be irrational. You are his. He needn't *care* in order to wish you an ornament on his arm."

Lady Serena's mouth firmed into a thin line. "I will not be a mere ornament. Cut my hair."

Miss Clapton shrugged. "Just so you know what you would do." She accepted the scissors and lifted Lady Serena's hair. Once again her eyes met Serena's in the mirror. "Certain?"

"Certain."

But when the scissors met and the first lock was laid aside, Serena felt a tightening around her heart. She couldn't bring herself to watch, closed her eyes, and waited. Finally Miss Clapton's wry tones told her she could look.

Opening one eye, Serena faced her new image. Her head felt so light she feared it might float from her shoulders. And, she discovered, the extraordinary length of the tresses had weighed them down. Freed, her hair rioted over her scalp and around her ears, elf locks curling forward to lie naturally against her cheeks. Was that creature in the mirror herself?

"Good heavens," she muttered.

"You didn't know?"

"It has never been cut," answered Serena. She patted a curl into place, tugged at a second. She turned her head from side to side. "It feels so different."

Miss Clapton went to Serena's sewing box. She bit off a length of thread before gathering up the long locks she'd so carefully set aside. "You keep these," she said in her usual caustic tone. "If you change your mind, you may take them to a wig maker."

Serena's chin came up. "I'll not change my mind."

"You will, happily and freely, take your new look down to the parlor for your husband's approval?"

"I care not if he approves or no. But it is," she added, "exactly what we must do, and instantly!" She rose to her feet. "I had not realized it was so late. Are you ready? Shall we go?"

"Of course," said Miss Clapton. "I wouldn't miss this for the world." Miss Clapton, who had come to Lady Serena for reassurance about her own appearance, was no longer in the least worried about her looks!

Contradicting her *words*, Serena's ambivalent *feelings* rasped at her nerves all the way down the stairs. Would Ian finally lose that unbelievably equable temper? Would he yell at her? Send her to her room? *Would he beat her?* But did it matter if he did? It was *her* hair. *She* wished it cut. Why should it be his business if she cut it or not?

But would he, *even if he should not*, feel anger toward her? Serena took her courage firmly in hand and marched through the salon doors opened for her by Ian's butler. She glanced around . . .

. . . and felt thoroughly deflated that no one was in the room but themselves.

"You looked just then," said Miss Clapton, "like a balloon when the air is let out. Have you seen one? I went to an ascension. Or"—she grimaced—"an attempt at one. The weather changed and they were forced to release the gas. The balloon slumped just as you did upon discovering that Mr. McMurrey is not yet down."

Serena ignored the wry teasing. "I have read about balloons. It is fascinating, the notion that one might soar above the world and look down on it all. I think I would enjoy a balloon ride."

"The going up, perhaps"—Miss Clapton's brows arched—"but what of the coming down?"

"One reads of bad landings when the basket is caught in a tree or comes down too quickly and crashes, but never does one hear of others which go up and down safely. That makes boring news!"

Miss Clapton chuckled.

"What makes boring news?" asked Ian arriving just then.

Miss Clapton watched her host approach his suddenly apprehensive bride. "We speak of balloons, Mr. McMurrey. Lady Serena thinks she'd enjoy going up in one, where I fear the problems of landing it." Miss Clapton's face wore that odd half smile so common to her, her eyes slightly narrowed.

"You cut your hair," said Ian.

Nothing but surprise could be heard in his tone. His hand came up and he rubbed his chin, staring at Lady Serena with his head tipped ever so slightly to one side.

"I like it. I cannot understand how you had the courage to do it, so beautiful it was, but it was an excellent decision, my dear." He frowned slightly. "Or perhaps it is that you have suffered from headaches, bearing the weight of so much hair, and therefore wished rid of it? I have heard cutting it is the only cure."

Serena bit her lip and tipped a quick look toward Miss Clapton, who, she discovered, suppressed chuckles. "I am glad," she said stiffly, "that you like it." The really confusing thing, Lady Serena discovered, was that it was true. She *was* glad he liked it! "It will be far more convenient. You have no notion how much time a woman wastes, caring for long hair."

Where, she wondered, had her original motives of defiance and rebellion gone? And why had she felt that way? She could not recall. Serena tucked the thought away for later cogitation.

Dinner was announced just then and soon over. Since they'd no plans for the evening, Miss Clapton and Lady Serena adjourned to her ladyship's favorite sitting room, where each occupied herself with her needle—and the exchange of tales about life under the thumb of a tyrant!

Off and on all day the story of the maggots which saved the life of that unknown soldier had entered Ian's mind, only to be firmly banished. Although undecided as to what he'd *do*, he had, before he and Lady Serena left to meet Miss Clapton, had words with the lad who worked in the kitchen.

Now, dinner finished, Ian could no long put off a decision. He asked that the knife boy be sent to his study, reassuring his butler that the servant had done nothing wrong and was not in for a scolding. He did not, however, satisfy Higgens's curiosity about his reasons for ordering the boy to him.

The lad carried a small tin with holes punched in the top. A rank smell hovered around him, and Ian wrinkled his nose at it.

"You were successful," said Ian.

"Yes sir. Found some good ones, I did. Lots of 'em."

"Very well. I promised you a shilling, I think, but if you have been forced to deal with that smell all day, you deserve more!" Ian pushed a crown across his desk, but the lad didn't reach for it. "What is it? Why do you bite your lip?"

The boy sighed. "Can't take it, sir. Hid the box outside, you see. Didn't suffer at all."

Ian chuckled. "Then have it for being honest, but be careful how you spend it. If Higgens finds you've visited the local ale house, you'll be for it."

"I ain't no toper," said the lad scornfully. "Besides, I've a brother in your school. M'family will appreciate the extra when I take 'em m'wages next week."

"Is it quarter day again? So it is." Ian settled back, ignoring as well as he could the stench. "Your brother is in my school, is he? Does he like it?"

The boy nodded. "He hopes to become a clerk. Or the guv says it is possible that Nobby might make a teacher, if he wishes."

"Do you, too have ambitions to better yourself?"

The lad cast him a scornful look. " 'Course I do." His chin came up. "I'll be your butler someday."

Ian refrained from smiling at the boy's dreams. "Perhaps you will," he said. "But you must read and do sums, you know."

"My brother will teach me. I already know m'letters."

"It must be difficult, with him in school and you working here." Ian eyed the lad. "Yes, quite difficult. I doubt that's the answer."

The boy's face fell for a moment, and then he squared his shoulders. "Here now, what's it to you?"

"What it is to me, my boy, is that I hate waste. You will join your brother at school. I'll see that a sum equal to your wages is sent your parents each quarter, and when you finish your schooling we'll discuss your future."

"Me?" The boy's eyes widened. "Go to the school?"

"Have you not wished to do so?"

The boy ducked his head, his toe digging into the carpet. "Couldn't afford to send the both of us. How will I pay you back?"

"Just don't waste this opportunity." Unable to stand the stench another moment, Ian opened the window, allowing cleaner air from outside to dilute the smell from the tin. "I'll write a letter you will take the headmaster once you've seen your family." Ian wrote the letter and folded it, sealing it with his signet ring. "And now a note for my agent so your usual wages are sent your parents." He looked up, catching and holding the lad's speculative gaze. "I will receive regular reports from the headmaster, boy, and if you do not make progress, or if you are a troublemaker, you will return to your work here. Do you understand?"

"I'll work hard, sir. Truly I will."

"Very well, and now"—Ian eyed the tin, a muscle working in his jaw—"*I've* work to do."

"Why you want those ugly things?" The question burst from the lad as if he could no longer contain it.

Ian stared at the box. "Want them? I wouldn't say I *wanted* them." He shrugged away his thoughts. "I doubt you've finished your evening's work. Off with you."

The boy, his curiosity unsatisfied, left the room. He was happy, however, that he'd not been reprimanded for impertinence. And his ecstasy at the opportunity to go to school had him feeling as if he were floating. How his friends would stare!

Ian wrapped the foul-smelling tin in a sheet of oiled cloth and then went off with it to a distant corner of

Green Park. There, swallowing bile, he lifted the lid. His lip curled at the stink, but, using his penknife, he carefully separated out the whitish maggots, discarding the foul-smelling meat.

Then, appalled that he might actually do something logic told him was far from sane, Ian caught a hack and rode to Lord Freeman's town house, where in due course he was admitted to Jack's room. His friend slept restlessly, his fever high. Jack's nurse, Lord Freeman's eldest daughter, was the only other occupant of the room. She looked exhausted.

Jack moaned now and again as the two spoke softly. With an ulterior motive he dared not reveal, Ian asked, "Why do you not go to your room, Miss Templeton? I've nothing else to do and will sit with Jack while you get what I'd guess is much-needed rest. I promise you I will not leave without sending to inform you."

Miss Templeton hesitated. "It is not right that you act his nurse."

"He is my friend, Miss Templeton. I will do my best for him if you will tell me his needs."

"What he needs most are liquids. Whenever he rouses enough to swallow, please try to get something down him." She gestured to the glass on the night table beside her. When Ian nodded, she rose tiredly to her feet and with an apology for deserting him, left the room.

Ian waited only until he was certain she would not return. Then he moved to the bed. His lips compressed when Jack shifted slightly and instantly, even asleep, attempted to suppress a moan of pain.

Still Ian hesitated. Say the maggots helped. Jack might never forgive him if, his life saved, the leg didn't heal properly. If he discovered he could no longer live as he wished . . . Still, even if he never rode again, there was much of which the man was capable, and Jack was intelligent. He would eventually discover new reasons for living, would he not?

Arguing with himself no further, Ian took out the tin and opened it. The decision made, still he shuddered when he saw the squirming maggots. But Jack was certain to die if *something* were not done. And if he were to die anyway . . .

. . . then, bad or good, whatever Ian did was irrelevant, was it not?

He shrugged and tossed back the light cover, baring the wounded leg. It was well bandaged, which was something of a facer. The wound would have to be revealed if he were to introduce the tiny beasties which, if Serena's story were true, would change things for the better. A muscle in his jaw working, Ian gently undid the bandage, but gentle as he was, Jack moaned and opened his eyes. "What . . . ?"

"Hush, Jack. It's just me. Ian. I'll get you a drink in a moment." Ian uncovered the wound in Jack's thigh. Pus oozed, and the stink of it was enough to make Ian fear he'd cast up his accounts then and there. He swallowed. Hard. Quickly, before he could change his mind yet again, he poured the maggots into the incision.

Ian left the bandages off and moved around the bed to raise his friend, an arm under his shoulders. He held a glass of a milky-colored liquid to Jack's lips. The smell said it was that staple of a sick room, barley water. Jack greedily swallowed the dribbles Ian poured into his mouth, and then suddenly his head lolled to the side and he slept.

Gently Ian laid him back. He stared at the pasty features, pain-contorted, and wondered if he'd done the right thing. Perhaps it would only prolong Jack's suffering. Or perhaps those terrible creatures would not stop with the eating of the rotting flesh but would continue their obscene dining on the healthy flesh surrounding the wound! For an instant Ian wished he had taken the time to discuss the "cure" with someone who might know something of it.

A doctor? No. Doctors scoffed at wise women. He needed someone with an open mind. . . . Wendover? No. *Merwin*, perhaps, but *not* Wendover!

Anthony Wendover would respond in one of two ways. Either he'd be sick as a dog or, alternately, thinking it a great joke, demand they proceed at once. There would have been no *thought* in either case: Anthony was a good man, but he tended to think with his emotions rather than his mind. Which was no help at all.

Merwin, on the other hand, would think *too* much. He'd analyze the situation, discuss it backwards and forwards, demand more information, and perhaps travel into the country to find either the woman to whom Lady Serena referred or the wounded soldier who had recovered.

All of which would take time. *And time*, thought Ian, looking down at their friend, *is something Jack does not have.*

Time! Ian pulled out his watch and discovered it was getting on for eleven. It occurred to him to wonder if Lady Serena would worry if he did not return at a reasonable hour.

He had been so preoccupied with what he meant to do that he had forgotten to tell her where he was going or how long he'd be out. Ian considered sending a message and then, shrugging slightly and with only a hint of bitterness, decided his wife was unlikely to care one way or the other. To care, after all, one must assume she noticed his absence.

And that was unlikely.

Depressed by the notion, Ian stayed where he was. If Miss Templeton were to fall deep into much-needed sleep, she should be allowed to sleep. She might not appear until morning . . .

. . . by which time he would, he hoped, have some clue as to how this obscene cure was working.

One way or the other.

Nine

A lamp, lit each night in the garden below, shone up through a young tree just coming into leaf and through Lady Serena's lightly curtained window. Serena lay stiffly in her bed, staring at the dancing light and shadow on her ceiling. She found pictures in the moving shadows, played games with them, and tried not to allow herself to wonder where Ian was. It was, she told herself, none of her business. Even if he stayed out the whole of the night it was not her business. And—

She tipped a look at the clock she'd moved to her bedside table.

—it looked as if he meant to do just that.

So . . . why did she care?

Because she did. Serena had admitted that some hours previously. But *why* she cared she did not know. She debated it again and again until, along with false dawn, came exhaustion which pulled her into a restless slumber.

When her maid came with morning tea, Serena pretended she did not hear. As soon as the chit left, she returned to sleep, hoping Ian had returned before the servants rose for the day, thus preventing escalation of the gossip which must be circulating in the servants' hall.

When she awoke the second time, it was to discover Miss Clapton seated near the windows, sewing. "Ah," said the companion. "I began to think you meant to sleep the whole of the day."

Serena yawned. "What time is it?" she asked when she could speak.

"After ten. Your husband came in while I ate breakfast under the frosty gaze of your butler. I don't think he approves of me."

"I'm unconvinced Higgens approves of *me*," retorted Serena, drawing a chuckle from Miss Clapton. "What do you mean, Ian arrived?"

"He was, or so he said"—Miss Clapton's brows arched—"sitting with a sick friend. All night. He looked it. Jack somebody or other."

"Jack . . . Princeton, I think." Serena yawned again. *Could it be the truth*? "Lieutenant Princeton came home from Portugal with a nasty wound and refuses to allow amputation. Ian says it will kill him."

Suddenly she recalled telling Ian Vicar Morton's tale of a similar case and what was done to save that man. Surely Ian had not tried . . . no, of course not. He would not take so disgusting and ill-founded a notion to heart.

Would he?

"You frown. You think, perhaps, he was *not* with a sick friend?"

At the sly note in Miss Clapton's voice, Serena glanced at her. She shrugged. "Frankly, I fear he *was*."

Another burst of that unexpected laughter came from Miss Clapton. "Incredible. Why does a wife, even one who is not *truly* a wife, prefer that her husband tell horrid lies about his whereabouts when he has been gone all the night *innocently*?"

"How did you know . . . ?"

"You are wife in name only?" Miss Clapton's brows arched. "Servants gossip, my dear. The whole world is likely to know." She tipped her head, a querying look in her eyes. "Now, this is a strange thing! I expected you to blush, and I do not understand why, instead, you look as if you were about to faint!"

"If my father hears such gossip . . ."

"You are married now." When Serena made no response, Miss Clapton added, "It is none of his business."

"He might guess . . ."

When Serena shut her mouth with a snap, Miss Clapton tipped her head and pursed her lips. "Guess . . . that you've no intention of making it a real marriage? Ever?"

"Do not say that aloud! Do not *whisper* it. I could not bear it if he discovered our plans. Not when I am so near to achieving my every wish."

"Your every wish. . . ."

Serena sighed, then glowered. "I have this strange feeling that I have already revealed too much."

"And you do not trust me." A sardonic quirk twisted Miss Clapton's lips but was almost instantly banished. "After all," she added, "how *can* one trust a fallen woman and promised murderess? Such a one must be untrustworthy in other ways as well, must she not?"

Serena pushed herself up against her pillows. "The strange thing is, I feel I can trust you, but it is not altogether my secret."

Miss Clapton nodded. "You are quite right that you may trust me, although I do not know how I might prove it. But it is also true you should not discuss a secret which involves another. I will contain my curiosity, which is my most outrageous trait. Perhaps I should inform you that your husband looked more than a trifle preoccupied when he arrived. Worried, even."

"Did he go to bed?"

"He was eating when I left the table. Oh! He said he meant to change and would then be at your disposal. He mentioned a school?"

"Oh, dear. I forgot we meant to go to his school. Have *you* an interest in the education of deserving youth?" she asked as she rose from her bed. Miss Clapton grimaced, and Serena smiled. "You do not and would be bored. I will give you coin and you may shop. You need day dresses and an evening gown or two. And chemises and . . ." She frowned slightly when Miss Clapton shook her head. "Not? You would say you need no new chemises?"

"Mrs. Strong found a length of lawn from which I cut several." Miss Clapton lifted her hands, showing Serena the one on which she worked. "Your Mrs. Strong was insulted that she must supply such as I with anything at all."

"She was impertinent?" Miss Clapton frowned, and Serena's forehead crimped into an answering frown. "If a servant treats you ill, then you must speak of it to Ian. He will see you are treated with respect."

"The respect I deserve, perhaps? But, my dear Lady Serena, is that not how they treat me?"

Serena cast Miss Clapton a severe look. "That self-mockery in which you indulge must cease. You agreed to your seduction, but you did not deserve your fate. Why should you be censured when the man who perpetrated a greater wrong by lying to you is *not*?"

A startled expression crossed Miss Clapton's face. Then she laughed. "I doubt others would agree with you, but if this school is important to you, then I would like to go"—she glanced up sharply—"unless I would be in the way."

"If you mean to accompany me when I attend committee meetings at Lady Cartwright's, then I think you *should* come." Serena adopted a mischievous look. "You see, my dear Miss Clapton, Lady Cartwright means to establish a girls' school run in similar fashion to this particular boys' school, although the subjects taught will differ. It would be as well if you and I had some notion of what is involved! Especially," she added, sobering, "since others will expect me to know the way of things at Ian's school."

"Which you do not?"

"I only recently discovered its existence. Lady Cartwright drove me by it one day, so I asked Ian about it. I do not understand him . . ."

"And look as if you wished to."

Serena felt shock rush through her. *Did* she wish to understand her husband? *Did* she want to know more about his strange ways? "Occasionally I do. And then again I only want the next months to pass so I can . . ." She glanced up, casting an accusing look toward her companion. "You, Miss Clapton, are far too easy a woman with whom to talk!"

"I am known to own an excellent shoulder on which to cry. All my friends came to me to pour out their troubles, and we discussed them to see if aught could be done. It is most amusing," she said with the mild sarcasm which colored much of her speech. "It seems I could help everyone but myself."

"With whom did you discuss your problems?" asked Serena.

For a moment it was the other woman's turn to look bemused. "You know, it never occurred to me to do so. Perhaps," she added caustically, "because I knew no one who would not be horrified by my situation—"

Miss Clapton seemed to collapse inside, and Serena knew what she had meant about a deflating balloon.

"—and rightly so," continued the woman stoutly. "Drat, drat, drat! I should not have agreed to come here. What was I thinking?"

"Perhaps that you had been offered sanctuary when you were much in need of it. Do not refine on such thoughts. I cannot tell you exactly why Ian made his offer, but I am glad he did so."

Miss Clapton bit her lip. "Those who were guests at

the house party will remember me. They may know I was sent from my home in disgrace."

"The party was long over when your grandfather sent you away."

"Or neighbors may come to town for the season. They will think badly of you for harboring me or think I lied to you . . ."

"Ian will know what to say."

"What to say! What *can* he say?"

Serena smiled broadly. One might even have called it a grin. "Why, that it is no one's business but our own."

Miss Clapton rose to her feet. "You have great faith in him, do you not?" She didn't pause for an answer but left the room, saying she would leave Lady Serena to prepare for their outing.

It was as well that Miss Clapton did not wish a response, because Serena was speechless. It was true she had faith in Ian. Trust. Where did it come from? How *could* she have come to trust a *man*? She shuddered. Then she squared her shoulders and quickly, without calling for her maid, dressed.

As she brushed her newly shorn locks, she smiled at her image. Even her mother would look twice in order to recognize her in this guise. What a difference the feathery curls touching her face made to her looks. Another thing about the short hair: She didn't require a maid to dress it. Before her marriage, she had braided it, coiling the plaits up and out of her way. Then, when they arrived in London, the abigail Ian had hired begged to do her hair, and she had begun wearing it in more elaborate styles.

But now! The sense of freedom that short hair gave her was amazing. No wonder her father would not allow his wife or daughter to cut their hair!

* * *

Lady Serena asked questions all the way back from their tour. Ian, tired but patient, answered as best he could. At one point he yawned, and for a moment Serena felt guilty for pestering him, but then another question occurred to her. They arrived home just as he ended his discussion about how students were assessed and whether charity students were dismissed if they did not apply themselves properly.

As they entered the house, Ian excused himself. He was headed for his room when Higgens stopped him, speaking to him in a soft tone. Ian, sighing, changed direction and went to his study.

Miss Clapton went upstairs, but Serena, preoccupied by all the things she'd seen and learned, followed Ian. She reached the doorway . . . and stared to see Ian and a stranger grinning at each other like idiots, tears running down the unknown's face.

"The doctor says he will recover. It is a miracle!"

Ian, catching sight of Serena from the corner of his eye, turned. "No miracle. Or perhaps"—he cast her a warm smile "—an angel had a hand in it. Come in, my dear. Templeton tells me Jack's fever broke late this morning and that his wound"—he gave her another, more mischievous smile, his brow quirked—"is clean and healing."

Serena hesitated, looking from one to the other. It seemed Ian had somehow managed the trick but didn't wish to admit it. "Lord Templeton?"

Rolly Templeton bowed. "Not a lord, my lady. Just an honorable. Or rather"—he flushed—"Lieutenant. I keep forgetting, you see, that I'm in the army now. I brought Jack home. He couldn't be sent by himself, and frankly"—his ears turned a deeper red—"I'm not much of a soldier. I'd a minor wound as well, and m'commanding officer was happy for an excuse to be rid of me."

"I was unaware the spring campaign was begun."

"Hasn't. Princeton led us out. Reconnoitering, you know. We ran smack into a French unit on the same business and, of course, we mixed it up a bit. Jack got that ball to his thigh, and a shot scored a path along the side of my head. Our fellows sent the French running and got Jack and me back. I'm all right now, but Jack . . ." He sobered. "Well, we didn't think he'd make it."

"His fever broke?" asked Lady Serena.

"His fever was bad when I left him earlier," said Ian. "Miss Templeton said she would have the housekeeper wash him down, trying to bring it down."

"Which she did. The doctor says it is impossible and that Jack should not have lasted the week." The young soldier chuckled. "He sounded vexed that Jack will *not* die!"

"The doctor's professional view of himself is no concern of ours." Ian thought of the maggots he had tossed from the window as it began to get light and hoped he'd gotten them all. He should have counted them. "Mrs. Strong will have set out a luncheon, Rolly. Will you join us?" he asked politely, wishing he could go to his room and sleep and sleep and sleep. The emotional energy spent on gladness for Jack was quite as draining as fretting over whether he'd lost his mind, when he'd actually poured *maggots* into Jack's wound.

"I'd like that if it won't put you out." Templeton looked beyond Serena toward where the click of feminine footsteps could be heard. "But if you've company . . ." His eyes bulged. He closed them, shaking his head, then opened just one, closed it. "No! Can't be." His hand came up, warding off . . . something. "You're dead. Deeaad," Templeton moaned as he slumped to the floor, his body folding as if it were boneless.

Serena, gaping at the fallen man, heard Miss Clapton's keening. Serena was pushed aside in her companion's rush to get at Rolly Templeton. Ian, quite as startled as

Serena, was nearly too late to prevent Miss Clapton from plunging a short-bladed knife into the lieutenant.

"Let me go." Miss Clapton struggled. "You said you would not prevent me!"

"But you, I think, promised to discuss the man with us. *First*."

Templeton groaned. He rolled onto his back. "She's dead. They told me she was dead," he muttered, covering his eyes with the back of his hand. "Blasted head wound! Seeing things. *Must* be seeing things." He opened one eye, stared up into Miss Clapton's angry-looking features, and shut it again. "Mad. I've run mad." He curled into a ball, his head hidden in his arms.

"Does that sound like a man who feels guilt? Or one who is horror-struck?" asked Ian quietly.

All the tension drained from Miss Clapton's rigid body. She passed the knife to Ian and dropped to her knees. "Rolly?" she ordered, shaking him. "Rolly, why did you not come back?"

"Did," he insisted and peeked at her. "You ain't dead?"

"You did not come. Not like you promised. It was *months* and you never came."

Templeton's ears burned red, and he sat up. "Well, I *meant* to come sooner. You know I did. But first it was a race and then it was a pugilist and then we went sailing and . . ." He shrugged. "Henny, you know I've never been any good at keeping track of time. That's why I make a bad officer."

"Officer?" She appeared to notice his uniform for the first time.

"I joined up when they said you was dead." He held out a hand to her. "You truly ain't dead?"

Miss Clapton laughed a short, sharp laugh. "There were times I wished it, Rolly, but I'm alive." Her soft, yearning expression belied the harsh laugh. "Damn you," she added, but there was no heat in it. She touched his cheek, pushed at a lock of hair . . . and discovered the scar left from his wound.

Rolly reached for her, and Ian, recognizing the look in his friend's eye, hurriedly removed Serena from the room. "I think it best if we leave them now. They've very likely a great deal to, er, say to each other."

Serena, her ears a trifle heated by her own suspicions, nodded. "Ian, where did that knife come from?"

He chuckled. "She was behind you, was she not? You did not see, as I did, when she lifted her skirt and pulled it from a sheath strapped to her leg! Cor-blimey, as they say in some circles. I wonder what she went through that she learned to wear a knife!"

"She lost the baby soon after I first saw her, and then she came to London." Serena frowned. "Ian, she wasn't holding the knife properly."

Ian remembered Serena on their wedding night. "You can give her a lesson later." A jaw-cracking yawn split his face. "Serena, I was up all night." He yawned again, trying without much success to restrain it. "Would you object if I . . . ?"

Holding the impulse back with some difficulty, Serena did *not* lay her hand against Ian's cheek as Miss Clapton had to Lieutenant Templeton's. "You go to bed. I had no breakfast, so I am hungry. I'll take a book and have a bowl of soup and perhaps a slice of ham."

Ian felt no reluctance to touch her and did so, running one finger along her jaw down to her chin. His finger resting there, he asked, "Has anyone ever told you what an incredible woman you are?"

"Nonsense." Serena felt a blush. "You rest," she said with a touch of Miss Clapton's caustic tongue. "You'll feel more the thing once you do so."

She felt his eyes boring into her as she stalked down the hall to the breakfast room. Ian, recalling that she usually laid her book on the side table in the small salon, ordered Higgens to retrieve it and take it to her so she could read at table as she'd wished.

And then, finally, he trod heavily up the stairs to his much-to-be-desired bed. And, for this once, he was glad it was empty!

Miss Clapton and Lieutenant Templeton left the McMurrey house not to return for several hours. When they returned, Ian, revived by his long nap, was sitting with Lady Serena in the salon. He set aside the book from which he'd read aloud while she sorted embroidery silks. Rolly was grinning widely, and Miss Clapton looked sleek and satisfied.

"We did it."

"You couldn't do it," objected Ian. "Not that quickly."

" 'Course we could," Rolly contradicted him. He squeezed Miss Clapton's arm and smiled down at her. "Bishop made no objections. Not once he'd heard the tale."

"Then you are married already?" asked Serena, rising to her feet. "Oh, dear. I have been concocting such wonderful plans!"

"Didn't say we were married," objected Rolly, frowning.

Miss Clapton gave her love an exasperated look. "What Rolly meant is that we purchased a license and will wed as soon as it is allowed. Three days, I believe."

Ian bit his lip. "Miss Clapton, may I make a suggestion?"

"Of course."

"I think we should do this with less haste and more propriety. There should be an announcement in the papers and a party in your honor, and then in a week or so, you may be wed from this house in good style. One cannot entirely avoid gossip, but I believe we may make a romantic tale of it rather than a farce or, alternately, a tragedy."

Miss Clapton and Lieutenant Templeton looked chagrined. "But . . ." she began.

Rolly put a finger to her lips, interrupting her. When she stilled, he asked, "You think it necessary, Ian? For Henny's sake?"

"Yes. Her family is unlikely to raise objections, but it is possible they will still treat her as an outcast—considering the sort of man her grandfather is. The *ton*, however, must be told some tale, and, quite obviously, the truth will not do."

"I see that," said Rolly. "Do hush, Henny. Ian is correct. I know we made plans, but we can change them so as to do right by your reputation. No," he added when Miss Clapton frowned. "I will not be ruled in this. Not when it is for *your* good."

Miss Clapton jerked his sleeve and, when he bent, whispered into his ear. Templeton turned bright red and tipped a quick embarrassed look toward Ian, but his mouth remained firm and he continued to shake his head at her. She sighed, compressed her lips, and then, finally, shrugged. "Very well, Rolly. Tell me, Lady Serena, what plans did you make?"

"First we'll hold a dinner? For friends and Lieutenant Templeton's family? And yours if they will come, of course. Then we must place an order for your trousseau, which"—Serena caught and held Ian's eyes—"we will pay for as our wedding gift to you." He nodded. "And finally, there must be the wedding and wedding breakfast and . . . and that is as far as I've gone. I've no notion what else we should do."

"Invitations must be printed up for the dinner," said Ian. "I know where that may be done quickly. And"—his eyes sparkled with humor—"just perhaps, Rolly should talk to his father and mother before we go much further?

I suspect anyone's parents would appreciate knowing their child is to wed! We will write Miss Clapton's family. I think I will do that in your place, Miss Clapton, since it is possible your grandfather would not open a letter coming from you?"

"I am dead to *him* at least. Now and again I have tried to get word to my mother by sending a note to our vicar, but that poor man is under my grandfather's thumb, so I've no idea whether he has dared inform her I am alive and well."

Ian nodded. "Once I put that letter in the mail, we must insert a proper notice in the newspapers. Rolly? Can you think of anything else?"

Rolly grinned and shrugged, smiling down at Miss Clapton. "All I thought of was getting the license so we could do the trick. Hadn't thought of anything else at all! I'll just toddle on and spout the news to the pater and the mater—"

"You will do it more tactfully than that, my lad!" scolded Miss Clapton. "Your parents believe me dead and will think you've run mad if you trot off home and blithely inform them we are to wed."

Rolly blinked. A smile slowly spread across his somewhat vacuous features. "Oh, but think, Henny! Wouldn't you like to see their expressions if I just tell 'em we've tied the knot?"

"Your mother would have a spasm if you did anything so cruel. Now, don't play the fool, Rolly, but think how to do it right."

The four discussed that problem and a few more things before Rolly reluctantly departed. When he was gone, Serena told Miss Clapton they would visit the modiste on the morrow.

Her cheeks just a trifle pink, Miss Clapton thanked her but warned, "I mean to go with Rolly back to his regiment. I'll not need frothy things but good, strong, sensible clothes, riding habits, a warm cloak perhaps . . . and not much of anything. Packing up when a woman follows the drum is sometimes, Rolly tells me, a hurried business indeed."

"You will not, then, remain in Lisbon as I understand many wives do?"

"No. I can manage Rolly. He's a bad soldier because he forgets things like duty rosters, not because he's a coward in battle. With me there, he will do very well." She smiled, that strange little half smile. "You will see."

"We should plan carefully then, exactly what you wish made up for you."

Ian rose to his feet. "You will not need me for that. Miss Clapton, if I did not wish you well, I hope you know it was not because I do *not*."

She grinned. "In fact, you will be rather glad to be rid of me, will you not?"

"How does a gentleman answer such a question as that?" teased Ian. "You are welcome for as long as you need a roof."

"But only just so long! You would be alone with your bride, would you not?" She stared challengingly at him, her brow quirked and her chin well up.

"I need not look at her to know you are disturbing that same bride, Miss Clapton," said Ian, less humor in his voice.

Incorrigibly, the woman added, "Yes, but that doesn't answer my question about *your* wishes, does it then?"

"I enjoy Lady Serena's company very much, as I hope she knows." He held up a hand. "And that, minx, is all the answer you will get." He grinned at Miss Clapton, gently touched his wife's heated cheek, and left the room.

"You shouldn't tease him so," scolded Lady Serena.

"Do you not wish to know if he loves you?"

"Do not talk nonsense. Love is a fairy tale for infants." Miss Clapton's quirky smile disappeared instantly. "It is you who speaks nonsense. I lost sight of it in my bitterness, but what Rolly and I have felt almost since we were in leading strings is *love*. It has changed over the years, of course, from what children feel to friendship and affection and finally to love as felt by adults. *But it has always been love*."

Serena resented the suggestion that love existed when she would never experience it. But if it *did* exist, then she wished to know more about it. "I," she challenged, "have always wondered why any woman is so foolish as to go into marriage voluntarily."

"If your father was anything like my grandfather, then I understand why you think as you do. I am lucky to have seen love elsewhere. My father and mother, for instance. *Despite* my grandfather, they loved each other. And Lord and Lady Templeton. They too have great and abiding affection for each other. As for Rolly and me? Just at the moment we enjoy a mostly physical love, but that too will change as we get older. What we now feel will grow into a more settled sort of thing which will include *all* the sorts of love we've ever felt for each other."

Startled, Serena blurted, "You *enjoy* . . . ?" She blushed. "Pardon me. I should not have allowed that thought freedom . . ."

"Why should you not be curious?" Miss Clapton described in far greater detail and a trifle more plainly than was necessary *exactly* what she had enjoyed with Rolly in the past, what she wanted of him now, and what she expected from him in the future. Despite some mild crudities, the picture she painted was as unlike the raw depiction Serena's brother had drawn as a perfect summer from a miserable winter.

"So you see," finished Miss Clapton, "it is something of a nuisance, this having to wait weeks rather than days in order to wed." Miss Clapton grimaced. "Ah, well. We were parted for months. I suppose today will satisfy us until our wedding."

"Today?"

"In the study," admitted Miss Clapton, grinning. "It was only afterwards it occurred to either of us that we were in the presence of others, which would have been embarrassing for all if your husband had not taken you off."

"And it does not . . . hurt?" asked Serena, thinking of her mother.

"The first time"—Miss Clapton shrugged—"a bit. After that?" She grinned. "In my opinion, the good Lord came up with a marvelous means of begetting children." The grin faded. "My experience, however, may not be that of all women. I understand that many gentlemen think a *lady* is born somehow different from other women; that they are more . . . delicate. They are not expected to enjoy it, or it is believed they are unable to do so or some such nonsense. So"—she cast Serena a challenging look—*"you* must see that your man comes to a proper view of things, assuming he has not!"

Serena blushed hotly. "Setting a man straight will not be my problem."

"I will not believe Mr. McMurrey incapable!"

The blush felt still more livid. "I wouldn't know. Since, as I thought you had guessed, we do not mean to remain married, we do not indulge in . . . that sort of thing. I'll never be in a position to know how he feels about his wife's . . . delicacy."

"Are you certain that is what *he* wants?" asked Miss Clapton sharply. "To sever your marriage tie?"

"How could it be otherwise?" Serena caught herself when she realized there was more than a little sadness in her tone. "He wed me only because his brother, who was my betrothed, died." She added, speaking more firmly, "Ian was unaware that James and I had an agreement that we would *not* wed. Thanks to our fathers, James and I were forced to rely on trickery to avoid marriage. I fear it was difficult for poor James to find believable excuses."

"So instead, he died? How agreeable of him!"

"Do not sneer. He took the smallpox. Ian told me he was recovering, but the pox weakened his heart, and he died." Serena sighed. "Ian did what he thought best, of course, but I do wish he had discussed it with me before we met at the altar. It is possible he too might have discovered reasons to postpone it as Jamie had done before him."

"Do *you* wish you had never met Ian McMurrey?" Miss Clapton chuckled. "You color up so prettily. You like him, do you not?"

"I don't understand him," said Serena, falling back on her favorite line. But she admitted, at least to herself, that she trusted him. And she had come to rely on him. But like him? It surprised her to discover she *did*. "Yes. I like him. A man! I cannot understand how it could have happened, but I *do* like him."

"Perhaps," said Miss Clapton dryly, "because he is a *likable* man." She smiled when Serena's cheeks colored. "He will make a good husband, and his children will be still luckier."

That was too much and Serena grimaced. "Good? Husband?"

"You still think that a contradiction, do you not? I, however, believe such men as my grandfather and your father are the exceptions. Actually, most men are just average, neither good nor bad. Rolly is that way. More good than bad, but he is nobody particularly special to anyone but me. Ian McMurrey, on the other hand, *is*. If I were you, I'd think twice about letting him go. You will never do better."

Serena's chin lifted. "I want my freedom!"

"With a man like Mr. McMurrey, you will have it—"
Serena stared.

"—Just so much as you will want or need." Miss Clapton rose. "Think about it. I'll make a list of what a soldier's wife needs. *You* be careful you do not make a fool of yourself, stubbornly certain you cannot be wrong."

Serena stared at the closed door for a very long time before her mind drifted back to Miss Clapton's vivid description of her feelings when making love with her lover. She felt herself blushing hotly at just the thought of the things Miss Clapton said they did with and to each other. Surely men and women would not . . . could not . . . did not . . .

But Miss Clapton said they did. And, against her will, Serena was more than half convinced her companion had not exaggerated. She pictured Ian. Such wonderfully gentle hands, but so huge. Such terribly broad shoulders. Such hard muscle she'd felt through his coat . . .

. . . but under that coat?

For the first time in her life, Lady Serena was curious as to what might be under a man's clothing.

Ten

The week drew on, but Serena could not forget Miss Clapton's descriptions of lovemaking. She could not forget the notion that perhaps such behavior was not as disgusting as she had believed. She was still less able to purge her curiosity about how it would be if *Ian* were to take *her* to his bed. On more than one occasion she found herself eyeing him, and *twice* he caught her at it.

"What is it?" he asked on this, the second occasion.

"What is . . . what?"

"What are you thinking when you look at me in just that way?" He tipped his head. "And do not," he continued after half a moment's observation, "ask me *what* way. That lovely color in your complexion tells me you know exactly what I mean."

The faint flush deepened to a blush. "I do know," said Serena, turning away. "But I cannot discuss it. Please do not ask."

He came to her and put a hand gently on her shoulder. She resisted his attempt to turn her. "Serena," he said, "I am your friend. I hope you know that."

"I believe it." The exceedingly strange thing was, she *did*.

"Friends can tell each other anything."

"Not everything."

He sighed. "Perhaps it is just that you have so little

experience of friendship, my dear. Please believe that I am here for you. That I will do anything—"

Serena choked back something which was halfway between a laugh and a sob.

"—in my power to make you happy." He forced her to face him. When she would not look up, he put a hand beneath her chin and gently pressed her face up. "Anything, Serena."

"No, no. It is nothing. You have promised the one thing which will make me happy."

"Your freedom." He sighed. "Serena, if I said I would give you the income from your fortune each year and permission to do with it as you liked, would you reconsider your need for an annulment? For . . . freedom? Would you remain wed to me?"

She tore herself from his gentle grip, moving backward. "But you did not wish to wed me. You too want to be free . . ."

"Do I? Perhaps, before I met you, I had notions I'd lose my freedom by wedding you, but, my dear, that was before I came to know you. Believe me, I will miss you a great deal if you insist on holding me to my promise." He watched her lips compress. "Say nothing now, Serena. But think about my offer. You may have your income just as you'd have had it if you had never married."

He eyed his wife. Poor dear. How could he tell her that, willy-nilly, she'd have those monies only if he settled them on her? And that assumed they managed to get the annulment she wanted, an impossibility unless he perjured himself, claiming impotence—and perhaps not then.

"Too," he continued when she did not speak, "you would find it an advantage to have my experience and backing when you do . . . whatever you decide to do."

"Set up a home for unwed mothers," she blurted. "For

women like Miss Clapton who are ejected from their homes and have nowhere to go." Honesty made her add, "Or as I thought Miss Clapton to be, ruined by force or by a man's trickery."

Ian frowned. "You might have to give up trying to distinguish between those who are forced and those who . . . cooperate in their seduction. It is a distinction often difficult to make."

"So I now understand. But even so, I do not know how to go about it." She swung around at a tap on the door.

Higgens opened it, cleared his throat, and announced Lord and Lady Freeman. Rolly's parents entered, identical frowns marring their brows.

"My lord. My lady, welcome." Serena breathed a relieved sigh that she and Ian could not now continue what was, for her, an exceedingly difficult conversation. "Higgens, please provide refreshment proper to the occasion."

Higgens bowed and closed the doors. Serena was pleased by the interruption, but Ian was not. Hiding his irritation that, just when Serena began speaking more freely, guests should arrive, he strode forward.

"My lady, will you sit here?" Ian escorted Rolly's mother to the most comfortable chair. "To what do we owe this honor?" he asked once Serena had the tea tray before her and he'd passed their visitors their cups.

"We *should* have come the moment Rolly told us. This Miss Clapton," said Lord Freeman bluntly; "you are *certain* it is she? We were told *by her family* that she had died. You see, Rolly returned from Portugal with a bad bang to the head, and frankly . . ." Lord Freeman paused as if frankness were beyond him.

"Miss Clapton did not die. She was ejected from her home, Lord Freeman, by her dreadful grandfather when he discovered she was . . ." It was Serena's turn to look anywhere but at her guests.

Ian chuckled softly at her embarrassment and received a glower in response. He turned to Lord and Lady Freeman. "Did Rolly inform you he and she had, hmm, indulged in illicit behavior during a certain house party?" Lord Freeman, spots of red on his cheeks, nodded. "Then you will understand that there were consequences."

Lady Freeman understood at once. "Oh dear! Why did the poor girl not come to me?" asked her ladyship.

Such a notion had never occurred to Serena. Now, she too wondered why.

"You may ask her," said Ian. "Shall I tell her you wish to speak to her?"

The door opened just then and Miss Clapton entered. "The tweeny said— Ah. My lady? My lord?"

Lord Freeman rose and bowed. "My dear, welcome to the family."

Miss Clapton eyed him as if she were not certain she should believe him. "Thank you," she said a trifle belatedly. Then, shyly, "My lady?"

When Lady Freeman rose to her feet and opened her arms, Miss Clapton, on a tiny sob, ran into the woman's embrace. Ian, touching his lordship's arm, tipped his head toward the door. Lord Freeman tugged at his cravat, nodded, and made for it. Asking silently for permission, Ian quirked a brow at Serena who made shooing motions. Gladly, Ian removed himself from what promised to be an emotional scene. He took his lordship to his study, where he supplied something rather stronger than the tea they'd been imbibing.

"There is a child? My grandchild?" asked Freeman as soon as they closed Ian's study door behind them.

"Should have been. She suffered rather greatly at the hands of her grandfather's sister. The great-aunt insisted she must give up the child, so Miss Clapton attempted to reach a grandmother who had died. Poor dear, she had not been informed of the death. So far as I can discover, she did not dishonor herself during the few weeks she was on her own. She made a living as a flower girl after the baby was born."

"Rolly didn't mention a child."

"Rolly," said Ian dryly, "may not know. Miss Clapton is not particularly forthcoming, believing the past should be forgotten. Rolly, being Rolly, is unlikely to have thought to ask."

"I make no excuses for my son, except to say that it must have been Miss Clapton's supposed death which sent him haring off into the army." His lordship drummed his fingers on the arm of his chair. "I hope," he added sharply, "that she is aware I will not allow him to sell out!"

"She will follow the drum, my lord. And"—Ian grinned—"she means to keep Rolly in line. She says he is no coward. With someone to see he remembers the duty roster, and where he is to be when, he will do very well!"

Freeman sighed. "He is a rapscallion, but there is no evil in him."

Ian saw a chance to change the subject. "In either twin, I think. I don't believe I have seen Alaric in town?"

His lordship sighed still more deeply. "Ally has gone into business. He is in Ireland with a friend who owns a small stud there."

Ian grinned. "He may fall into debt, but it is likely to be far less than if he were running free here in London with nothing to do!"

Freeman smiled at that. *"Children.* They are one's greatest delight and one's greatest bane. Thank heaven my heir is a rock-steady sort of man!

In the salon Miss Clapton confessed to losing her child and proceeded to mop up her future mother-in-law's tears. "My first grandchild," wailed Lady Freeman. "In a pauper's grave!"

Serena saw her companion's lips tighten. "Is that where the infant is buried?" she asked gently.

Miss Clapton stared into the distance, her features hard and cold. "She is on a hill top under an apple tree. I buried her myself."

"My dear . . ." Lady Freeman's expression became one of horror as she understood. "Oh, my poor dear child, you were alone, were you not? You suffered the child's birth alone and were alone when you discovered she was dead and . . . Oh, you poor dear! Why, oh why, did you not come to me?"

Miss Clapton looked startled at the notion. "Frankly, it didn't occur to me. Then too, my grandfather, when he discovered my plight, locked me in my room, so I'd have been unable to do so if it had." They were silent for a moment before Miss Clapton drew in a deep breath. "Well, in any case, as soon as I could"—Miss Clapton continued with that bitterness which Serena guessed protected her from strong emotion—"I wrapped her in my shawl and buried her under that gnarled old ap . . . ap . . . apple tree." The starch went out of her, and this time Lady Freeman wiped away the young woman's tears. When both were calm, Miss Clapton added, "I laid stones from an old wall over the grave."

"We will discuss a proper burial with my husband, my dear, and then you need not think of it again." Lady Freeman patted Miss Clapton's hand, drew in a deep breath, and, with a brightness she obviously didn't yet feel, said, "Now tell me what you've planned. I will help in any way I can."

Lady Serena detailed their ideas. She finished, "Your note said you will join us for the announcement dinner. Because of that, I assumed you were agreeable to the marriage."

Lady Freeman's ears grew rosy, and she darted an apologetic glance toward Miss Clapton. "It was only today I wondered . . ." She paused in embarrassment. "Rolly was so very happy, finding her here, but a *head* wound." She shook hers. "He had terrible dreams when he first came home. It occurred to me to wonder if this Miss Clapton was a figment of his imagination. Not that a woman didn't exist, you see, but that it might not be *our* Miss Clapton."

"You mean you feared some vixen had imposed on him," said Miss Clapton. Lady Freeman nodded. "I will allow you the vixen bit, which I can be when need be, but I will not allow that I've imposed!"

"Of course not. He confessed he meant to wed you long ago, and that he only went off on that walking tour because it was already planned. He'd meant to come back directly and make everything official. Except then—"

Miss Clapton touched her finger where the ring, which previously hung around her neck on a cord, now rested. "Then it was one thing after another for the poor boy," she interrupted. "He never was much good at saying no, was he?" Miss Clapton drew in a deep breath. "Well, for my part, I am only glad we have discovered each other again. We will forget the months between and go on from here. It is best that way."

"Rolly may feel differently, my dear," said his mother hesitantly. "About the baby, I mean. He may wish to help rebury it."

"Rolly doesn't know about the babe," said Miss Clapton and bluntly added, "I would rather he never knew. Or at least, not until we've half a dozen more so he'll not have time to think too much about the first."

Lady Freeman frowned, a sad look back in her eyes. "You have become a trifle hardened, have you not?"

"Which," suggested Miss Clapton, "may be just as well, may it not? If I am to follow the drum with Rolly,

I'll need everything I've learned and perhaps more." She flashed a sudden grin, her eyes twinkling with humor. "Lady Serena is teaching me how to use a knife properly. In case some Frenchman catches me up, you see."

"Lady Serena is . . . A *knife*?" Lady Freeman turned a wide-eyed, astonished gaze on her hostess.

Serena blushed rosily. "When my brothers were bored they would teach me things a young lady ought not to know. I'm a good shot, too. But that is not relevant. What *is*, is whom we invite to the wedding. My lady, you asked if you could help. We desperately need a proper invitation list."

"I will make one up immediately. If you've not ordered the invitations, then I can do that as well. Only tell me how they are to be engraved." Lady Freeman turned to Miss Clapton. "Is your mother coming up to town, or will you return home . . . ?" She stared at Miss Clapton's suddenly blank expression. "Oh, dear. Oh no! Surely your grandfather could not . . . Surely he would not . . ."

Serena knew Miss Clapton wished her mother's presence and cast an anxious look her way.

A muscle worked in Miss Clapton's jaw. Finding her tongue, she spoke caustically. "You forget, my lady. I am dead. He has said so. Surely you do not suggest a mother could have anything to do with the wedding of a dead daughter."

"Your grandfather should be taken out and shot," exclaimed Lady Freeman. She rose to her feet and turned toward the door as her husband and Ian entered. She held out her hand to his lordship, who came to her instantly. "You will not credit it," she said. "Miss Clapton's grandfather has not acknowledged her engagement, so her mother likely knows nothing of the wedding and will not be allowed to attend!"

Lord Freeman cast Miss Clapton a commiserating look, took his wife into a warm embrace, and, over her head, cast a resigned look toward Ian. "You've received no response to the letter you mentioned?"

"None."

"I will write him." His lordship settled his chin on his wife's head and smiled a wry smile. "It is an excuse to tell the old curmudgeon exactly what I think of him and his rigid morality. *And* his selfishness. It is wrong of him to keep Miss Clapton and her mother apart."

Soon the Freemans left and Miss Clapton removed to her room. "I saw your expression when Lord Freeman comforted his wife, Serena," said Ian. "Why were you so surprised? But I need not ask, need I? Again it is that you think all men are as cruel and insensitive as your father."

Serena sighed. "It is very difficult to change the beliefs of one's whole life. I am trying, but I am still surprised, shocked even, when my beliefs are so thoroughly contradicted by the evidence before my very eyes. Not only did he comfort her, but he did so in public. Before strangers." Serena shook her head. "Ian, how *does* one go about changing one's thinking?"

"With great difficulty, I would guess," he said in a kindly tone which hid his relief that there *was* some change in his wife. "If you are trying, then that is all anyone can ask, is it not?"

"I am having little success, but I *do* try! Ian," she added quickly, "before the Freemans arrived . . . I don't understand what you said about giving me my income but not an annulment. Why would you suggest such a thing?"

Ian eyed her, wondering if he dared tell the truth. No. He did not. "Perhaps," he said slowly, "I have gotten used to having you around? I would miss you if you were to leave me?" He drew in a deep breath when she merely frowned. "Serena, I want you to know that, whatever happens between us, I will see you've the funds necessary to starting the sort of home you wish to establish. Much thought needs to go into its organization, but something of the sort can be done and done well. We will see to it."

"You'll see"—her eyes widened painfully—"that I have funds . . . ?"

"Bloody hell," he muttered and turned away. "Serena, your fortune is mine. There is nothing I can do about that, but I *can* cede you the income." He swung back and was shocked by her pallor. "Dammit, Serena, it is the law."

"You could not give it back?"

"It may be possible." Ian sighed. "I will have my solicitor check. But, my dear, if you *do* get it back, who will see to your investments? Can you guarantee you will not be cheated?"

"Cheated?" Serena sighed. "Why is everything so complicated? All I ever wanted . . ." She snapped off the words and turned to the window. "Day-to-day living is far more difficult, with far more to see to, than I ever thought it to be. *Would* I be cheated?"

"It would depend on who managed your fortune, would it not?"

"Then Father was right in that I could not look after my money myself."

It was not a question, and Ian smiled at her resigned tone. "As you say, life is complicated. Intricate. You simply do not know enough."

"You would say I am stupid."

"I would not! Never would I suggest such a thing."

She turned, struck by his vehemence.

"Serena, it is not true. What I *would* say is that you've had no opportunity to learn, have not been taught even the most basic things a person must know to handle such a fortune as was left you."

She remained silent for a long moment. "Could you teach me?"

"I might." He stared at her rigid spine. "I'm not sure, however, that I know where to begin."

She turned, a small smile tipping the corners of her mouth, but a rather sad look shadowing her eyes. "At the beginning perhaps?" she asked. "Is that not where one is always told to begin?" She stood more straightly still. "But not," she added, "until after the wedding."

"No. Nothing may be done until then." He stared at her, wearing a warm, gentle expression she didn't understand. "About anything," he added softly.

She cast him a curious look. There had been a rather odd emphasis on those last words, had there not? She was about to ask, having come to the conclusion Ian did *not* mind questions, when once again they were interrupted.

This time when Higgens entered to announce a guest, Ian found the intrusion as welcome as Serena had when the Freemans arrived. He had been, he feared, about to rush his fences and tell Serena how much he'd come to love her! Had wished to press her into allowing him to show her . . .

"I go out of town for a few days," said their visitor plaintively, "and come home to find all turned topsy-turvy!"

"Alex!" Putting all such thoughts from him, Ian walked toward Lord Merwin. "You have heard the good news, then?"

"That Jack is recovering? Yes. I also heard that you came to his room, spent the night at his bedside, and in the morning, he was well on his way to good health. Now, my boy"—he poked Ian in the chest—"I demand an explanation and you will not put me off! As you know, I am not one to believe in miracles, whatever Jack's doctor says."

Serena excused herself, leaving Ian to decide whether he would confess or continue to pretend innocence.

* * *

The men reminisced about their friend with no mention of Jack's inexplicable cure. Finally Alex broke into a story of a time Ian and Jack had walked into the hills and a sudden fog trapped them there. "I know the tale," said Merwin, waving it away. "What I want to know is what magic cured our friend so that he may, someday, be lost in the Highlands all over again."

Ian sighed. "Let it rest, Alex."

"Then you *did* do something."

Ian's lips compressed. "Alex, I still cannot believe I did what I did and, even less, can I believe it *worked*. I'd rather not discuss it!"

But Alex would not let it lie, and in the end Ian repeated his wife's tale and explained how he'd acquired the maggots. "I told you to leave it be," finished Ian, chuckling. "You, my friend, look a trifle green!"

"Yes, well, I wish now I had *not* insisted on knowing. I wonder . . . do you suppose one could start a business in maggots?"

Ian laughed. "Alex, you think of a means of promoting such a gruesome cure and I will back you, but only if you prove we would not be tilting at windmills like that fellow in that Spanish story."

"Windmills." Alex sighed. "A particularly stubborn windmill, I fear. Now, tell me what is bothering you, because it cannot be Jack, who is recovering with surprising swiftness. And do not," he added when Ian shook his head, "attempt to convince me you are not bothered. By something."

"Alex, you have the longest nose of any among my acquaintance!"

"And would, you would add, put it where it is not wanted? Are you certain you do not wish to speak of it?" For a moment he was watchfully silent and then added, "Whatever *it* may be?"

"You never stop digging, do you?" Ian sighed when Alex merely grinned. "Then, if you must know, it is the prospect of perjuring myself before the Archbishop of Canterbury, swearing I am incapable and that my wife should therefore be freed of our marriage."

"An annulment? But you told me you had fallen in love with her. Surely you do not want an annulment."

A muscle jumped in Ian's jaw.

"Do you?"

Ian heaved a short sharp sigh, and a resigned look crossed his face. Still he did not respond.

"But why?" asked a bewildered Lord Merwin. "The lady is a delightful woman, or so I thought on those occasions I have enjoyed her company. She is attractive and, I believe, has better than average intelligence?"

"It would never occur to you, of course, that it might be she who wishes the annulment?"

"Well"—Alex actually boggled, his eyes bulging—"*no*. Why should it? She has wed one of the marriage mart's most popular bachelors, to say nothing of one of the richest. And, if that were not enough, one of the nicest and most generous of men. She has a comfortable home, children to look forward to." He threw up his hands. "*I* don't know. Tell me why she would wish rid of a situation most women would come near dying to achieve?"

"Thank you for bolstering my confidence, Alex. I needed that. I had begun to wonder if she was right and I wrong, and I the monster she thinks any man must be. Alex, I once told you, did I not? She would be free of *any* man."

"She isn't . . . ?" Lord Merwin's brows arched. "*You* know."

Ian shook his head. "She is not a lover of ladies, if that is what you would say."

"Have you seduced her?"

"Alex . . ."

"Oh, damn your overly developed sense of honor," said Alex crossly. "You have promised her you will not?"

"Not exactly. But I let her believe I will seek an annulment, and if she is not a virgin . . . well, that could cause difficulties, could it not?"

"She is ignorant and believes her virginity sufficient?"

"Yes. But proof she is untouched could be demanded."

"So"—Alex eyed his friend—"you will perjure yourself."

Ian grimaced. "I hope it will be unnecessary."

"Bah! Seduce her. Make love to her until she wishes you never stop."

"She also thinks *I* wish to be free. And she has more than a modicum of honor, although where she learned it, given her father, I haven't a notion. Perhaps from the grandmother of whom she has spoken on occasion . . ."

Alex ignored Ian's digression. "What you would say," he asked, "is that, even if she changes her mind and wishes to remain married to you, she might not tell you?"

"Not an impossibility."

"Ian, you ass, tell her the truth."

"No. At least . . . not yet."

Again Alex eyed his friend.

"No," said Ian sternly. "Promise you will tell her none of this."

"Oh, all right. But I think you are behaving idiotically if you allow her to go on believing a falsehood. She should know exactly what is involved, know how it will affect you to do what she wants done. What she *thinks* she wants or what she may, before the time comes, *not* want but will insist be done anyway. You are a blockhead, Ian, if you go on in such a way."

"Perhaps." Ian cast his friend a bitter look. "But for

now I prefer to be thought an idiot, ass, or, er, blockhead to being known as a manipulator who merely comports himself more smoothly than her father would do." Ian snapped his fingers. "Which reminds me, I forgot to write her mother, inviting her to London for a visit. Serena says her father will not allow it, but the invitation must be sent or he cannot refuse."

"You *wish* it refused?"

"It is a necessary first step before I do something to detach Serena's mother from her situation. A legal separation may be more than I can manage, but something must be done so that Serena has one less worry on her mind."

"Has Lady Serena asked that you do something?"

"We haven't discussed it except the once when I told her we would make it possible for her mother to escape if life became too difficult for her. We discussed the invitation at that time."

"Ian, a moment ago you mentioned that odd book about a ridiculous Spanish grandee who tilted at windmills?"

"I enjoy it and have reread it on occasion." Ian actually grinned. "You, I suppose, will insist this is another windmill? Alex, my wife's peace of mind is not a windmill."

"No, but the notion that a man such as you described will allow his wife to escape him *is!*"

Ian's grin turned a trifle sardonic. "I know a ferret who has a knack for discovering secrets a man most wishes hidden. I must discover if he is employed at the moment."

Alex's eyes widened. "You would stoop to blackmail?"

"I would do a great deal to free Lady Dixon. Her freedom is, in part, a selfish thing, Alex, *not* a case of simple generosity. I am in a battle for my life, and overcoming Lord Dixon could bring Serena to surrender."

"Did that make sense?"

"If it did not—" Ian's lips compressed and he sighed. "Alex, I can explain my feelings no better."

"I'm sure you could if you tried." Alex thought about what Ian had said. His brows arched. "You think of your relationship with Lady Serena as a *battlefield?*"

"You might have come up with the same analogy if, when you went to your bride's bedroom on your wedding night, you found yourself faced by a determined woman with a knife in her hand." Ian grimaced. "A knife she knew how to use."

Alex blinked. His eyes widened. Then he shouted with laughter. Ruefully, Ian joined in.

"Yes, all very humorous," said Ian, "but not if I had gone to her bedroom for the expected reason! Only because I meant to suggest we wait to share a bed until we knew each other better can I see the humor. Or perhaps I can laugh because I convinced her of my true reason for coming."

"And too," suggested Alex slyly, "because you look ahead to better times?"

"I once told you to keep a civil tongue in your head when speaking of my wife, Alex. I will tell you only this once more, and the next time I will succumb to a far more uncivil means of convincing you."

"But, Ian, I said nothing uncivil!" Alex's eyes were opened to their fullest extent, an expression Ian recognized as one of devilment.

"Yes, well, don't *think* such things, either," grumbled Ian. "And," he added when he saw his friend would speak, "you need not say that I may not govern your thoughts, for I know it!"

"You can't, of course, but I will attempt to do so," conceded his friend. Alex rose. "I must go. Will you write Renwick or shall I?"

"About Jack?" When Alex nodded, Ian said, "I mean to invite the Renwicks to Rolly's wedding, although I doubt they'll attend. It is impossible for Jase to travel with any comfort. Since I must write anyway, I will tell Jason about Jack's recovery. *You* mean to attend Rolly's wedding, do you not?"

"Try and prevent me!" Alex was gone on the words.

Eleven

The next day, when Lady Serena and Miss Clapton returned from a visit to Mirabele's where Miss Clapton had had a fitting, they were met at the carriage door by one of the footmen. He handed Lady Serena a note. "I'll read it once we are inside, James." Serena reached for his hand for help in descending.

"My lady," he responded politely, and equally politely pretended he did not see her extended hand, "I was told to say you are to read it *before* you descend."

Serena's eyes narrowed and her lips thinned. Then she recalled she was doing her best to overcome her tendency toward instant, unthinking, and obstinate resistance to anything a man told her she must or must not do. She colored as she realized she had actually believed herself growing beyond that reaction, and then frowned slightly as it occurred to her that, with Ian, she had.

"Will you not see what is said?" Miss Clapton suggested diffidently.

"Yes." She sat back, opening the note. "Oh dear."

"Is it terrible?"

"Not for me, Miss Clapton. It is your grandfather. He is here. Ian asks that we not return home, but that we go directly to Lord Freeman and remain there until he sends word or comes himself."

"My grandfather . . ." Miss Clapton paled and then

squared her shoulders. "Grandfather Clapton detests London. If he has come to Town, it can be for no good. Please. Let us go."

Serena's frown deepened. "I've things to do before this evening's dinner and there is no reason why *I* should avoid my home, but it is best to discover what he wishes of you before you show yourself. Perhaps he has come for your wedding? Is it not possible that he wishes to see you married before he forgives you and allows you to speak with your mother?"

"Possible . . . but I do not believe it." Miss Clapton trembled.

Serena grasped her companion's gloved hand and folded her fingers around the note. "You give this to Lady Freeman. It will explain why you have so unexpectedly arrived and must stay beyond what is proper for a morning visit. We will apprise you of what has happened as soon as may be."

When Serena entered the front door, she saw Higgens standing outside Ian's study. The butler held a poker from the parlor's fireside. She wondered at it . . . until she heard an angry roar, a stranger's voice.

"I will know where the lying wench is to be found, and you will tell me!"

"I have said you will not discover it from me," she heard Ian answer.

"My granddaughter is dead. This impostor will be brought to court and sent to Botany Bay where liars and cheats abound."

"Mr. Clapton, I do not see how the man she is to wed, that man's father, and his mother could all be wrong about the identity of your granddaughter. They have known her from childhood and agree it is Miss Clapton."

"I have said she is dead. She is dead."

"Let me understand you. You decreed she was dead, therefore she *is* dead?"

Lady Serena heard a judicious note in her husband's voice. His voice was different. Dangerous sounding . . .

"I have said it, have I not?"

"You are, perhaps, God?" asked Ian.

There was a moment's hesitation before the old voice spoke in more normal tones. "Not God, but the head of my household." The voice firmed. "I tell you she is dead."

"You selfish, unfeeling, heartless bastard!" Ian's voice rose with each word. "You have not a thought in your head except for yourself, your reputation, the gossip which might concern yourself!" His anger exploding, Ian roared more loudly than his guest. "You announced that Miss Clapton is dead and now, once the fact becomes known she has married, it is *you* who will be called the liar. You cannot bear that others might find you less than rigidly upright and morally correct! You are a sorry excuse for a man, Mr. Clapton, and I will not have you under my roof. Go. Now."

I'll not leave without I see that lying, cheating witch punished for foully misrepresenting herself as another *who is dead*."

Silence followed Mr. Clapton's announcement. Serena discovered she shook nearly as badly as Miss Clapton had trembled when receiving the news her grandfather was in London. Serena had nearly come to believe her husband incapable of anger, but now she saw he could, after all, lose his temper. She wrung her hands. What would he do?

It is Ian, she told herself. *He'll do no more than throw the old man out.*

"Mr. Clapton," said Ian quietly, "I am almost prepared to believe that *you* believe your granddaughter dead."

Serena collapsed against the hall wall. Was this a trick? Surely he could not have controlled himself so quickly!

"*Why* do you believe it?" Ian asked.

"If it is any of your business, which it is not, I know she is dead because my sister wrote and told me so. I told the world the whoring chit was dead even before I had that letter, because to me and mine she was. But for near two months she has been dead to the world as well, and I will not have some female use her name to fool Lord Freeman into complacency."

"Mr. Clapton," said Ian softly, "has it not occurred to you that the liar is your *sister*? That *she* lied to you when your granddaughter could no longer bear her cruelty and ran away from her? Miss Clapton attempted to reach her mother's mother—"

"Nonsense. Her maternal grandmother died a month after I discovered Henrietta's whoring!"

"I understand that, but Miss Clapton was not informed of the circumstances."

Again there was silence. "Bah. Nonsense," blustered the old man. "M'sister would not lie to me. She would not dare."

"You sound less than certain. Mr. Clapton, would you recognize your granddaughter if you saw her?"

Serena bit her lip. She knew Miss Clapton did not wish to see her grandfather. Should she interfere? Dared she?

"I don't know," said Mr. Clapton more quietly than previously. "Surely, if it *is* her, harsh experience will have changed her, and not for the better. There is a baby . . . ?"

"She lost it."

Again there was silence. "My great-grandson."

"Her daughter."

"Oh, well. A girl child."

Serena heard a sneer in the old man's tone, and a touch of that frightening anger was again evident in Ian's. "I suppose," he said, "you think that not so bad, that she lost a female child rather than a male?"

"Of what possible use is a girl? I might have raised a boy to be a better man than was my mealy-mouthed, namby-pamby son!"

"You assume the child's father would allow you to raise it, which I doubt. Mr. Clapton, this must be settled. If you will not accept Lord and Lady Freeman's word that she is Miss Clapton, you must see her yourself—"

Serena stiffened. How could he!

"—but I cannot allow that without her permission."

Serena, digesting Ian's caveat, was surprised when his sour laugh burst upon her ears.

"You stare, Mr. Clapton. Why? Because I will not go against a woman's wishes? Because I will protect your granddaughter and not allow her to be harmed?"

"Females have no rights. Why pretend they do?"

"Because that is untrue. A woman has the right to dignity and fair play. And protection, of course. What she has *not*, and this only because men have taken to themselves the power to enforce it, are *legal* rights."

"A woman hasn't the sense to come in out of the cold. How would one dare give her the responsibility for running her own life? Boy, you speak utter nonsense."

"I know many well-educated women who are sensible, and capable of running not only their lives but their estates. They regularly make difficult legal decisions. *As you know yourself, if only you would admit it!* The women who *cannot* are unable to do it because some men, you for instance, will not allow them to learn those things necessary for the running of their lives. I myself am in the process of contriving a set of lessons for my wife. She is an heiress and has plans for her income, but—"

"*Her* income?" inserted Mr. Clapton, sneering.

"—her father is very like you, Mr. Clapton. He forbade her the knowledge she needs to be comfortable in making decisions. And *her income*, sir, because I'll decree it so. Which is wrong. It should be unnecessary for me to interfere. The fortune was left her and should *be* hers."

"Bah!" Serena heard the old man's arrogance. "Things are as they are because that is the way they should be."

"Should *not* be! We will not agree and have," said Ian, sternly, "drifted from the subject, which is your granddaughter. Why are you reluctant to take Lord and Lady Freeman's word for Miss Clapton's identity?"

"*You* think I merely insult his lordship, but he will ask for a dowry, will he not? Ha! Didn't think of that, did you? I won't hand it over for just any light skirt to misuse."

Serena heard Ian sigh. "More insults. Is it your way, when you are in the wrong, to fall back on insults?" The old man blustered until Ian cut him off. "You may return home with a quiet heart," said Ian in a soft but dangerous tone. "No one expects you to cede the girl's rightful dowry. But there is one thing I insist you *must* do."

"Don't you go telling me what I must or must not do!"

Ian ignored him. "You must allow your daughter-in-law and your granddaughter to write each other. Freely, without interference. Nor may you insist you see the correspondence."

"*Not read their letters?* More nonsense! How do you think you are to control your womenfolk if you allow them such freedom?"

"I do not."

"You . . . *what*?"

There was shock in the old man's voice, and Serena heard Ian chuckle. "I trust to their good sense. Since I will see they have the education necessary for making decisions, then I *may* trust them, may I not?"

"And what," sneered the old man, "if you find they are unworthy of that trust, *as my granddaughter was,* and that they have gone against your wishes and done something you must then undo?"

"Against my wishes? But have I not said—" Ian paused. "No, perhaps I have not said. You see, I expect *no one*, including my wife, to agree with me *on every point*. As long as Lady Serena has good reason to believe or to act as she does, then that is quite all right by me."

"More nonsense."

"If," continued Ian doggedly, "she were to act thoughtlessly in some particular situation, then I would explain the problem as I see it so that she might think about it. But that she follow my every wish? That her thinking match mine in every respect? How utterly boring. I can look in a mirror if I wish that sort of mindless sameness!"

Serena frowned. Ian sounded sincere. Unaware she listened, he could not be speaking for her ears. Her mind in a whirl, Serena could bear no more. She removed quietly to her room. Once there, she did no more than untie her bonnet before plopping into the slipper chair by her window. So much to think about. . . .

First: Ian McMurrey lost his temper. Finally. Just as she had known he would. *But* his anger was *not* directed toward herself, a woman, but toward another man *and in defense of a woman.*

Second: Ian regained his temper very nearly instantly. He controlled his anger, subdued it . . . Impossible, she'd have thought, but he did it. He *said* he would never hit her, never show brutality to wife or children. Dare she believe him?

Third: He told that awful man he meant to teach her about money, teach her the proper use of it. Why? Because she had asked him to and he would indulge her? Or because he truly believed she had the capacity to learn and *should* know? She could, of course, and would . . . but *he* believed that?

Fourth: Did he actually expect to wring a promise from that terrible man that Miss Clapton could freely correspond with her mother? Hah! In *that* he would fail. Serena knew, through and through, men like Mr. Clapton!

Fifth, and most immediately important. Did he actually mean to ask Miss Clapton's permission before confronting her with her grandfather? And if he did, what— Serena shuddered—would he do if the young woman said no? Oh! He would *not* be so unfair as to become angry with her. Would he?

Serena's mind would not settle. It skipped from one question to another with no logic or control, back and forth, circling this way, skipping that. She was still sitting there dazed when, after a knock she barely heard, the door opened and Ian looked in.

"Higgens said you were home." He entered. "My dear?" he asked, obviously alarmed. "Are you unwell?"

"What? Unwell? Why do you think me unwell?"

Ian visibly relaxed. He smiled. "The fact, perhaps, that although you arrived some time ago, you sit staring at nothing at all while still in your pelisse and still wearing your bonnet. Do you think it possible that *might* have something to do with it?"

Serena raised her hands to her head. She blushed. "I . . . well . . ." Quickly she removed the hat and laid it in her lap. She stared at it, wondering what she could possibly say to explain behavior he found puzzling.

"Serena," he said gently, "Higgens also let slip that you heard part of my conversation with that unbearably self-righteous man. Did something we said bother you to such an unbearable degree that you appear near to swooning?"

She cast a glance his way. Higgens had. . . . "Yes," she admitted.

"If something we said upset you, I am sorry. But perhaps it is also that you are recalling your father, who must be very like Mr. Clapton?"

"*Very*."

"My dear," he asked gently, "will you not talk to me? Ask me the questions I see going round inside your head?"

"Did you send him off to see Miss Clapton?"

"Heavens, no. I must discuss that with her first, must I not?"

"You did not believe him when he insisted she is dead?"

"What I believe is that his sister lied to save her own skin when Miss Clapton ran away from her, er"—his lips compressed for an instant—"her *care*. It is possible, of course, the woman herself believed it. She might assume that, penniless, her great-niece could not survive childbirth so *must* be dead. Whether or not she believed in Miss Clapton's death, I would guess she is so puritanical a woman that she believes her great-niece would never dare to show her face where anyone might recognize it. For the shame of it, you see."

"Does Mr. Clapton accept that reasoning?"

"He didn't admit to it, but I believe, deep down, he accepted it."

"Have you sent word to Miss Clapton?"

"No. When Higgens informed me you were home, I came to see if you would like to go with me to talk to her."

"Did he agree to correspondence between Miss Clapton and her mother?"

Ian sighed. "I have yet to achieve that goal. He insists that until he knows it is his granddaughter, he cannot make such a decision. He will discuss *nothing* until he has ascertained the truth for himself."

"Ian, when I first arrived, he was saying he would

prosecute Miss Clapton. Might he bring Bow Street Runners with him to a meeting with her?"

"We may easily prevent her arrest. I can guarantee *that*, at least."

"But how?"

"Lord Freeman will swear it *is* Miss Clapton, and her mother may be brought forward to identify her. We can also threaten Mr. Clapton with being sent to Bedlam if he persists in insisting she is *not* his granddaughter when everyone else insists she *is*." He smiled a smile which was not quite nice. "He will, I think, find it believable that his family would jump at the chance of being rid of his hand on the reins!"

"As I would. I often thought my father insane. It was easier than believing him merely *mean,* which is such a petty thing."

Ian chuckled but made no comment. "Will you come with me to discuss the situation with Miss Clapton? And with Rolly and Lord and Lady Freeman, of course?"

"Yes, please. Ian, will that awful man not follow us?"

Ian's laugh was filled with more humor this time. "I had him followed, my dear, my footman making no attempt to hide himself. Mr. Clapton is aware I'll go nowhere near his granddaughter while he is by, and since we will, in this one visit, have her yea or her nay, it makes no odds. Later he may have us followed with our goodwill."

"Very well." Mentally and emotionally drained, Serena rose awkwardly and moved, for her, in a listless manner to her mirror, where she replaced her bonnet without really seeing what she did. "Let us go, please."

Ian promptly offered his arm. She accepted it in the same lifeless manner. He frowned to see it. Serena would have stared to see his expression of deep caring and to know of his concern.

* * *

With what seemed to Serena more than a touch of bravado, Miss Clapton suggested that an invitation to that evening's celebratory dinner be sent to the small hotel her grandfather patronized. "He will hate it," said Henrietta, a malicious sparkle in her eye. "By his presence, he will give support to my engagement, but he *will* come because he will tell himself he must ascertain if it is truly me."

"Oh, but, my dear," exclaimed Lady Freeman, "you have not thought! You will unsettle Lady Serena's seating plan!"

"Actually," Serena contradicted her hostess, "she *settles* it. I did not think of that problem when I invited Lady Cartwright. We met at the modiste's this morning, and when she gave Miss Clapton best wishes on her engagement, I made the invitation, apologizing for the short notice."

"Then of course it is a proper notion to invite Mr. Clapton," said Lady Freeman. "It was very bright of you to think of it," she added, turning to her future daughter-in-law.

Rolly and his twin entered just then, startling Serena by their identical looks. Miss Clapton, however, went directly to the twin on the left, who enfolded her in his arms. She whispered in his ear, and he blanched. He whispered back, urgently. His twin, overhearing, burst into laughter.

Rolly, without releasing Miss Clapton, scowled at his brother. "Ally, you fool, you know the curmudgeon! Would *you* wish to have him there acting as if he were eating funeral meats rather than participating in a celebration?"

"But think of the tale you may tell when—"

"That is enough," interrupted Lady Freeman. Her resigned tone indicated she was used to the twins' bickering. "Bring Miss Clapton here and yourselves as well. Alaric, when did you arrive?"

"An hour ago."

"It is a truly unexpected pleasure! But you *are* here, and you too must attend this evening's dinner." Her Ladyship cast an agitated look toward Serena. "My lady, your table is once again unbalanced."

"I will ask Lord Merwin to bring his grandmother," said Ian. The soothing rumble of his voice seemed to work on Lady Freeman as easily as it did on everyone else. "If I might borrow paper and pen . . . ?"

"Yes, and Rolly and I can deliver your notes," said Ally.

"You do it," said Rolly. "I will not leave my Henny's side until we know what that blasted man means to do!"

"Rolly, I would very much appreciate your scrubbing my back"—Miss Clapton grinned when Lady Freeman gasped at her outrageous suggestion—"but I think others would be less tolerant and not show proper understanding of such improper behavior. Mr. McMurrey will see that I am safe, so you and Ally can deliver the notes to the Merwins and my grandfather." She chuckled when Rolly blanched. "My love, just pretend it is a French regiment you face and you will do very well."

Rolly squared his shoulders. "Yes, of course. But I worry about you."

Miss Clapton's hand drifted to her thigh. "I think you need not concern yourself, Rolly."

It was the first Serena knew that Miss Clapton still wore the knife that had been secreted beneath her skirts when the woman planned to kill Rolly. She glanced at Lady Freeman and breathed more easily upon discovering her ladyship, occupied with Rolly's twin, had not noticed. She feared her ladyship would *not* approve such hoydenish behavior.

Serena looked around the salon at the milling guests. Everyone had arrived but Mr. Clapton, who either was late or had, after all, decided not to come.

Had he changed his mind? Would he remain away so that he need never admit his granddaughter still lived? Serena could see her father making such a decision, although he was unlikely to state the case in quite that way. Serena glanced across the room to where her husband spoke with Lady Merwin and one of Rolly's aunts. Ian bowed and moved on to a group of people which included Lady Cartwright, Lord Merwin, and Lord Wendover, who laughed at something Rolly's twin, Alaric, said.

Rolly himself and Miss Clapton strolled up to Serena. "It is going very well, is it not?" asked Henrietta.

"Everyone appears to be enjoying themselves."

"They are," said Rolly, his arm around his fiancée's waist. "You don't know how unusual that is. Events such as this which are family and ceremonial are often dreary beyond belief."

"It is because it is *not* entirely family," said Henrietta. "You were very wise, my lady, to include the leavening of a few friends."

"Mr. McMurrey suggested it. Except for Lady Merwin, you had met them all. They liked you, so it seemed proper they should help us celebrate."

Behind her, Higgens cleared his throat. Serena turned. There, a scowl pasted firmly on his wrinkled features, stood a slender-boned old gentleman who must be Mr. Clapton. Serena found her feet glued to the floor and was astounded when Miss Clapton, pulling her lieutenant with her, went directly over to him.

"Hello, Grandfather. I hear you insist I am dead."

"Impertinent wench." He stared down his nose at her.

Miss Clapton chuckled. "For saying the truth? You have an odd notion of impertinence!"

Her grandfather gave her a baffled look. Bafflement changed to anger. "I will speak with you later." His thin mouth thinned still more. "Alone."

"Never."

"What!"

"I said *never*." Henrietta smiled sweetly. "Never again will I suffer your cruelty. You sent me away, and I will not return. Will you, by the way, allow my mother to attend my wedding? Or will you expend your anger that you have lost control of *me* on *her*? Poor Mother. She never could withstand your vicious tongue as I could do."

Miss Clapton sighed dramatically, and Serena realized the room had become exceedingly quiet as everyone listened avidly. Serena signaled to Higgens, who recovered his poise. "Dinner," he intoned, "is served."

The line formed quickly. Serena found Lord Freeman at her side offering his arm and saw Ian offer his to Lady Freeman. Behind them, others paired in proper order of social standing with only one minor squabble between two of Rolly's elderly cousins. She later learned they always feuded over precedence.

Everyone adjourned to the dining room, where the table was extended to its greatest possible size. Even then, the diners were a trifle squeezed, and the footmen had difficulty serving properly. Serena almost wished the table were set in the old-fashioned way, but it would not do. A return to older forms would label her a county mouse undeserving of her position as Ian's wife.

Lady Serena put the thought aside and turned to Lord Freeman, who sat on her right, and asked if he had taken his seat in the House of Lords this year. He discoursed for some time on Lord Liverpool's speech on the security of the Coast, and went on to comment on the sorry situation between the Princess of Wales and her daughter, the Princess Royal.

"I," Lord Freeman said, "have some sympathy for Prinny's feelings in the matter, but I fear he goes too far in trying to separate the two entirely. Princess Charlotte has too much proper feeling for her mother not to resent his high-handed attempts to exclude Princess Caroline from all decisions concerning her daughter."

Those nearest Lord Freeman took up the discussion, to Serena's relief. Her emotions concerning high-handed fathers were overly intense, and she dared not comment on the Regent's behavior. She turned to Rolly on her other hand.

Rolly lectured her on Wellington's latest strategy, including a discourse which obviously echoed what the lieutenant had heard from older officers about Wellington's policy of retreating until certain of his ground before engaging the enemy.

"It is, you see," said Rolly earnestly, "that we are nearly always outnumbered by French forces. His Lordship must take care to have some other advantage."

"That makes a great deal of sense, Lieutenant," said Serena. "Are you prepared for your wedding to Miss Clapton?" she asked, hoping to turn the conversation to something less likely to do damage to her appetite.

Rolly grinned. "I have been ready anytime this last year! And longer." His smile faded. "I wish I had known—"

"Shh! This is not the time for such thoughts," whispered Serena, fearing Rolly meant to say something he should not with Mr. Clapton seated only two chairs beyond him.

The meal continued smoothly until, just before the sweet course, Ian rose to his feet. He offered a toast to Miss Clapton and Lieutenant Templeton and all good wishes for their future. Everyone raised their glasses . . . except Mr. Clapton, who sat silent, a stony look on his face. Serena looked from the old gentleman to Ian, who shook his head slightly.

A second toast was offered by Lord Freeman, and another by Rolly's twin. Through it all Mr. Clapton neither moved nor spoke. Ian signaled for the last course, which, again, Mr. Clapton ignored.

Serena had grown steadily more anxious from the moment Mr. Clapton refused Ian's toast to his granddaughter, but the meal ended without complications. She rose, thankful she could signal the women to leave the table. Perhaps, if there *were* to be unpleasantness, it would occur when the women were absent and only men in the room . . .

. . . but her hopes were shattered when, at that moment, Mr. Clapton rose to his feet and glared at her.

"Sit," he ordered. "I have a few words to say." He glared around the table. "I am not happy. My granddaughter is a sinner. She should suffer for it, not be rewarded by marriage. And what sort of man *would* wed her? He"—Mr. Clapton pointed a bony finger at Rolly—"is a fool for accepting ruined goods."

"*You* fool." Rolly rose and went to Mr. Clapton, pulling him away from the table and around to face him. "She is *my* goods, and if it were not for *you,* we'd have married months and months ago. But you, you sanctimonious old fool, had to pretend she was *dead*. It is *your fault,* all of it, and don't pretend otherwise. I just wish you were young enough I could treat you as you deserve to be treated!"

Rolly's hands, fisted into the old man's lapels, hinted at how he believed Mr. Clapton should be treated.

"So," finished the lieutenant, giving the man a slight shake, "if you cannot keep a civil tongue in your head, get out. We don't need you." Rolly rounded the table and stood behind Miss Clapton, who put a hand over his which rested on her shoulder. "I," continued Rolly, "have wished to wed my Henny anytime these past ten years, but first we were too young, and then, Mr. Clapton, she worried about her mother, who cannot stand up to you. For *her* sake Henny would not say me yea. Finally she agreed to wed me and then"—he frowned—"everything went wrong. But"—the frown deepened to a scowl—"my Henny is a wonderful woman, and anyone who says differently must answer to me."

"Or me," said his twin, rising in a rather laconic manner. "I've known Henny all those years as well. She's a right one and will make my twin a good wife." He lifted his glass toward Miss Clapton, who smiled at him through the tears running down her face.

"Bah!" said Clapton. "I grant you one thing, McMurrey. It *is* Henrietta and not another doxy pretending to be her, so that much is settled."

After a fierce glare all around the table, he stalked from the room. Silence followed. And then Serena heard her husband swear softly. Fluently.

So did everyone else hear him, of course. Ian's ears turned bright red. He cleared his throat. "Mr. Clapton managed to have the last word after all," said Ian, forcing a smile. "Which is too bad, since *I* had words to say to him over and above what Rolly said so well." His smile softened when his gaze settled on Serena. "My dear, if you and the other ladies wish to adjourn to the salon, I promise we men will join you very soon."

This time when Ian raised his glass, it was to his wife.

Twelve

Mr. Clapton made no more difficulties. Although he didn't attend the wedding, he did bend to the demand that he allow at least a limited correspondence between his granddaughter and her mother. That they achieved even so much surprised everyone, especially Henrietta.

The wedding itself was intimate, with few guests beyond family. The less exclusive wedding breakfast which followed was long and joyful, the couple's obvious love for each other drawing tears to Lady Serena's eyes.

Love. Serena had had no belief in love, but watching the young couple made it impossible to deny. At first Serena did not understand the hot, dark emotion marring her enjoyment of the day. Then she did. Jealousy. *Green jealousy*.

"Some will say he could have done better, but I believe she'll be the making of him."

Lord Freeman spoke in Lady Serena's ear, a welcome interruption to hateful thoughts. The party had moved into the salon after dining, and his Lordship's words forced her to turn her mind to her responsibilities as hostess.

"I wonder where I can find her like," His Lordship mused. He glanced down at her, chuckled at her startled expression, and added, "For my *other* sons, of course."

Lady Serena felt chagrin for misinterpreting his lordship's comment. "I have only just met your elder son, my lord, and haven't a notion what would suit him. But do you truly think Mr. Alaric Templeton would be tolerant, in a wife, of the new Mrs. Templeton's outspoken ways?" Serena made the objection without thinking and then tensed, awaiting an angry response, perhaps a blow.

But Lord Freeman merely barked a sharp, *"Ha!* You've the right of it, my lady! For Rolly's sake, Alaric will say nothing, but one night when he'd imbibed a glass too many, he admitted he has never understood his twin's attachment to Henrietta. Or, for that matter, what *she* sees in Rolly. But, he explained to me in that overly careful and insistent manner of the inobriated, the two were as one from the moment they met as children."

" 'Twas meant to be, as a poet might say," responded Lady Serena and was surprised to realize she was more than half serious.

"That"—Lord Freeman's fond gaze shifted to where his wife stood beside the new bride—"was exactly what I felt when I first met their mother."

Serena couldn't think how to respond to that. Thankfully, no response was required. Lord Freeman abruptly excused himself and removed to his wife's side where, resting a hand on her shoulder, he joined the conversation.

Ian took his place. "You look a trifle bemused, my dear."

Startled, she looked up at him. "I am sorry."

"Sorry you look bemused?" he asked, a teasing quirk to his brow. "What did his lordship say that has left you gaping nearly as badly as when I once suggested that you close a fishlike mouth?"

Serena flashed a quick smile at the memory but, in answer, merely said, "It was nothing." When more seemed needed, she repeated Alaric's comment that Rolly and his bride seemed fated to be a pair from their first meeting.

"Gothic nonsense," said Ian. For once he was out of tune with his wife. "Ally has spent too much time with his Irish friends." Before she could think how to respond, Ian said, *"I don't believe it."*

Serena was justly irritated by Ian's rude reaction to the emotion which she was just coming to accept might be real. Real for others, at least, if *not* for herself. But even as she formed a retort, he excused himself and moved away. Serena watched him bow to Rolly's sister, Miss Templeton, before turning to a haggard-looking man seated in a bath chair.

"Princeton!" exclaimed Ian joyfully. "Is this wise?"

"Probably not," said the convalescent soldier with husky-voiced humor, "but I could bear the four walls of my room no longer." The man was skin and bones, but there hung about him the remnants of dark good looks and a sense of authority. "Where is Rolly's bride?" he asked. "I would wish her well before I am so impolite as to collapse."

Serena realized that Ian's irritating words had referred to Princeton's arrival and were not, after all, a response to her comment. Her annoyance evaporated, and she rejoiced in Ian's happiness in his friend's recovery.

But it will be, mused Lady Serena, eyeing the new arrival, *outside of enough if the foolish man overextends his strength and suffers a relapse!*

She joined the tall young woman with worried eyes who hovered near Lieutenant Princeton. "Miss Templeton?" said Lady Serena. She introduced herself and then offered a suggestion, pointing discreetly toward a small room opening off the one they occupied. As she explained her plan to rescue him from overexertion, she watched Princeton. He listened to friends, a smile playing about his lips, but even though he enjoyed himself, stress deepened the lines around his eyes and mouth with every passing moment.

Miss Templeton nodded at Serena's proposal to rescue him from overexertion. "An excellent notion." She bit her lip. "If only I could convince him."

"We will not be so foolish as to try," said Lady Serena, her eyes twinkling. "He is trapped in that chair, is he not? I will have Mr. McMurrey push Lieutenant Princeton into the next room, and you, Miss Templeton, may guard the door against too many visitors!"

Later, as they took their leave, Jack thanked Lady Serena for what she had done. "Miss Templeton warned me how it would be, but I insisted, willy-nilly, I would come. I forgot how very tiring friends can be. Far worse than facing the French, you know." He grinned an odd half-grin revealing excellent teeth. "The French don't make one laugh."

Lady Serena chuckled. "Perhaps we could send a corps or two of them to Spain. A secret weapon, perhaps? The French could laugh themselves to death!"

"Hah! Excellent! I will suggest it to Wellington"— Princeton hesitated half a moment, and his next words couldn't hide a touch of bravado—"when I return to duty."

Princeton was very tired, and Lady Serena tactfully urged him and Lord Freeman's daughter out of the house. A frown etched tiny lines between her brows as she watched Jack being helped into the carriage. She'd no notion what Lieutenant Princeton felt for Miss Templeton, but she strongly suspected Miss Templeton believed herself in love with the lieutenant.

What, she wondered, would happen to the woman if Princeton healed and rejoined his regiment? He'd go with no thought for those left behind. Miss Templeton's future looked dim indeed. Serena sighed.

"What," asked Ian from behind her, "did that mournful sound signify?"

Serena told him her observations.

"It is doubtful Jack will recover sufficiently to return to his regiment," said Ian. "Even when healed, his leg is unlikely to regain full strength, and he will never ride in his old manner. Which is too bad. He was never truly happy except in a saddle." Ian too uttered a soft sigh and stared after the departing carriage. "Did I do wrong? Should I have refrained from interfering?"

"Life holds much of interest besides riding. Perhaps this happened to the lieutenant so that your friend would be forced to discover it."

"Do you believe that?" Ian studied her, his head slightly to one side. "That there are reasons things happen as they do?"

She stared down the street after the carriage, remembering something Rolly had said. Miss Templeton, long ago, made a decision she'd not wed, insisting that her family gave her all she wished from life. Serena doubted the woman would hold to that vow if the lieutenant asked for her hand. So perhaps it was meant she must nurse Princeton in order to discover a love beyond love of family? "I think I must believe it . . ."

"Perhaps then, my dear, you might consider the possibility there was a reason we are wed." Softly he added, "You might spend a little time determining what that reason is."

Ian turned into the house, leaving a very startled woman staring after him.

Serena discovered she'd no choice but to ponder the point. The notion would creep into her head at the oddest moments. It woke her from sound sleep. It left her sitting motionless at table, her fork halfway to her open mouth.

It was most particularly apt to arise when Ian walked in on her unexpectedly, as he'd a habit of doing . . .

. . . and as he did just then. "Serena, I have a letter here from Renwick. He suggests that you must be tired from all the fuss and bother of the wedding, and wonders if you would care for a week or two in the country?" Ian grinned. "Reading between the lines, my dear, I believe that, now Jason has come out of seclusion and rediscovered he enjoys company, he thought up this excuse to supply himself with some! *Do* you feel like a repairing lease? Would you enjoy a period of quiet with Lady Renwick, who, I think, would be your friend?"

"I am not tired—"

Ian wondered what had caused her recent lassitude if it were not that. She was so quiet, listless almost . . . he missed her quick step and bright eyes.

"—but, although there is much to enjoy here, I find I prefer the country for everyday living."

Biting her lip, Serena cast him one of those quick looks he had decided were a check on whether her words had roused him to anger. Often he could actually *see* her relief that she had not. She did it less often now, but would she never fully trust him? Ian knew he was impatient for that day to come or, alternately, sometimes feared it never would!

"Visits are one thing," she continued, "but actually living in London! Well, others find it just the thing, but I am glad for that invitation."

She bit her lip again as another thought crossed her mind. She looked up at him with that faintly worried expression he hated seeing but which appeared in any situation in which she feared the reaction of a man to her words. It was especially upsetting since, in all other circumstances, she was wise and decisive . . .

"That is," she interrupted his thoughts, "if *you* need not remain in town?"

"I have done all that is required of me for the present. When we came up from the coast, there was a bit of a problem concerning one of our more brilliant students at the school, but that is settled and I am free to go. And you?"

"I offered to write letters for Lady Cartwright, for her new charity effort, but I've a list and may do so from Lord Renwick's estate as easily as here."

Ian's eyes danced. "Oh, my dear! Far *better* there. Those who receive your letter will be more disposed to give it a thoughtful reading." Serena cast him a look of confusion. "Because, my love," he explained, "Lord Renwick will frank your letters and you will save the recipients the cost of the post, which they will appreciate!"

"Lord Renwick write out a frank? But he is blind . . . !"

"He invented a tool to help him place his signature where he wishes it to go. As you appear to know, he is *supposed* to write the whole address, but that detail is overlooked by the authorities more often than not. You will see. That is, if it is truly your wish we go?"

"Oh, yes, *please*."

Now, what, wondered Ian at the unusual emphasis she gave the word, *did that signify? Panic? Surely not. But why. . . .*

Serena again interrupted his rampaging thoughts, her words tumbling one over the other. "I would very much like this opportunity to know more of Lady Renwick."

Ian hesitated, wondering if he dared probe, but her expression settled into that closed look which told him he'd get no answers. At least, none which were helpful. He nodded. "I will write the Renwicks that we arrive on the . . . eleventh? Will that suit you?"

Serena nodded and watched him leave the room. She struggled against another surge of something very like panic. For some time she'd known she must accept a long and lonely future. All would be different after the annulment, and she wanted, she discovered, to meet as many people as she could before then, to enjoy their company while she could.

Besides, Lady Renwick's letter to her when she was first married had left her much intrigued. She had not exaggerated when she told Ian she wished to know her ladyship better, and consideration led her to believe the panic was due to a fear that another opportunity would not arise before her birthday and the dissolution of her marriage. It was essential to grasp this one, and she had feared that Ian would deny her the treat if he knew how much she wished to go!

Serena grimaced. That was her old self reacting in her old way. When would she accept that Ian did not, *would* not, behave like father? A rueful chuckle escaped her as it crossed her mind she would very likely manage the trick just about the time it was no longer necessary: just when the marriage was over and done . . .

The laugh turned to a sob, and Serena fought to contain her tears. She would not give in to self-pity. Ian had asked her to think why they had been meant to wed. Her chin came up, and she straightened her back. Well, it was obvious why, was it not? It gave her the opportunity to discover that the world contained good men as well as evil. Commonplace men as well as extraordinary.

And *loving* men as well as those who could only seem to hate.

It was a much-needed lesson, she told herself, and there were few months left in which to learn it. Once the annulment was attained, most people would no more wish to know her than they would acknowledge a divorced woman. Serena swallowed hard at that thought and, for a long moment, again fought back tears. *Why,* she wondered, *am I turning into the sort of teary-eyed woman I despise? A watering pot!*

Again she stiffened her spine. She would *not* succumb to self-pity. A good man had promised to see that she achieved her heart's desire, and she had no reason on earth for self-pity!

So why—Serena paused on her way to her room—*does achieving my freedom and the means to fulfill my dreams seem so pointless?*

When no answer occurred, she continued to her room, where she and her maid began packing. When they came to London, Ian had insisted on extensive improvements to her wardrobe, so getting ready to leave would take several days. Gowns, rich in flounces and lace and other decorative features, could not be hastily folded and pressed into a single trunk. There was need of blue paper and extra care. And now, besides her trunk, she had band boxes, hat boxes, and glove boxes to fill, and other boxes she had not previously known existed.

Not until Ian had widened her horizons. *Dear Ian*, she thought, a tenderness filling her. *He has been such a very special force in my life.*

Serena, bent over a gown laid out on her bed, straightened so suddenly she had to grab for the bed post to steady herself.

"Dear Ian?" she muttered.

"Did you say something, my lady?" asked her maid from across the room.

"Hmm? Oh. Just talking to myself."

Serena bent back to her folding, but worked more slowly as she pondered the strange emotion she had just experienced. The warmth, the happiness, the . . . the love?

Again Serena straightened. She stared at nothing at all and then, without a word to her maid, left the room, removing to the privacy of her small parlor. There she paced and paced, becoming more and more irritated by the lack of space. When again she approached the window onto the back garden, a movement caught her eye. She paused to determine what it was, wanting, *needing* distraction from the *dismay*, the *anxiety* filling her with a now panicky fear of her lonely future.

"Ian?" she breathed when, reaching the end of the path, he turned toward her. Why did Ian pace the garden paths as she paced this room? The nice *long* garden paths . . .

Serena recognized a touch of jealousy. *How ridiculous*, she thought, *to envy him the space in which to pace properly*!

But why did *he* pace back and forth . . . back and forth . . . back and . . . ? Serena watched for a long time. And then turned abruptly. She had, she realized, been feasting her eyes on him! Filling her mind and memory with the sight of him!

Was this terrible emptiness, this longing for something, this feeling of fear, was *this* love? Surely not. According to the poets, love was a wonderful thing, a joyful thing. Then she recalled a sentiment in a poem she'd read many years previously. She sighed. Because it was not *love* she experienced. It was *unrequited love*. For the third time that afternoon, Serena felt tears welling.

This time she allowed them to fall.

The newly acquired understanding of her emotions unsettled Serena. For the few days they remained in London, she did her best to avoid Ian, finding reasons to leave the house early and twice managing to stay away through dinner, sending messages that she had been detained and would return later.

The first day of her desertion Ian excused on the grounds of last-minute errands, those bits and pieces of shopping and visits to friends which took up so much more time than one expected. The second day he wondered . . .

The third day he lay in wait.

"Serena?" He came from his study as she entered the house. He had been frowning slightly, but at the sight of her he drew nearer quickly, concern for her making him reach for her. For once he ignored her attempt to avoid his touch but held her in a gently firm hold, searching her features for clues. "My dear," he finally asked, "what is it? What has you so upset?"

"Upset? Why should I be upset?"

"I do not know, do I? It is why I ask."

Higgens cleared his throat, drawing Ian's attention to the fact they were not alone.

"Higgens," he said, putting Serena gently under his arm, "bring a tray to my study, please. I think her ladyship has not dined?" He glanced down and noted her blush. "A bowl of Cook's excellent broth and perhaps bread and cheese if none of the roast is left."

Then, ignoring Serena's muttered protests, he led her to his study, where he removed her bonnet and began unbuttoning her pelisse.

"Ian, I can do it—"

"Shh. You are exhausted. I haven't a notion what you've been doing, but you are wearing yourself out. Can I not help?"

Serena dropped her gaze from his to stare at the floor.

"I would do anything to see you happy," he added gently.

Still she did not respond.

Ian sighed, which brought her eyes back to his face. "My dear, is it something so terrible you cannot tell me?"

She started to shake her head, then nodded; then, looking helpless, her features marred by a pained expression, she met his steady gaze.

He squeezed her shoulders gently, but even that encouragement brought no words, so he led her to a chair. When she was seated, he returned to his desk and the letter he'd been penning, casting her a quick look now and again. Something bothered her deeply. He must discover what it was.

The food arrived, and Ian was pleased to see her eat every bite. She was almost greedy about it as if she had not eaten for quite some time, and if, as he suspected, she'd had nothing since the biscuits and tea she'd taken before rising that morning, then it was little wonder she was famished now.

When she finished, he wiped his pen and laid it aside. "My dear, we said we'd leave tomorrow, but if you have not finished your errands, we may postpone our going. It is not as if there were some important dinner at which we must arrive at some particular hour."

"I've no reason to delay our departure," she muttered, but would not look at him.

Ian waited a moment. He stifled another sigh at her refusal to allow him to help her. "Then," he decided, "we leave as planned. Cook is to pack us a breakfast which we will eat at a spot I know not too far south of the river. A pleasant view in a quiet place where we may be at peace."

Now, why, he wondered, *did she cast me such a look as that?*

Serena said nothing, however, so Ian continued. "It should take us little over seven hours to reach Renwick's Lair even stopping to rest the horses. I wish to use my own, you see, rather than hire strange teams from posting houses. We will lunch at an inn in Tunbridge Wells. . . . Serena, are you quite certain you are ready to leave London?"

Serena nodded.

"My dear," he said after eyeing her for a long moment,

"can you not tell me what has you so worried and anxious?" He waited. "Is it," he then asked, "your mother, perhaps?"

Serena looked startled at the thought, so Ian knew it was not that.

"You have, perhaps, discovered another woman who needs such help as Mrs. Rolly needed?"

She shook her head.

"Then what?" Again he waited. "Serena, I cannot help if I've no clue to your problem."

Agitated, Serena rose to her feet. "It is nothing. Nothing at all. Time will see everything right. It will, it *must* be all right. In time . . ."

Without so much as a good night, she hurried from the room. Ian, his lips tightly compressed and brows lowered over deep-set eyes, stared for a very long time at the door she had closed with careful control.

Thirteen

Her maid was in her room, so Serena moved directly to the window, keeping her back straight, her body erect.

"My lady?"

"You may go," said Serena abruptly. "I'll not need you tonight."

"Yes, my lady," said the maid. She cast her mistress an odd look as she left the room.

Serena neither knew nor would she have cared that her maid suspected her mistress and master had argued. Nor, at that moment, have cared that the question was hotly debated in the servants' hall. At any other time she'd have been embarrassed, but her mind was far too preoccupied with the coming day.

How, she wondered, could she endure seven hours in the carriage alone with Ian? The thought chilled her. How to cope? How to be with him for so many hours and not reveal her love for him? A love unwanted by either of them!

Serena discovered that by angling around the bed, she actually had more room for pacing here in her bedroom than any other place available to her. With roiling thoughts, sore heart, and the journey looming, she paced until deep into the night, when she could walk no more. But, undressed and in bed, her sleep was once again disturbed. She tossed and turned, dozing, dreaming, occasionally awakening to wonder what was to become of her. She could not, it seemed, think of anything but Ian.

She stared at the shadow pictures on her ceiling. The tree leaves outside her window were mature now, the splotches of shadow larger, more interesting—although *nothing* held her interest for long.

Except Ian.

Recalling the preceding day's committee meeting at Lady Cartwright's, she felt a wry smile twist her lips. Someone asked her a question and she'd not heard it. Then, once they had her attention, she found it impossible to comprehend what was wanted. Lady Cartwright, fortunately, saved her from embarrassment, but it was another indication that loving Ian had destroyed her capacity to function.

Love! How wrong the poets! *Not* beauty, peace, and gentleness but obsession! And such obsession with the loved one was unsettling, even destructive!

Toward morning Serena fell into the first true sleep she'd had since she'd admitted the state of her emotions. Therefore she was not happy when her maid insisted she rouse and dress, that the carriage would be at the door very soon.

Ian awaited her in the entry hall. He took note of the dark circles under her eyes and gave Higgens a quiet order. Then he helped Serena into the carriage, but he stood on the pavement, looking toward the house. Very soon a footman appeared, carrying a pillow filled with lovely soft goose down and a light carriage robe over his arm. Ian tossed them onto the forward seat before climbing in beside her, but before giving the coachman orders to proceed, he turned to her.

Serena felt deeply cosseted when he tucked the pillow behind her and wrapped her in the robe, and she fought against sudden tears.

"You have not been sleeping well, I think. I recall that

you prefer to nap when you travel. I will wake you when we reach our picnic spot," he said and touched her cheek gently as had become his custom. Taking a book from his pocket, he settled into his own corner.

Serena watched him from behind barely slitted lids. Such a strong and caring man. Such a thoughtful man. So controlled. So kind. So intelligent. Serena repressed a sigh. That last was the problem, was it not? If he were more obtuse, he might not guess at her love for him. So . . . if he *did* guess, what would he do?

He would not wish to hurt her, so he might suggest they remain wed, that they make theirs a true marriage. But for him it would be merely one of convenience, and that Serena could not bear. To love him and know he loved her not? Impossible. What was she to do? It occurred to her that what she *should* do was enjoy each and every moment she was to have with him. That she must gather up memories for those days, weeks, *years* when she would be alone.

But not just yet. Not until she could control her emotions. Which she could not. Serena turned her back to Ian and pressed her face against the pillow.

It would never do for him to see her cry.

They arrived at Renwick's Lair somewhat early, since Ian did not awaken her for the picnic. With great self-restraint, he'd allowed her to sleep. She had looked so fragile there in her corner, so much in need of a hug, of strong arms holding her. But he had not dared to touch her.

What, he wondered, was upsetting her? He might, perhaps, ask Lady Renwick to discover what she could. A cold fist clenched around his heart as it occurred to him that Serena might have met somebody, fallen in love with another man. Perhaps she wished her freedom *now*, did not wish to wait until after her birthday. The cold spread . . .

When Lady Renwick took Serena off to her room to wash the travel dust from her face and hands, his lordship and Sahib led Ian to the study. As Ian poured them each a glass of claret from the decanter on the sideboard, Lord Renwick asked, "What is wrong? Why are you not yourself?"

"It is so obvious a blind man can sense it?" asked Ian with a touch of wry humor. "How can *you* know, my percipient friend?"

"Sahib told me," said Renwick with a quick smile. "I have learned to read him, and he *is* showing concern for you, is he not?"

"It appears to be true," said Ian as he looked down at the tiger settled next to his chair. The beast stared back at him with huge, burning eyes. "But how do you know that?"

"He is not at my side, so I knew he had gone to you."

"He lies at my feet staring at me. It is disconcerting, to say the least."

Jason chuckled. "As I said. He worries. So, Ian, what is wrong and how may I help?" His brows arched over his blind eyes. "So Sahib may cease his worrying, of course!"

Ian didn't so much as smile. He sipped his wine, his gaze unfocused. "I doubt," he finally admitted, "that anyone can help, although I wondered if your lady wife might discover Serena's problem. My wife won't discuss . . . whatever it is. Do you not think the odds are better that she will talk to another woman?"

"Hmm. Is *your* problem that *your wife* has a problem?"

Ian smiled. "It sounds a trifle nonsensical, but, yes, that is exactly the situation. Or part of it," he added in mutter. Then he said, "Serena has run herself ragged or days now, and I've no notion why."

"I will ask Eustacia to discover what she can," said Renwick. He sipped his wine. "In the meantime, tell me about Jack . . ."

So Ian exchanged his most urgent worry with the esser but still pressing concern he had for Jack's deteriorating state of mind.

While the men talked about their friend, Lady Renwick watched her guest remove her bonnet and pelisse. She noted tired eyes, and that Lady Serena had lost weight. Even as her ladyship wondered what might be wrong, she talked of nothing at all in particular, her wonderful voice calming her guest.

"Are you like me, Lady Serena? When one has been cooped up in a carriage for hours, a walk seems just the thing? My husband's aunt's rose gardens are particularly lovely just now."

"I would like that." Serena reached for the discarded pelisse and bonnet.

Eustacia led the way. As they strolled, she continued to prattle in a fashion quite out of character for her, but, as Lady Serena responded with no more than monosyllables, it was difficult to do otherwise.

"Oh," said Serena, her attention finally caught, "is that not an exceptional color?"

"I am particularly fond of that lovely deep pink rose and steal the blooms more often than the gardener likes. You must tell Jase's Aunt Luce you like it. She will be pleased at the compliment. She planted the gardens when Jase returned home blind. For the scent, you know."

As she spoke, Eustacia realized Lady Serena had again disappeared into her own mind. This would not do. This was not the same woman who came from her wedding.

That woman had been apprehensive, but certainly not mute. Something terrible must have occurred.

Eustacia drew in a deep breath. "What is it?" she asked. "What has you in such a pother? Tell me and I will see what I can do. . . . Oh, dear! I did not wish to make you cry, but I cannot bear it." Eustacia put her arm around Serena and drew her toward a bench under an arbor where climbing roses bloomed in profusion. "Sit here, my dear, and tell me the whole story. Or," she added, "do *not* tell me, but believe I will do anything I can to help you if you will only allow me to know what I may do."

"There is nothing anyone can do. It is stupid. Impossible. I have been a fool."

Gambling debts, perhaps? Eustacia waited, but Serena only stared into some invisible distance seeing what no one else could see. "A fool?" repeated Eustacia gently. *Or had Lady Serena, in a few short weeks, fallen deeply in love with some man?*

"I've no notion how it happened. Such a gradual thing . . ." Serena drew in a deep breath. "But it is nothing. Truly. Time will solve my problem."

"You do not know me yet and are not comfortable with me," said Lady Renwick slowly. "I have jumped into deep waters in my usual impulsive fashion, saying things others would know they should not say. Aunt Luce blames my tendency to frank speaking on my father, who was a vicar, but I think it is more that I am impatient of many of society's rules. Believe me, Lady Serena, you may trust me. If ever you wish to talk to me, that is. You needn't, of course, but I hope you will allow me to be your friend, to help . . ."

When Serena didn't respond, only giving her hostess a helpless look, Lady Renwick chuckled. "Oh, dear, I am doing it again. I will say no more just so long as you understand that if, at any time you wish it, I've an excellent shoulder on which you may cry." Eustacia rose to her feet. "And now, instead of probing where I should not, why do we not continue our walk and then return to the house for tea? And in the meantime you must tell me all about the wedding and Lieutenant Templeton's bride and also, if you will, about this other lieutenant, Jack Princeton, about whom my husband is so concerned . . ."

With unexceptional things to discuss, Serena managed to put aside her apathy and, as they talked, become more her old self. She discovered she liked Lady Renwick, who had sensible things to say and did not talk nonsense. Long before their walk ended, they were fast friends.

Several days passed in simple country pleasures. One day it rained, but then the sun shone brightly and Lady Renwick planned picnics and suggested a riding party, which she immediately canceled when she learned Lady Serena did not ride. Instead she suggested they surprise Ian. Serena would have riding lessons as she did herself.

Eustacia ruefully admitted that she was no more than a novice and had much to learn if she were to come up to Prince Ravi's standards. The East Indian prince was also a distraction for Serena. She enjoyed talking to the boy about life in his homeland. What he told her intrigued her, and for the first time she grew curious about other peoples, other ways of living. *Perhaps*, she thought, *I will travel before I settle down to planning my home for betrayed women.* But it was merely a notion and she did not consider it seriously.

The riding lessons remained secret for only a few days. One morning, as Serena was walked her mare around a training circle and Lady Renwick practiced very low jumps, the gentlemen appeared. Sahib was in his cage, and the men were strolling and talking when they came upon the two women and their grooms.

Ian, seeing them, put his hand on Jase's arm. "There

is a lesson in progress. Do you think we should go away?"

"Who? Doing what?"

Ian described the scene. "Serena is doing surprisingly well for someone who has never ridden. At least, she told me it was one thing her brothers were forbidden to teach her."

"And my wife?"

Ian glanced toward his hostess. "Taking her jumps like a trooper." But he wasn't interested in Lady Renwick's prowess. He only had eyes for Serena. "How lovely she looks," he muttered. "I must order her a habit. That one doesn't fit properly."

"She looks lovely in an ill-fitting habit? My friend, you *are* in love, are you not?"

"I assumed you knew," said Ian. "Yes. Of course. Almost from the beginning."

"And have not told her."

Ian was silent. "Jase, did I never explain this marriage?"

"That you were forced into it by your father? That it was arranged for your brother and you were the substitute groom when he died?"

Ian chuckled. "Reluctant groom, you mean! How quickly that reluctance faded." He sobered. "Unfortunately, I made an agreement with Lady Serena that we would terminate the marriage."

"Terminate it! Ah. But then you changed your mind, of course."

"Oh, no. Not at all."

Lord Renwick frowned. "So . . . why are you still wed?"

"What? Oh." Ian explained Serena's problems with her father and how she must be of age before attaining her freedom.

"But you love her."

"Yes."

Ian filled his eyes with the sight of his bride, noting her serious mien as she concentrated on sitting properly and holding the reins as she should.

"Ian, you fool, you cannot simply decide to end a marriage—"

"No."

For a long moment Jason remained silent. "That is all? Just no?"

Ian cast his friend an impatient glance. "Surely Alex wrote you the details."

"Of course." Jason grinned. "I merely thought you might not like it that I knew"

Ian managed a wry chuckle. "Jase, how long have we both known Alex?"

Lord Renwick also laughed softly. "Of course. You knew when you told him he would pass on the word. Ian, I can see why you do not tell her you must perjure yourself in order to free her, but why have you not told her you love her? Has it not occurred to you that, if *you* fell in love, *she* might also? She would be still more diffident to admit it, would she not?"

"Love me?" Ian's heart pounded at the notion, but then he sighed. "Unlikely. Jase, can you begin to imagine her feelings toward men? Any man? I told you about her family. Her father."

"Distrust. Fear, perhaps?"

"Definitely fear, although I believe I've pretty well convinced her she need not fear me. I am far less certain she *trusts* me."

Lady Renwick turned just then. "Aha! Serena, we are discovered!"

Lady Serena glanced around, and her cheeks filled with rosy color. "So I see." She pulled up her mare. "I had hoped," she said in a slightly scolding voice, "to manage more than walking this poor patient beast in circles before you discovered what we did."

"Should we go away and come again when you are more proficient?" asked Ian. "We can forget we ever saw you."

"Can you?" she asked.

"Never," he said softly—but vehemently enough that his wife heard him. "We will leave you to your practice."

"Sahib must be wondering if we forgot him," added Lord Renwick. He tapped the path with his long cane, oriented himself, and set off toward the tiger's cage.

Ian smiled encouragingly at his bride, nodded toward Lady Renwick, and followed after.

Lady Renwick trotted up. "My dear Serena, do close your mouth. My stepmother always said I would trap flies if I did not close mine. I disliked her taunting tone, but I now see what she meant."

The men disappeared, and Serena turned toward her hostess. "Ian has another notion. He says I look like a fish trapped on shore and gasping for breath."

"*Why* are you emulating a gasping fish?"

"You were farther off. Did you hear Ian's response to my question?"

"As to whether he could forget we were practicing until we were ready to show off our skills?"

"Yes. He said *never*."

"So?"

"It was the *way* he said it."

"You mean as if he spoke of something else?"

"Yes . . ."

Lady Renwick eyed her new friend. "Serena, I do not know Ian well yet, but I do know Jase considers him the deepest of his friends. The one who has the greatest sensitivity to others. And the one most in need of gentleness and love. Do you think he has fallen in love with you?"

"Ian . . . ?"

Eustacia chuckled softly. "Ah, yes. *Exactly* like a fish."
Serena closed her mouth with a snap. "No. It is impossible."

"That he might fall in love with you? But why not?"

"With me?" Serena shook her head. "No. Impossible,"
she repeated.

Eustacia considered adding more, but there had been
the most trifling hint of a question in that last as if Serena
might just possibly be thinking about it. Perhaps it was
best to let her think. For the nonce . . .

"I will," she said, "try that jump three more times
before we go in."

"And I will walk this beast once again around our
circle. If Riggs has the time for it, of course." She mo-
tioned to Lord Renwick's head groom, who had taken
himself beyond hearing.

Riggs approached and led the mare back into position.
Before he let her begin, he reiterated the principles he
was teaching her that morning. Serena set the mare in
motion and, quite proud of herself, made it all the way
around without a single correction.

Ian spent as much time as he could manage with
Serena. Finding occasions to be with her wasn't easy,
although Serena discovered he was very nearly as adept
at tracking her down as she was at avoiding him. When
they did manage to do things together, she enjoyed it
and, each time, reminded herself she wished to have
every moment with him she could manage.

But then she'd forget and do her best to disappear when
she knew he searched for her. The fear that he discover
she loved him drove her to it. She could not bear the
thought that he'd give up his freedom for her if he knew
her feelings for him, that he would remain married to
her only because he was too good a man to hurt her by

getting the annulment she had once believed she wanted more than anything in the world.

Oh, if only he loved her too! But even that thought frightened her. *If* he loved her, would he continue to do? And if he did not remain in love with her, would he resent the fact they were still wed and no longer had a means of ending it?

Serena, her head and her heart embattled, lost still more weight.

Ian, noting it, tempted her whenever he could. He carried small tins of biscuits in his pocket and shared them with her when they walked. He offered her tidbits from his plate at mealtime when there was no company to be shocked by such behavior. When the evening tea tray came in, he would, himself, load her plate and take her her cup and saucer.

"You must eat more," he told her one evening when she demurred, saying it was far too much.

"I've no appetite, Ian."

"I wonder if I should have the doctor in," he mused, staring at her, worried about her.

Startled, Serena, who had avoided looking at him, glanced up. She was still more startled by the caring she read in features. For an instant she wanted to touch him, rub away those lines in his forehead, tell him there was no reason for him to worry about her. "I am fine, Ian, I have always been overly slender, you know."

"You had begun to put on a few pounds when we went to London," he retorted.

"You wish me to get *fat*?" she asked, trying to make a joke of it.

"Not *fat*," he said and sighed. "Please try to eat a bit more, my dear. To make me happy?"

So Serena forced down another of the tasty tarts, washing it down with another cup of tea.

"Thank you," he said softly and took the plate from

her. But he set it on a table within reach of her fingers before moving away to speak to Jase. He kept an eye on her and was exceedingly pleased when, involved in a conversation with Lady Renwick, she absently picked up another tart. Before the evening ended, she had cleaned the plate. Ian wished he'd put one or two more of the thin, crisp, lemon-flavored biscuits on it.

Lady Renwick had talked of the region, the people who were invited to the dinner planned for two days hence. "You will like the squire's wife. And the vicar's. The curate isn't married, although more than one lady has attempted to find him a bride. I wish he *would* wed. It might take his mind from trifling faults among the congregation and instill in him a little more understanding."

"The vicar where I grew up is unmarried," said Serena, "but is a wonderfully understanding man. I wonder if marriage would solve that particular problem."

Lady Renwick chuckled. "Very likely it is a false hope, but you will understand when you meet him why we are willing to attempt most anything in order to make him something less of a stick! A disapproving stick."

"You should think, instead, of the woman who would be forced to endure him if he did *not* change," said Serena, her voice dry as dust.

"Ah! You have put your finger on a flaw in our plans. I will nip in the bud any further efforts along those lines. Are you," she added, "feeling forced to endure?"

"Hmm?" Serena, who had been staring at Ian, turned. "Forced . . . ?"

"You are unhappy," said Eustacia, "and I cannot put *my* finger on why. You will remember, when you first arrived, I pressed you to confide in me, but it was too soon. Do you feel, now, that you might do so? Perhaps there is a solution you cannot see because you are too close to the problem."

"I"—Serena cast a glance toward the men—"will think about it."

"Ah! I have been maladroit. You fear Ian might overhear."

Just then the men excused themselves. They would walk Sahib and, by the way, indulge themselves in the disgusting habit of smoking a cigarillo.

"Fate has taken a hand," said Lady Renwick when the door closed, leaving them to themselves. "Will you not tell me?"

Serena took a deep breath. "It will sound absurd, I fear. You remember I was engaged to Ian's brother?"

Lady Renwick nodded.

"James and I had an agreement. We would avoid a wedding until I came of age and the engagement could be broken."

"So?"

"My father was determined to marry me off before then. You see, I'd a rather large inheritance which I'd have come into and I could have escaped his control."

"But you did that by marrying Ian."

"No. I lost my inheritance by marrying Ian."

Lady Renwick frowned.

"I am still under a man's control," said Serena gently. "I am not free."

This time her hostess blinked.

Serena sighed. "And that is the problem."

"That you are not free?"

A wry smile twisted Serena's features. "No. That I *will* be." She pursed her lips, staring into the small blaze in the fireplace lit not for warmth, which was unneeded, but because it was pleasant. "And," she said finally, "I am no longer certain I wish to be."

"Ian . . . ?"

". . . will request an annulment when I pass my next

birthday. Once I am twenty-five, my father has no reason to force me into another marriage."

"But has he reason *now*? Is not your fortune in Ian's hands?"

"Yes, but I feared that if Ian got the annulment immediately, my father might demand my inheritance be returned and he would then wed me to some man over whom he had control so that he would lose neither me *nor* the money."

"Why, I wonder, did he not do that in the first place."

Serena chuckled softly. "My guardian angel must have looked into my future. I was engaged to James before I inherited my fortune. I suspect my father attempted to break that agreement, but Ian's father would not allow it. After all, a fortune from which his son would benefit!" The chuckle was followed by a bark of laughter. "If James had *not* found a means of avoiding our wedding altogether, why, I would have gone to him merely to spite my father!"

"But this annulment. On what grounds will Ian manage that?"

"The marriage will not have been consummated," said Serena placidly.

"I thought . . ." *Was* Serena's virginity sufficient . . . ? Lady Renwick drew in a deep breath. "But," she continued, changing what she'd been about to say, "if you no longer wish it, why do you not tell Ian so?"

"He was forced to wed me. He cannot wish to remain wed to me. I will not allow him to sacrifice himself for me."

"But if it would be no sacrifice?" asked Lady Renwick gently.

"Not . . . ?"

"My dear, the two of you are obviously in love with one another. The *mistake* will be if neither of you finds the courage to tell the other how you feel and he goes through with . . . whatever it is he must do." As she observed Lady Serena's expression of horror, Lady Renwick reminded herself to ask her husband exactly what Ian must do. If he must . . . If it were what she feared . . . No, she could not recall that long-ago conversation with her father. Not in detail. "Let us have one more cup of tea and we will call it a night. My dear, I will only repeat that I am not a gossip. Although I am certain you know it, I repeat it to reassure you."

Serena ignored that. "How can you say we are in love with each other?"

"How? But it is true, is it not? You have fallen deeply in love with him. Which is no surprise, of course. I thought you would, once you discovered what a wonderful man he is."

"But he does *not* love me!"

"Does he not? I suppose you would know? And I note that you do not deny you love him?"

"I have been so afraid he would guess, and now you tell me it is obvious and I am right to fear it."

"Oh, not obvious unless one looks for clues. You watch him, for instance, with your heart in your eyes. But you are careful to do so only when he looks elsewhere. You wish simultaneously to be with him and to avoid him, another clue, my friend."

"A clue?"

Lady Renwick handed Lady Serena her cup with two more biscuits set on the edge. She smiled. "Unacknowledged love is always full of contradictions. You wish to be with him because you love him. You avoid him because you fear his knowing why. As you said."

"How did you know Lord Renwick was in love with you?"

"Oh dear. How *did* I know?" Lady Renwick settled back into her chair, a musing look on her face. Her hand lifted to touch a small heart-shaped birthmark which

marred her complexion. A secret smile tipped her lips.
"Ah, yes. You see, I had always believed I was too
flawed"—she pointed to the birthmark—"to satisfy any
man. Poor Jason believed his blindness a major hindrance
to any woman wedding him. When we each understood
the other's fears, we concluded we were meant for each
other. He could not see my flaw, so I could face him
unafraid. But, of course, by that time we already loved
each other to distraction. As so often in such situations,
the both of us had been far too cowardly to admit it."

"How can I admit it when Ian will stay wed to me,
willy-nilly, whether he wishes or no? How can I know
he stays with me because he *wants* to?"

"My dear, believe me. He looks at you just as you
look at him. Only he does his looking when *your* attention is elsewhere!"

Lady Serena set her untouched cup aside. She twisted
her hands in her lap, staring into the fire's embers. "He
cannot love me."

"Why can he not?"

"Men don't love me. I was verging on spinsterhood
when Ian wed me, and no man has ever in all those years
loved me. Not even my father or my brothers. Of course,
that would be a different sort of love."

"Something I recall you saying just after your wedding . . . were you *allowed* to know any men? Young,
personable men?"

Serena blinked. "Well . . . no."

"Then tell me how anyone could have fallen in love
with you?"

Serena frowned.

"Only occasionally is falling in love an instant sort of
thing. Normally, one discovers another's character slowly
The pair find interests in common. They discover they
are a trifle short of breath whenever the object of interest
appears, and that they wish the other to touch them but

they feel strange when it happens . . . and eventually, my dear, they realize it is love."

"Love. Love is very odd, is it not?"

Lady Renwick nodded. The two stared at the dying fire as Lady Serena drank her tea and, much to Lady Renwick's satisfaction, nibbled around the edges of another biscuit.

Ian looked down at his wife. Jase had forced a promise he'd tell her he loved her, but dared he? He sighed and then abruptly, almost harshly, said, "Love makes one do odd things." A muscle jumped in his jaw. "As I have done . . ."

"You have . . . ?" He loved? But whom? Did he mean to tell her he wished his freedom even sooner than she'd expected?

"I love you, Serena."

Despite Lady Renwick's encouragement, she could not comprehend his meaning. Not immediately. When the words finally registered, her eyes widened in shocked surprise. *Ian loves me?*

"I do not tell you in order to burden you, my dear. You must not feel sorry for me or go against your own desires or needs. I merely inform you of it because you should know. In case it is relevant to . . . any decision you will make."

Decision? But their decision was made, was it not? And yet, did this not change everything? Assuming she believed him. Assuming Lady Renwick had not, after all, passed along her knowledge of Serena's love for Ian.

"You suggested you behaved oddly because of it?" she asked, putting aside the fact itself for later thought.

"Yes."

"In what way?"

"You need not know *that*, my dear," he said with a quick, almost puckish smile.

"Why do I not?"

"Because knowing might interfere with your decision as the other will not."

"That you love me will not influence me?"

"It need not. This other?" Ian thought of his decision to perjure himself for her sake and internally cringed. "It might." When Serena would have questioned him further, Ian held up his hand. He hid his disappointment that she had not responded in kind and dreaded that his speaking made everything worse. "I merely wished you to know, and we need discuss it no further. . . . Will you walk with me to the stables? Jase's groom has bought a new mare for Lady Renwick's use. I would see her."

He held out his hand and, hesitantly, Serena laid hers in it. The warmth of his ungloved hand through the thin cotton covering hers startled her. *What*, she wondered, *would it feel like if I were ungloved? Would I feel still odder sensations? Would I sense still more strangeness?*"

"What are you thinking?" asked Ian.

"Thinking? I don't know that I was thinking anything at all."

"Feeling, then?" he asked, amusement in his voice.

"Feeling . . ." Her voice trailed off.

"You *were* feeling something?"

Serena remembered Lady Renwick's caution that she not throw away what might be through simple cowardliness. "I like your hand holding mine. I wondered," she went on bravely, "what it would feel like if I, too, were not wearing gloves."

Ian turned her toward him. He bent over her hand and undid the tiny button holding the glove to her wrist. Very slowly, very gently, he pulled the glove from her fingers and stuffed it in his pocket. Then he held out his hand. Serena stared at him, found him staring back. She wished she could read his mind, could know what he was thinking . . . feeling. Slowly she raised her hand and laid it in his. His fingers closed about hers, and she bit her lip, her eyes widening.

"I like this very much," he said softly.

Serena swallowed. "I . . . too."

He smiled at her and, hesitantly, she smiled back. His fingers squeezed hers and, turning, he strolled on toward the stables.

Dare I believe he loves me as I love him? she wondered.

Dare I hope? he wondered.

. The following day Ian went to where Lady Renwick and Lady Serena practiced their riding under Riggs's watchful eye. When the lesson ended and the horses walked toward the gate, he approached.

"You are doing very well," he said. Then he glanced at Lady Renwick, his ears coloring slightly. "The both of you." Turning back to Serena, he added, "I must see to buying you a mare of your own." He walked beside her until they reached the stables and then reached up for her, lifting her down. "Such a little thing," he said, his hands still at her waist.

"Not so *very* little," she contradicted him. "It is merely that you are so large!"

She placed her hands over his. For another long moment they stared at each other. Then Serena, embarrassed, glanced around. The groom had disappeared. Lady Renwick, well along the path to the house, had not even bothered to say good-bye. She and Ian were alone!

"Walk with me?" he asked.

She plucked at his fingers and he released her. Then, perversely, she wished he had not.

"There is a pond beyond the rhododendrons which,

he gardener tells me, is starred with water lilies." He gestured to a low rise covered with dark leaved shrubs. "Shall we see?"

Serena bit her lip. In the long night hours when she had wakened and dozed only to waken again, she had sworn to admit her love to Ian. But now the opportunity was here, she was afraid. Still, it must be faced. And sooner rather than later . . .

"Serena?"

Or perhaps not *quite* yet? "Yes. I would like to see the lilies."

Ian did not turn, however. Instead he lifted her hand and carefully removed the thin leather glove Lady Renwick had loaned her for riding. When he held out his hand, Serena placed her bare palm against his, and again that wonderful but unnerving sensation skittered up her arm and down her spine. *Could this be,* she wondered, *he sensation Miss Cla . . . No, Mrs. Lieutenant Templeon described?*

"There is a path, I believe, off to the right. As I recall, the ground rises on all sides of the pond except at the far end. The rhododendrons were planted many years ago and in the spring provide an amazing combination of colors."

Kind Ian, thought Serena, *to talk of unimportant things.*

"I was here when we were schoolboys," he continued. "Jase's father was already allowing the grounds to go to the devil, but we didn't mind. It made playing at wild Indians or armies all the more exciting. We need not, you see, worry about tearing through a flower bed or, that we break a tree limb. I remember finding this path, running along it until I"—he pulled her to a stop—"reached this point. I stopped dead. Serena," he said, "can you imagine coming out from under dark trees into a sea of sun-bathed color?" He swept his free arm in an arc, indicating the basin before them. "Even at that age I was shocked into silence by the beauty."

"There are a pink and a white rhododendron in our village. The bushes become one huge bloom in the spring." Serena tried to imagine the slopes surrounding the pond covered in blossoms.

"Here there is every pink imaginable. Some deep and vivid. Some so pale as to be nearly white. And the darkest blossoms are planted to form streaks, rather like those running through polished marble. It was glorious."

Serena gestured. "Now the lilies are in bloom. Perhaps it is well the rhododendrons are over or the delicate water lily would not show to advantage."

"I see a wisp of purple along the banks here and there. Shall we investigate?"

"Yes, please."

Ian started down the path, pausing at the steeper parts to be certain she had no difficulty. Even though she knew she could manage easily, she liked his care and consideration. One more small bit to add to the scales already weighted in his favor. Ian was not her father. He would never be anything like the man she was forced to call Father.

"I plan," said Ian, as if reading her thoughts, "to take you to your old church this coming Sunday. We must rise early to be on time for the service, of course, but I thought perhaps you would like to see your mother . . . ?"

"Seeing her in church where the neighbors will see how my father behaves? A masterful notion! Yes, thank you. I will like that."

A bench was situated at a strategic point along the shore, and Ian turned her toward it. "Will you sit for a bit?" he asked.

"Yes, please."

"You are exceptionally docile, my dear." He spoke

with that touch of humor she loved to hear. "You worry me!"

"I . . . I lo . . ." Serena drew in a deep breath. Slowly she let it out. In despair, she gazed up at him. "I am such a *coward*!"

Fourteen

"A coward? Ha! *That* doesn't sound like my Serena!" He sobered. "My dear, are you about to tell me you still wish your freedom when the time comes? I told you you were not to allow my feelings for you to interfere in what you need. What you want. It will be all right, you know."

"No! Not at all right!"

"My dear—"

"Shh," she interrupted. "I must say words I never expected to say."

After a glance at her stern features, Ian remained silent. He felt as if his heart were being torn in two, hopes and fears playing tug of war with the strings.

"I love you," she finally muttered, the words not only spoken quickly but so low he had difficulty hearing them. "I didn't mean to," she continued only a trifle more firmly. "I didn't even know I could." She stared out over the lily-dotted water. "Love anyone, I mean. I didn't believe there was such a thing as love . . ."

Ian placed his hands on her shoulders and turned her to him. When she didn't raise her head, he put a thumb under her chin and very gently pushed until she stared up into his steady gaze. Then, very slowly, he dipped toward her. Very gently he pulled her nearer. And, as soft as a butterfly's touch, he touched his lips to hers.

Then, nearly convinced such self-denial might cause

him an injury, he sat back. "You love me?" he asked, wishing to hear the words again.

For half a moment she stared at him, bewildered by the sensations the feather-light touch roused. Then her lips compressed . . . but, finally, she nodded. Once. Firmly.

"My dear, if I love you and you love me, where is the problem?"

"Me. *I* am the problem. I have no notion what to do. I don't know how to behave. And . . . I'm afraid."

After a moment's thought, Ian smiled. "May I make a suggestion?"

"Please do."

"Might I perhaps court you as I would have done if I'd met you, say, at Almack's one evening, and fallen in love with you? Might we pretend we've just met and I will call on you with trifles and take you for walks and we can talk and perhaps, when no one is looking, hold hands as we've done twice now?" He lifted her bare hand and engulfed it in both of his large, warm palms. And he stared at her. Seriously. Solemnly. Waiting . . .

She stared at him. Then a short sharp laugh escaped her. But then she sobered again. "I *should* find that ridiculous when we have been wed for more than two months now, but . . ."

A wistful expression reminded him of her odd shyness which he'd found rather delightful, assuming it didn't become a permanent part of her! "But you do not?" he asked.

"No." She stared at him, feeling her hand in his and liking the feeling, remembering his lips on hers and wondering if he might kiss her again. She looked at his lips. Might he *really* kiss her? I think," she said shyly, "I would like to be courted."

"Then we will seal the bargain," said Ian. This time

when he kissed her he allowed his lips to cling for a moment. He was relieved when she did not pull away.

But, he told himself sternly, he must remember this suddenly shy lady was unlike the competent and able Lady Serena who could handle a household or defend herself with a knife. He must not allow his passions full rein but must go slowly with her.

Which, as he'd suggested, meant he must court her.

Except for the Sunday they drove over to see her mother, the following two weeks passed in a golden haze for Serena. For hours at a time she even set aside her concern for her mother, who had, she'd thought, looked a trifle peaked.

Ian, too, had thought his mother-in-law was not quite up to snuff and contrived a moment to have words with a ferret-faced little man who sidled up to him when he went to the local tavern with his youngest brother-in-law.

"Nothing?" Ian asked the man.

A smirk creased the man's face. "See for yourself," he said, and a paper changed hands. "No proof, though," he warned. "Not yet."

Ian, when they returned to Renwick's Lair, studied the laconic report and frowned. He went to find Jase and explained what his investigator had discovered.

"Do you think it can be true?" asked Jason, shocked.

"If it *is* true, then I've means to force the bastard to separate from Serena's mother."

"Yes, but *is* it? And, Ian, think. It means your wife is a bastard!"

"That is unimportant. And," he said warningly, "something she must never know. In fact, it would be best if her mother remained in ignorance of her situation. Her father will say nothing. To acknowledge it disinherits his current heir and puts a half-wit son by his real wife in what is now a mere lout's place!"

"I wonder why I get the impression you do not care for your brothers-in-law."

"There might be hope for the youngest . . ."

When Ian didn't continue, Jase asked, "The first wife has willingly kept his secret all these years?"

"According to my ferret, the woman thinks herself a widow."

"Can you trust your informer?"

"Oh, I trust him. I just wonder if he has made an error in this particular case." Ian rubbed the folded edge of the paper back and forth against his chin, his deep-set eyes almost lost below lowered brows.

"What will you do?"

"Do?" Ian chuckled. "Why, continue to court my wife, of course. Jase, she is like a child who has a birthday every day! You cannot see her, but have you not heard it in her voice?"

"Eustacia tells me about her," said Jason, smiling. The smile faded. "Ian, you cannot fob me off. What will you do about Lord Dixon? You cannot simply forget this."

"No, but I must be *absolutely certain* before I confront him. I must have *proof*."

When Ian said no more, Jase spoke warningly. "When you *do* confront him, don't go alone."

"Shall I take you and Sahib?"

"Yes. And perhaps Merwin. Not only is he active in politics where he has influence, but he is handy in a scrap, if it comes to that."

"Very well. But I'll do nothing until I am certain, so do not hold your breath. Lady Renwick is not a happy lady, but I do not believe Dixon will do her permanent harm." For a moment Ian's lips compressed, and a cold, hard glitter turned his blue eyes nearly gray. Then, glancing at the clock, he put such thoughts aside and smiled.

"And now, if you will excuse me, Serena is about finished with her lesson. I go to meet her."

"I will go with you, if you've no objection. Eustacia and I mean to take a gentle ride over to one of my tenants who has a complaint with which I must deal."

Sahib was put in his outdoor cage before the men strolled to the stables. Jase's placid hack was saddled and waiting. Hearing the approach of two horses, his lordship turned. Ian, smiling, walked toward the women and lifted Serena down, never allowing her eyes to stray from his. He allowed his hands to cradle her waist a trifle longer than was strictly polite, but she made no objections. In fact, she got that dreamy expression in her eyes for which he watched. Then and there, he decided he'd put his luck to the test.

Their walk that day took them to a sort of summer house with latticed sides covered in vines. Inside were a table, chairs, and cushioned benches.

"It is warm today. Will you rest here for a bit?" he asked when she tripped up the three steps to explore.

"Lady Blackburne should make a habit of designing gardens, should she not?" asked Serena, turning toward Ian. "She has a delightful way of hiding surprises here and there. Like this little house . . . Ian?" she asked a trifle warily as he approached her.

"Shh," he whispered. "Let me kiss you, Serena . . .'

She did. In fact, she more than allowed him to kiss her. She cooperated fully, her lips willing if untutored.

He lifted his head, tipped it back, and, closing his eyes groaned softly. "My dear . . ."

"Shh." She tugged him closer. "Again."

Serena learned quickly, and enjoyed every moment of the lesson which followed her demand. But when Ian's emotions heated up and his hands roved where another's hands had never before touched her, Serena realized that if she did not somehow bring the experiment to a halt she would learn far more than she was quite ready to know!

Only her hands in his hair, pulling him away from her, finally brought Ian to a realization of what he had thoughtlessly almost allowed. Actually, he mused ruefully, he'd been incapable of thought! He stood across the small room from her, staring through the lattice. "Should I apologize?" he asked.

"Heavens no! It is just that . . . that . . ." He turned, and bravely she added, "that when we make love for the first time I would rather it be safely in our room with the assurance we will not be disturbed."

Ian was relieved he'd not frightened her. "My dear, I have had a thought . . ."

"Yes?"

"My love, if you look at me in quite that hopeful manner, I may forget what I was about to say and you will find that, even when one is not *safely* in one's room, love can be a delightful pastime!"

Serena blinked and then seated herself on one of the small chairs. She folded her hands. "Ian, will you please tell me your notion?"

Her eyes widened when he approached her and went down on one knee before her. He reached for her hands and held them gently, looking squarely into her eyes.

"Serena, my love, will you marry me and be my loving wife?"

"But . . ."

He smiled. "You would say we are already wed. My dear, when we said our vows before Vicar Morton, I doubt either of us was in quite the proper frame of mind. I would like to say those words again. And mean them." He drew in a deep breath, "So, my dear, will you wed me?"

"*Can* one? I mean, is it allowed to be married all over again?"

"I think the vicar here would accommodate us if we explained."

"Can you explain? I mean without embarrassing yourself?"

He smiled. "Oh, I think so. Will you wed me?"

"Yes."

His smile broadened. "Just yes? No coy and demure disclaimers? No ifs, ands, or buts? No maidenly hesitation?"

Serena flushed slightly at that last. Because even though his passion had frightened her, it had also intrigued her and she was almost certain he would, as Mrs. Lieutenant Templeton had explained, make the experience a joyful and enjoyable one. But he was such a large man it was frightening. So, even though she *knew* he would never treat her as his father treated her mother, she was feeling that maidenly hesitation of which he spoke, because, if she were wrong and he did mistreat her, she would be unable to defend herself . . .

"My dear, you've a most expressive face. I think, when we finally do come to our marriage bed, that you should place your knife under your pillow. Then if you feel you must fend me off, you'll have a weapon with which to do so." He chuckled at her expression of shock. "All I ask is that you try not to cut me in any vital way!"

"A penknife, perhaps," suggested Serena.

She was so relieved her eyes twinkled, which delighted Ian to the point he pulled her near for a hug that rather engulfed her and left her breathless when he set her away from him. "You, my dear, are a joy and a constant surprise. I wonder how I survived so long not knowing you."

"James said he would keep his family away so there would be less embarrassment when, finally, the engagement was broken."

"So that explains . . ." Ian's shaggy brows drew together and then relaxed. "He was wild, unpredictable, and the most splendid of brothers, but he was also a trifle secretive and more than a bit sly. I never wondered too much why he put us off meeting you, but I see he was more sensitive than I knew. More careful of your feelings."

Serena chuckled. "You misunderstand. It was, I think, *his* embarrassment he wished to avoid rather than mine!"

"Minx."

"Occasionally. Do you mind?"

There was just a hint of her old concern in that. Ian spoke promptly, hoping to bury it once and forever. "Not at all. I *like* it." He was pleased when the tiny frown lines faded from her brow. "And now, my dear, if you will excuse me, I've a wedding to arrange!"

"I will, happily, if only you will walk me back toward the house, first? I paid no attention to where we wandered and, frankly, I doubt if I could find my way."

They were in the midst of a small woods when Ian's brother Aaron and Prince Ravi appeared. The boy, pouting, looked up. "Ah, Mrs. McMurrey, do you know this plant which my stupid tutor cannot name?"

"Do not tell him, my dear sister. Please. It is not that I do not know but that I wish him to find it in his book there. My student is lazy, you see, and will not work if he can find someone to do it for him."

"I will be Rajah one day," said the boy, his nose in the air. "It is unnecessary that I work."

"Is it?" asked Ian, his brows arching. "How boring."

"Boring?" The boy stared arrogantly at his tutor's brother.

"Oh, I think so," said Ian. "To have every whim gratified very nearly before one has voiced it? To have no way of passing the time since all is done for one? How could life be other than a bore?" Another moment passed, Ian's frown mirrored on the prince's fine-boned features.

"Bah!" shouted the boy and ran off.

Aaron chuckled. "That is always his answer when he can think of no better. Ian, thank you. I have tried and tried to explain that very thing to him but never succeeded. You have convinced him with only a few questions."

"I am glad to have been of help." Ian glanced at Serena. "Aaron, must you chase after him?"

"No. Later he will appear in the schoolroom, contrite and apologetic, and very likely knowing the name of the plant we studied."

"Then, if you are returning to the house, will you escort Lady Serena? I've an errand and if I follow the path Prince Ravi traveled, I will be well on the way."

They took their separate paths, and Ian, after twenty minutes walking, came to the rectory where he arranged to bring Serena on the following afternoon. Then, when the tea tray arrived that evening, Ian, who had discussed it with Serena earlier, invited Lord and Lady Renwick to go with them when they reaffirmed their wedding vows.

"What a wonderful notion," said Lady Renwick, but she cast a curious glance toward Serena. She smiled when Serena blushed. "Jase, might we too . . . ?"

"Of course"—he dropped his hand to Sahib's nape, scratching lightly—"but let us wait until the anniversary of our original wedding to do so. We need not impinge on our friends' day."

When she finally stood before the vicar, Serena realized that what she was about to do would tie her to Ian forever. *Was* this what she wanted? For a moment she froze. Then she glanced up at him. Big. Solid. Trustworthy and kind. And *not* like her father.

Yes. Yes, it was exactly what she wanted. Her shoulders relaxed and, only a trifle hesitantly, she groped for Ian's hand, slipping hers into his and squeezing gently.

"Ready, my dear?"

"Yes," she said and smiled a glorious smile which had the vicar beaming back at her. "Oh, yes, please."

That evening, trying not to think of the hours to come, Ian took a glass of wine with Jase while he waited until he could go up to join his wife. In her room. In her bed . . .

"Have you done anything more about her father?" asked Lord Renwick.

"I have sent my ferret word he must find proof. Solid proof."

"Do you know how the man discovered what he has so far?"

Ian smiled. "He is not one to reveal his methods. I would guess it involved an uninvited sojourn in Dixon's study."

"Would his lordship retain anything so dangerous to him?"

"It may be nothing a normal person would find of interest. A single name in an odd phrase would lead my ferret onward. And if the name led to a married lady who thought herself widowed?" Ian shrugged. "He will have been to the church and checked the register, but two men may have the same name. I don't know how he will verify that Lord Dixon and the seeming widow's husband are one and the same. He *must* document it." Ian sighed. "Still . . . it all takes time. There will be links difficult to establish . . ."

"Just remember," warned Renwick, "you are to take some of the Six with you when you confront Dixon. He must know that more than you alone are aware of the situation."

"I'll not forget." Ian raised his eyes to the ceiling as if he would look through to the floor above. "I believe I can wait no longer . . ."

"Besides, it is often nice to play lady's maid to one's

wife," said Jason with a sly smile. "In fact, I believe I will take myself off and do just that! Sahib. Come."

Ian watched Jason walk with a firm stride to the door, grasp the handle without fumbling, and open it. He disappeared down the hall, Sahib at his side. Ian shook his head, amazed at the confidence with which his blind friend moved about his home.

Ian started for the door himself and was halfway there when he spun on his heel. He went to the decanter and poured another glass of wine, which he downed in a few gulps. Now the time had come, now he was finally to join Serena in her bed, *now* he found he was as nervous as any bridegroom!

It occurred to him that Serena would be still *more* nervous. The knowledge soothed him. Ian was always at his best when helping others. In this case he must set himself to calming his wife, to loving her, to moving her to love him in return, *to want him as he wanted her*.

And he would.

What is more, he did.

Dear Reader,

We aren't entirely finished with Lady Serena. With luck, Ian may succeed in his attempt to make his wife's mother happy, too. However, perhaps not in my next book, which is *The Christmas Gift*.

This is Lieutenant Princeton's story. As Jack recovers and realizes he will not die, he loses all patience with Lady Anne's mothering. He hires an ex-sergeant who was wounded in the same battle. The man helps him escape to a hiding place where Jack has little success in his attempts to come to terms with his useless leg.

Jack's friends do not allow him this reclusive life. They bring him to Lord Merwin's estate where Merwin's widowed cousin lives. Patricia Haydon remembers Jack from when they were all much younger. Unhappily looking forward to a marriage to an older man chosen by her parents, Patricia grew infatuated with Jack. Now, years later, she looks forward to meeting him again and is *not* pleased to find him so changed.

Patricia cannot stand by watching a man drift into self-destroying bitterness. Unlike Lady Anne, who wishes to cosset Jack, Patricia uses every possible means to make Jack see that the world is not so bad after all. She dares him, nags him, and makes jests which allow him to laugh at himself. Then she discovers the cure for his bitterness: A means by which he can ride again!

Best of all, they fall in love with each other.

I would enjoy hearing from you and may be contacted via E-mail at JeanneSavery@yahoo.com or by snail mail, in care of my publisher.

Cheerfully,
Jeanne Savery

BOOK YOUR PLACE ON OUR WEBSITE AND MAKE THE READING CONNECTION!

We've created a customized website just for our very special readers, where you can get the inside scoop on everything that's going on with Zebra, Pinnacle and Kensington books.

When you come online, you'll have the exciting opportunity to:

- View covers of upcoming books
- Read sample chapters
- Learn about our future publishing schedule (listed by publication month *and author*)
- Find out when your favorite authors will be visiting a city near you
- Search for and order backlist books from our online catalog
- Check out author bios and background information
- Send e-mail to your favorite authors
- Meet the Kensington staff online
- Join us in weekly chats with authors, readers and other guests
- Get writing guidelines
- AND MUCH MORE!

**Visit our website at
http://www.zebrabooks.com**